"Do you know who I am?" a soft voice murmured in her ear.

Her heart began to bump.

"Because I know who you are."

Melanie turned her head. He was smiling at her, eyes gleaming.

"You're the Raven," she said.

He leaned closer, and heat curled inside her like melting toffee.

His mouth brushed hers, barely a touch at all, but she felt it to her toes.

"I'm going to kiss you," he murmured.

"Oh, yes, please . . ."

There was a thud.

The horse vanished and, with it, the man. Melanie opened her eyes and found she was alone in the four-poster bed at Ravenswood.

She rubbed her eyes and sighed.

She could still feel him, she could even taste him, and she had really, really wanted that kiss.

By Sara Mackenzie

SECRETS OF THE HIGHWAYMAN
RETURN OF THE HIGHLANDER

Coming in December 2006

PASSIONS OF THE GHOST

SARA MACKENZIE

SECRETS OF THE
HIGHWAYMAN

AVON BOOKS

An Imprint of HarperCollinsPublishers

This is a work of fiction. Names, characters, places, and incidents are products of the author's imagination or are used fictitiously and are not to be construed as real. Any resemblance to actual events, locales, organizations, or persons, living or dead, is entirely coincidental.

AVON BOOKS
An Imprint of HarperCollins*Publishers*
10 East 53rd Street
New York, New York 10022-5299

For my husband,
who makes everything possible.

Prologue

The Sorceress made her way through the stone halls of the great cathedral. The shadows were cool and deep, and the air held a tantalizing memory of flowers and incense. There was no sound but the swish of her cloak—deep red and bright as the flame of her hair—and the soft breathing of the warriors who rested here.

Each awaiting his turn.

With a smile of anticipation, the Sorceress turned through an archway decorated with twining stone vines and carvings of odd little creatures. This was just one of many chapels, each one occupied by a warrior. A beam of sunlight shone through the tiny round window high above, illuminating the face of the sleeping man who lay like an effigy on top of his own tomb.

For a moment the Sorceress studied him.

Brown hair with a touch of gold, long and falling untidily across his forehead. A strong masculine face with the mouth now relaxed rather than curved in its usual cynical curl. Hazel eyes hidden beneath closed eyelids and almost feminine lashes. Handsome, yes. In his day the Raven was renowned for capturing the hearts of the women who crossed his path.

The Sorceress recalled the words spoken of him by his friends: dashing and reckless, brave and true. They were words any man would be proud to own. And yet on his headstone were a very different set of words:

NATHANIEL RAVEN
HERE LIES THE INFAMOUS RAVEN
WHO PUT FEAR INTO THE HEARTS
OF ALL WHO TRAVELED
THE HIGHWAYS OF CORNWALL,
AND WHO WAS SHOT DEAD,
IN THE YEAR OF OUR LORD 1814

So what had gone wrong?

How had Nathaniel Raven, gentleman, ended so ignominiously, shot down in the act of highway robbery, dying on a lonely stretch of road in Cornwall without anyone to mourn his passing?

Briefly, she touched his cheek, her fingers light, but even that soft touch made him stir. As if he felt the power in her fingers, as if he knew his time had come. He would need help, but the Sorceress had found a suitable mortal. It might be tricky, and they all might fail, but that was not up to her.

"It is time, sweet Raven," the Sorceress whispered.

She lifted her arms and began to chant the ancient incantation of waking, her words growing and growing, until the sound of her voice echoed like thunder in the silence of the chapel, and the very air crackled and sparked.

The Raven opened his eyes.

One

Melanie slowed the Aston Martin, creeping along the narrow lane. The vehicle almost brushed the hedges growing on either side, reducing her vision to the depth of the headlights forward or the taillights backward. She felt like she was in a tunnel, with only a strip of dark, star-strewn sky above. Was she even going the right way? The last sign was miles back.

She had never felt so completely alone.

Maybe she should turn back. There'd been a pub at the crossroads, and the thought had crossed her mind to stop and stay there for the night, but then she'd decided it would be best to just get to her destination. She could wake up tomorrow morning at Ravenswood, ready to begin work.

Now she regretted that she had been so dedicated.

She longed for her neat, familiar office with an actual physical ache. Melanie Jones, twenty-nine, solicitor with the firm of Foyle, Haddock and Williams, had a reputation for getting things done in an orderly fashion.

Everything in its place, no surprises, everything . . . comfortable.

People said that about her. You knew where you were with Melanie Jones. Others, less kind, called her a control freak. Melanie preferred to think that she lived her life just as she wanted it, the rough edges smoothed off, every possible deviation noted and sidelined. Her childhood had been a nightmare of doubts and uncertainties and, when she left home, she had promised herself she would never have to worry about the inconsistencies of life again.

And now here she was, deep in Cornwall, driving a car she loathed because her Ford Escort was being repaired and her boss had insisted she take his car, an Aston Martin. Sensible Melanie, driving a car made famous by James Bond, into the dark depths of Cornwall.

The car crept forward and abruptly the hedges gave way to a grey stone wall on one side and a dense wood on the other. She hit a pothole, and as her headlights tilted, there was a brief view over the wall and across a field, and then the road widened a little, enough to make her feel less claustrophobic.

Maybe it would be all right after all. She'd keep going until she found a signpost, then she'd decide whether to continue or turn back to the pub. Maybe there'd be another pub close by. With luck, the worst was behind her, and Ravenswood was just around the next bend.

Melanie sped up a little in anticipation, just as something big and black ran out in front of her car.

She slammed on the brakes and was jolted violently forward, bruising herself against the seat belt. The car engine stalled and for a moment Melanie sat, stunned, wondering what had run out in front of her and whether she had hit it. She blinked to clear her vision, and peered through the windscreen.

A dog. A hound. Bigger by far than a Great Dane, and coal black. It sat on its haunches in the middle of the lane, facing the car, ears pricked, perfectly still. It was looking right back at her, the gleam of the headlights reflecting in its oily dark eyes.

Melanie couldn't move.

There was something strange about the hound, something frightening. Its size was intimidating, but there was a stillness to it. And the way it stared straight back into her eyes, as if it was aware of her as a person. Melanie became conscious of the utter silence all around them.

Maybe I'm imagining it.

She blinked again, but the hound was still there.

Waiting.

The thought popped into her head. It *did* look as if it was waiting for something. She cast a nervous glance sideways at the woods. The trees were close together, twisted, bending, like old widows gossiping, they formed a wall of blackness. Anything could be in there, watching her, preparing to pounce.

One thing was for certain—she needed to get out of here.

Melanie gave the car horn a long blast. In the eerie silence the sound was very loud, but the black hound didn't even flinch. Her heart thumping, her hands shaking, she sounded it again. Still the thing wouldn't move.

"All right then, if that's the way you want it." She fumbled with the ignition key. The powerful motor started. The black hound didn't take its eyes off her as she began to inch forward toward it. The car moved closer, and the animal still didn't move. The big black head was higher than the hood of the car, high enough that the gleaming eyes were on the same level as her own.

This was worse than before, when at least there had been some distance between her and the hound. Now it loomed over her.

"Good God, what now?"

The car bumper must be almost knocking against the animal's body. She braked with a gasp.

"Will you please go away!"

A whistle came from the woods.

The black hound's head snapped around, and then it was on its feet. With one gigantic leap, it cleared the lane and vanished into the thick wall of trees. And just like that it was gone.

Melanie ran a shaking hand through her short blond hair.

So it must have been a real dog, she told herself with relief. Only a real dog responds to a whistle . . . doesn't it? For a moment there she had been wondering if the hound was something else. Something like Conan Doyle's creation. Hadn't she read somewhere that he'd taken the "Hound of the Baskervilles" from west country folklore? The ghostly, demonic black hound that ran across the moors in the night, seeking . . .

"Seeking what?" Melanie muttered. "London solicitors

traveling in Aston Martins on business to out-of-the-way places? It's probably someone's pet."

With her hands still shaking, she drove forward again, this time picking up speed. There was a sense of relief when the woods tapered off. Less atmospheric wilderness was just fine with her. Soon she was in open meadows, with only a stone wall continuing to keep her company on one side of the lane.

No houses, no lights. And no road signs. She'd have to turn back after all, Melanie told herself. The idea wasn't a comfortable one; it would mean returning to the spot she had just left. Even the thought of a good night's sleep and proper directions wasn't enough to raise any enthusiasm for that.

"Then I'll keep going, there must be something up ahead."

Clearly the caretaker at Ravenswood hadn't been up to the task of giving sound directions. Eddie, was that his name? He'd sounded about a hundred years old on the crackly phone line, as old as Miss Pengorren when she died in the London nursing home and left her personal affairs in the hands of Foyle, Haddock and Williams. Melanie, as their junior representative, was here to unravel those affairs.

Anyone else would have jumped at the chance for a week in Cornwall, but Melanie wasn't looking forward to it at all. Her life was just as she wanted it, and now she was being sent into unknown territory where anything might happen. How could she maintain her timetable? Well, she'd just have to try. And it was a brilliant opportunity to impress. From the day Melanie joined the firm of Foyle, Haddock and Williams, she had planned to make her future there. The traditional, slightly old-fashioned firm and unexciting clientele suited her perfectly. Nothing much happened, each day was similar to the next, no *surprises*—

A flicker of movement at the edge of her vision jolted her from her reverie. She turned to look, the horrible thought flashing through her mind that it was the black hound.

But no. It was a man. A man riding a horse beside her car. He was on the other side of the stone wall, in the field, and all the color had been leached out of him. As if he were drenched in moonlight. Except there was no moon; the night was particularly dark.

Shock made her cold as her eyes took in the details while her brain floundered to make sense of them. The rider was bent low over his horse's neck, and he wore a cloak that flew out behind him like wings, a tricorn hat, and a mask covering half his face. As Melanie stared, he gave her a quick sideways glance and kicked his heels into his horse's sides. It was almost as if he were enjoying himself. As if they were having a race.

The car shuddered, and Melanie swiveled, fixing her eyes unblinkingly on the road ahead. This couldn't be happening. First the black hound like something from a horror movie, and now this.

She glanced sideways at the man, hoping he was gone, and instead found he was almost up level with her car. Something else caught her attention, and she realized it was the black hound. It was loping along behind the man and horse.

The whistle from the woods. It must have been . . . this was its master . . . they were connected, the two of them.

Melanie moaned and did the only thing she could. She put her foot down hard on the accelerator. The motor roared, and she shot forward. Now she couldn't hear anything but the sound of the car, but she had a shaky feeling that there wasn't anything else to hear. No hooves striking the ground, no snap and flap of the rider's cloak, no breathing of man and beast. Nothing. Her companions were completely silent, as if they didn't really exist.

Incredibly, he was edging in front of her.

Panicking, she glanced at him again and realized he was looking right back at her. His eyes through the slits in the mask were brilliant, warm, dangerous, and he grinned as if he were enjoying himself. Melanie found that her own heart was racing, but whether from sheer terror or a strange and unfamiliar excitement she didn't know. Whatever it was, she felt incredibly *alive*.

The road was far too narrow and the surface too rough for her to be driving this fast, but, recklessly, Melanie accelerated again, speeding forward, trying to stay ahead of him.

The rider spurred his horse and, stooping even lower over its neck, prepared to give chase. A few strides, and he was level with her again, and then he was in front. She could see the back of his head beneath the tricorn hat, as well as the ponytail he'd made of his dark hair. Beneath the cloak he was wearing an old-fashioned jacket and breeches. And then, with a final burst of strength and power, he outpaced her. He made it look breathtakingly easy instead of completely impossible.

She thought he'd ride off then, leave her behind. Instead she watched in horrified fascination as he eased up on the reins until he was level with her again. He looked at her, directly into her eyes, and that's when he did it. Winked.

Melanie gasped.

His teeth flashed white. He lifted one gloved hand and blew her an extravagant kiss.

Melanie slammed on the brakes but even as her instincts reacted her brain was telling her they were already gone. The road was empty.

For the second time tonight she sat in silence, heart pounding, hands clenched on the wheel. She tried to see where he had disappeared to, peering into the darkness, but there was nothing. All about her was absolutely nothing.

He must have ridden across the field on the other side, she thought desperately. He must have escaped that way. But she knew he hadn't. One moment he'd been here, beside her, grinning into her eyes like a madman, and the next . . . he'd gone.

Melanie started the car again, and as she did so she saw there was a signpost almost level with the bumper. The paint was fresh and new and easy to read, and it was pointing ahead.

RAVENSWOOD 2 MILES

Two

There was no light. Ravenswood was completely dark and, seemingly, completely empty. The relief Melanie felt on finally reaching her destination turned to anxiety when she realized there was no one to greet her or help her get inside. She fumbled with the heavy keys she'd brought with her from London, wishing she'd also brought a flashlight. The door clicked at last, and she pushed it open in relief, half-surprised it didn't creak in the time-honored manner.

Nothing would have surprised her after all that had happened to her so far.

Everything was still and quiet, and there was a musty smell. Melanie felt along the wall and found a light switch and flipped it. A feeble bulb high above blinked on. She sighed and looked about her. A wide area immediately inside the door gave way to a grand staircase rising to a gallery on the upper floor and beside it a narrow corridor heading into shadows at the back of the house. Doorways were mostly closed, the rooms within secretive and silent. Although Melanie knew Ravenswood hadn't been used in a while—since Miss Pengorren went to the nursing home in London—the furnishings were still in place as was all the bric-a-brac that makes a home. As if the owner had simply stepped out for a moment.

The impression was misleading. Miss Pengorren would never return, and she'd been the last of her family. In her will she'd instructed Mr. Foyle that her house was to be sold, along with the furniture, and the money to go to charity. Everything, her personal items included, would have to be cataloged beforehand.

Organization. That was Melanie's job, and she had been sent by the firm because she was so good at creating order out of chaos. Not the sale itself, that would be handled by one of the partners, but the so-called boring stuff was all Melanie's.

"It will probably take you all week, but you can go back down there after that, if necessary," Mr. Foyle had informed her. "Just call if you have any difficulties. We're relying on you, Melanie."

He'd made it sound as if it was a test, and if she passed it, she would win a prize. A partnership in the firm? Mr. Williams had retired six months ago, and his name was yet to be removed from the letterheads and his place filled. Melanie had hopes, she was the most dedicated underling, and she had been there the longest. Perhaps Miss Pengorren would see her finally reach that pinnacle.

Foyle, Haddock and Jones.

With a smile she set her cases down on the marble floor.

She'd ring Mr. Foyle tomorrow and tell him she was here.

There was a sound. It took her a moment to realize it was the sea. She hadn't known Ravenswood was so close to the coast, although Cornwall was a narrow peninsula, making the sea only a few hours' drive from even the most isolated village. She hadn't been to the beach in years. Before she knew it, her mind had drifted back to childhood.

The warmth of the sand between her toes and her pleasure in building a sand castle, complete with turrets and a drawbridge. She'd worked hard for hours on that castle, carrying water, patting the sand into shape, carving the windows and doorways and heraldic crests with the sharp edge of her little spade.

Solemn, her blond hair tugged back into a neat ponytail, her skinny legs covered with goose bumps from the chill wind, Melanie was already on the path to being the determined overachiever she turned out to be. Suzie, her elder and only sister, was utterly different. Suzie had been there at the beach with her latest boyfriend, and they'd been wrestling and giggling in the way young lovers do. Then, for some reason, Suzie's boyfriend had jumped up, maybe Suzie was teasing him, and backed away from her, not looking where he was going. He stepped right in the middle of Melanie's castle.

Melanie still remembered the anguish, and the fury.

"You've ruined it!" she'd cried, hot tears spilling down her cheeks.

Suzie had made sounds of sympathy, but her eyes had been laughing. She didn't care. No one cared. Melanie's life was in the power of people who simply didn't care. Well, things were different now. Melanie was strong and tough and in complete control of her own destiny, and she meant it to stay that way. This job was important to her, and there was no one to mess it up as Suzie's boyfriend had messed up her sand castle. She would succeed; failure was not an option.

A salty breeze stirred her hair, reminding her she was standing in the empty hall and had left the front door to Ravenswood open at her back.

There was a footstep.

Someone was standing behind her.

Melanie spun around.

A thickset man her own height, smelling of damp wool, stepped back in surprise. "Sorry, love," he said. "I thought you were burglars."

His accent was English west country, pleasantly burred.

"Burglars?" she repeated, exasperated. "I rang to let you know I was coming. I'm Melanie Jones from Foyle, Haddock and Williams, Miss Pengorren's solicitors. We'll be handling the sale of her house. You're the caretaker?"

"That's right. I'm Eddie." In the dim light he looked fortyish, his dark hair turning grey, and carrying a few extra pounds beneath his old woolen sweater. He certainly wasn't the old man he'd sounded on the phone.

They shook hands solemnly.

"You're late," he said mildly. "You said you'd be here this afternoon. I thought you must be staying somewhere else overnight."

"I'm sorry, I got lost, and then . . ." She hesitated. It had been so real and so strange, and she knew from experience how it would sound to a stranger. People tended to scoff at ghosts. But Eddie was waiting, and she had an uncharacteristic compulsion to share at least some of it with him.

"There was a man on a horse, riding beside my car."

Eddie stared at her, and then his mouth widened in a delighted smile. "Oh-ho, then you've seen the Raven! At least, that's what they call him hereabouts."

Her relief was muddled with confusion. "The Raven?"

"Nathaniel Raven."

"As in Ravenswood? Then he's real? He lives in this area?"

Eddie laughed at her, but it was meant kindly. "Nathanial Raven's been dead for years. He's a ghost. You've just seen the Raven's ghost, Miss Jones."

Melanie felt dizzy. She'd known it, of course she had, she hadn't forgotten how it felt to see something supernatural—although she'd tried. And no living man could look and act like that. She'd known it, and yet to hear it said like this aloud, so matter-of-factly, didn't make it better. It made it worse.

"Nathaniel was a highwayman," Eddie continued,

"back in the old days. He was no direct relation to old Miss Pengorren. He used to live here, in this house, long ago, before the Pengorrens took it over."

"Have you seen him?" Melanie glanced about her at the shadows and shivered. "Does he, eh, appear often?"

"No, unfortunately." Eddie shrugged, as if ghosts were commonplace to him. "There have been dozens of stories about him in the village and roundabouts. It's coming up to the anniversary of his death, you see, although I never heard of him appearing before. Maybe something's stirred him up, turned him restless. Could be because of you coming to sell the house."

"Wonderful." Melanie gave a tight little smile. "Well, unfortunately, I have no choice. My job is to get the house ready for sale, and I intend to do it. Now, I think I'll go up to bed so that I can get an early start. Is my room ready, Eddie?"

"Yes, I saw to it myself."

"You're here on your own?"

"I used to have a wife, but she's gone now."

"I'm sorry," thinking he meant she was dead.

"Don't be," he said cheerfully. "We're divorced and she lives in Arizona and she's very happy. Hated this damp place, she did. I stayed, though. I'm related to the Pengorrens, you know. Wrong side of the blanket." He grimaced, but there was a gleam in his eyes, as if he enjoyed his murky family tree.

Eddie led the way up the grand staircase, producing a small flashlight from his pocket. "Had the electricity turned off when the house was empty," he explained. "I had it switched back on again when you said you were coming, but some of the wires are dodgy. Best to have a flashlight or a candle with you, just in case. The hot water is on, but it's been playing up, and you probably won't get any until the morning. The kitchen stove is working—it runs on bottled gas—and there's an electric jug if you wanna cuppa."

"Thank you, but it's okay. I ate earlier. I just want to go to bed. It was a long drive and—"

"There he is." Eddie interrupted her.

He pointed with his flashlight. Melanie blinked, wondering who *he* was and what she was supposed to be looking at. There was a large painting hanging on the wall above the staircase. A portrait of a man. He was standing against a background of sea and sky and cliffs, his head lifted proudly, a slight mocking smile twisting his aristocratic lips.

Melanie peered more closely. He wasn't wearing a cloak or a mask, but there was something in that smile that she recognized. A reckless enjoyment of life. A devil-may-care attitude.

Another shiver ran through her.

"The Raven, I presume," she murmured.

"The painting was up in the attic for ages, but Miss Pengorren had it brought down. She went a bit strange in her last year here, kept saying she shouldn't have the house, that it was all wrong, and Nathaniel Raven had more right to hang on the wall than any Pengorren."

"I think I'd prefer him back in the attic."

Eddie sniggered. "You don't want to antagonize him like that. He was a bit of a bad lot. You never know what he might do." And with that partly humorous threat, he led the way up the remainder of the stairs.

Melanie's room was old and had seen better days, but it was clean, and the four-poster bed, when she tried it, was comfortable. Eddie busied himself making a fire in the hearth while Melanie went to the window and peered out. The panes were small and warped, the glass very old, and there were shutters that could be closed in bad weather. She could see an area of flat and treeless land, and beyond that the sea.

It looked restful tonight, flat and smooth, with barely a hint of froth on the waves. From somewhere in her memory she dredged up pictures of wild storms and foundering ships and innocent souls cast onto the rocks. Wreckers had once set out false lights, to steer their prey onto reefs. Smugglers had been here, too, probably. This was Daphne du Maurier country, and anything was possible.

"There you are."

Startled, Melanie turned. Eddie was wiping his hands on his sweater. Briefly, she felt disoriented, unlike her practical herself, but it was only for a moment. Annoyed, she forced her romantic thoughts back where they belonged, locked away, kept in check. She'd decided long ago that there was no place in her life for romance and adventure. Melanie had no intention of giving herself as a hostage to fate, a whimsical leaf on a breeze to be blown one way and then another.

Eddie was giving her a strange look. "Are you sure you'll be all right here all by yourself?"

"Of course," Melanie replied in her briskest voice. "I'm not the nervous type. I'm here to do a job and I plan to do it."

Eddie didn't say anything to that, only pointing out that he'd left her the flashlight, in case, and wishing her good night as he closed the door after him.

Melanie went to the fire and warmed her hands, listening to the stairs creaking as Eddie made his descent. The front door closed with an echoing bang. Melanie was alone in Ravenswood.

The haunt of the Raven.

And she knew she wasn't going to sleep a wink.

Nathaniel Raven stood and looked up at the lighted window. Absently, he rubbed the head of the black hound, scratching his ears. The animal pressed against him, clearly enjoying the attention. He wasn't sure whether Teth had found him or he had found Teth, but somehow they had come together in the between-worlds and now the black hound was his constant companion.

A shadow passed before the window.

The woman, Melanie Jones.

After he had raced her on the road, he had watched her from the shelter of the trees as she cautiously made her way up the driveway to Ravenswood, and then unlocked the door. Fair hair cut short, the trousers and jacket loose but not quite disguising a slim, female shape. Her eyes were blue and slanted a little, and her mouth was full but unsmiling, unyielding.

Nathaniel had always preferred to find humor in a

situation and to run where fate took him; his paramours had certainly gone with him willingly—and smiling.

Was this really the woman who would help him? Give him his second chance? She looked like she didn't laugh much, as if life for her was full of serious matters and predestined appointments. But for a moment when their eyes had met, he had thought . . .

The light in the window went out.

Nathaniel sighed. He didn't really have a choice. He needed her, and somehow he had to persuade her that she needed him. Well, persuading women was one of his most developed talents.

Three

She was riding. On a horse. Melanie was ambivalent when it came to horses but this time she didn't mind, because someone was riding with her. She could feel a strong arm about her waist, a body behind hers, and it was most definitely a "he." They rode through the night, the moon above them like a grapefruit.

His breath brushed her hair, her cheek, as he leaned forward. His gloved hands were strong on the reins. In control.

Melanie found that a turn-on.

"Do you know who I am?" a soft voice murmured in her ear.

Her heart began to bump.

"Because I know who you are."

Melanie turned her head. He was smiling at her, eyes gleaming through the mask. An old-fashioned tricorn hat sat on his head, and a black cloak flowed out behind him.

"You're the Raven," she said.

He leaned closer, and heat curled inside her like melt-ing toffee. His mouth brushed hers, barely a touch at all, but she felt it to her toes.

"Oh yes, please . . ."

Did she really say that? Well, it was a dream . . .

There was a thud.

The horse vanished and, with it, the man. Melanie opened her eyes and found she was alone in the four-poster bed at Ravenswood. She must have flung out her arm—to embrace the Raven—and knocked her cell phone to the floor.

Melanie rubbed her eyes and sighed. She could still feel him, she could even taste him, and she had really, really wanted that kiss.

The old house seemed less *Rebecca*-ish in the daylight. Melanie washed hastily in tepid water, dressed casually in baggy old jeans that hung from her slim hips and the *I fought a bull and won* sweatshirt Suzie had brought her back from her holiday in Spain last year. It had shrunk last time she washed it, so the fit was a bit snug, but it was comfortable. Melanie went downstairs to see what she could find to eat.

Eddie had left a loaf of bread and a carton of juice on the table in the kitchen, which was a huge room with a high ceiling and dusty shelves. Melanie imag-ined that it must once have been full of the servants who were needed to put food on the family's table, but now there was something poignant about the empty space. Like the shell of the great *Titanic,* lying forlorn at the bottom of the ocean.

She toasted a slice of bread in an antique-looking toaster, spread it with some delicious marmalade she found in the equally antique-looking refrigerator, and drank some cold juice and hot instant coffee.

There was a door in the kitchen leading out onto the side of the house and an old walled garden. The stonework was crumbling in places, and the neat rectangles where flowers and herbs once grew were overrun with weeds, but Melanie found herself surveying the spot with dreamy eyes, imagining a tangle of sweetpea and honeysuckle and the buzz of bees.

There's going to be a storm, and the old oak tree in the park is going to fall over.

The words rang in her head like a wake-up bell.

It was a long time since something like that had happened to her—daydreaming was bad enough, but premonitions? She thought she'd outgrown them. Her lapse irritated her, but more than that, it frightened her.

Pushing it from her mind, Melanie finished her coffee and washed up her few dishes, set them to dry in the plastic drainer, and began to explore the house. There were plenty of rooms, some with dust sheets thrown over the furnishings, others left as they must always have been. Everything would need to be cataloged and valued before sale. It might be simpler to contact a reputable antiques' dealer or an auction house. Get it done professionally. Melanie did not pretend she was an expert or even a well-read amateur.

There must be someone suitable in Plymouth, or Truro, or one of the tourist traps like St. Ives or Mousehole?

"Phone book," she murmured, glancing about the room she was in. It was on the upper floor and in a large room, with mullioned windows from which she could see the park, and a high grey stone wall dividing what had once been gardens from the open fields to the east. Fields, that is, apart from an odd conical hill, rather like a small Glastonbury Tor, which rose dark against the morning sky, with a standing stone perched on top.

Melanie was drawn to the windows and stood, peering at the hill, aware of a disturbing tingle beginning deep inside her. As if something were trying to get out. A memory? Perhaps she had seen a picture of this place before. Or was it more a sense of unease?

Stay away.

She shook her head, again refusing to listen, but her eyes remained fastened on the silhouette against the grey April sky. The stone was sitting on the very top of the hill, and there seemed to be a hole in the middle of it, an eye, so that it was almost as if it were looking back at her.

Her sister Suzie had been through a phase where she'd believed all that New Age stuff about the magic of ancient stones and megalithic sites. She'd traipsed all over the countryside, taking part in half-baked rituals and dancing in flimsy robes in the freezing dawn of the midwinter solstice. Melanie had shaken her head at her sister's antics, and then gone back to studying, to getting her degree, to making something of herself.

But now, looking at the hill, she suddenly understood a little of the fascination and awe Suzie must have felt. The tor was so completely alien to the surrounding landscape that she could not help but wonder who had made it and why. What rites had taken place there? What creatures had been summoned?

Had the earth opened like a ripe plum and its contents spilled out?

With a shudder Melanie turned away. "Phone book," she said loudly, returning her thoughts firmly to the task at hand. "I need to look up some names and make some inquiries. Get the ball rolling."

Surely there would be lots of interest in Ravenswood when the locals knew it was on the market? Historic landmarks like this didn't come up for sale every day.

But when she finally found a phone book, she glanced at her watch and realized to her dismay that it was still only 7:00 A.M. Far too early to ring anyone up yet.

With a sigh, she headed over to the large desk she had noticed by the wall and opened some drawers, picking up papers and reading them at random. At least she had found Miss Pengorren's "office." There were bills here, some of them second and third requests, and unanswered letters from friends. The elderly lady had let things slide before she made her final journey to the nursing home.

Ignoring the stuffing spilling from one corner, Melanie sat down in the comfortable old leather swivel chair and prepared to discover the worst.

Miss Pengorren's handwriting was wavery and sometimes difficult to read, but her forceful personality came through in her choice of words. *"Get Eddie to see to the taps in the bathroom. No excuses."* The note to herself made Melanie smile, it was like something she herself would write. *"Why hasn't the loose board in the attic* been attended to? And no, I'm not too old to be up there, thank you, Eddie!" Miss Pengorren's requests seemed small enough but they were the symptoms of a house in decay. It must have been frustrating for her, particularly as Eddie didn't seem in any hurry to carry out her orders.

Melanie looked up and noticed a row of leather-bound diaries stacked neatly on a shelf. She slipped one out and opened it. The date was ten years ago, and it seemed to be a brisk and informative record of daily life at Ravenswood. She put it back and found the most recent one. Miss Pengorren's busy writing filled the pages. Pleased, Melanie spent a moment reading some of the pithy comments Miss Pengorren made about her neighbors, and her concerns about a world that seemed to be changing too quickly for her to keep up with it. *I have outlived my usefulness,* she had stated bleakly.

Flipping to the end of the diary, Melanie saw that the handwriting deteriorated along with Miss Pengorren's health. She rambled, sometimes beyond understanding. There was talk about the house not being hers. *"A monstrous injustice,"* Melanie read aloud. *"I wish I could restore Ravenswood to its rightful owner."*

That was the final entry.

With a sense of unease, Melanie closed the book and put it back where it belonged. Was this some legal matter she should look into? Or was it just the restless maunderings of an old lady whose mind was beginning to deteriorate? She would have to read all the diaries, she supposed, and if necessary ask the advice of Mr. Foyle. And there were the upper rooms and the attic to explore, as well as the old stables and outbuildings.

The extent of her task weighed heavily on her for a moment, but she shrugged it off. One thing at a time, that was the trick. Organization. Lists! Melanie was a great one for making lists whenever possible.

But instead of reaching for a pen and paper, Melanie pushed the chair back and stood up. She felt edgy and anxious. Her gaze slid to the window, to the mini-tor, but she refused to be drawn back to stare at it.

And then she remembered.

At home in London she went running every morning. She was missing her routine run. She'd feel better once she'd stretched a few muscles and whipped up a few endorphins.

Outside on the looped driveway the air was fresh and clean, and she gulped it in with pleasure. Last night she hadn't been able to see much, but now she turned in a circle, looking about her. Ravenswood had been built in the fifteenth century, and although it wasn't one of the larger stately houses—only nineteen rooms—it was imposing enough. The grey granite had been softened by time and climbing plants, and the mullioned windows on the upper floor reflected the light. It was clearly in need of maintenance—the tiled roof was sagging in places, and there was a worrying hint of damp in some of the rooms, but surely a true lover of historic houses would overlook that?

Melanie turned around again. There were the remains of an extensive garden in front of the house, the shrubs long overgrown, the flower beds choked with weeds. Big old trees blocked any view toward the road she had traveled down last night, and what had once been tree-studded parkland was now densely cluttered with saplings and suckers.

There's going to be a storm and—

Melanie immediately blocked the image of the fallen tree, the broken branches, the smell of burning in the air, before it could take hold.

She'd had practice enough.

Instead, she told herself that although the park might look uncared for, even neglected, the land was probably worth a great deal. Melanie was surprised it hadn't been sold off ages ago for holiday vans or cottages. A place like this must eat up the money. She'd have to ask Eddie about that.

Eddie from the wrong side of the Pengorren blanket.

Melanie grimaced. Did people really say that anymore? And why did Miss Pengorren feel she had no right to the house; why had she returned Nathaniel Raven's portrait to its place above the stairs?

The Raven.

Thoughtfully, Melanie began her warm-up stretches.

She had taken another look at the portrait of Nathaniel on her way downstairs. She hadn't meant to, but something had insisted she turn and gaze into that smiling, dangerous face. Perhaps it was the lingering effects of her experience of last night or her dream from this morning.

Nathaniel Raven's eyes were hazel, and they stared back at her with more than a hint of teasing laughter. He was a flirt, a ladies man, a heartbreaker, and not to be trusted. The sort of man cautious Melanie automatically avoided.

Her gaze had slid to his hand. He wore a broad signet ring, made of silver, and probably complete with the family crest, whatever that was. He was pointing with his forefinger, and she could just see the misty, vague representation of Ravenswood to one side. He looked very much like one of the local gentry, born and bred into the English upper classes, secure in his position within the society of the times.

Why had he turned feral?

Melanie finished her stretches. "It's none of my business," she murmured, and set off purposefully along the track that ran through the overgrown garden, toward a gate set in the high stone wall. When she unlatched it and peered through, she saw that another, far-less-defined path, led across the fields toward the steep rise of the tor.

The sense of unease returned, but Melanie refused to allow her imagination to rule her. *I control my body, it does not control me; I control my mind so that it works for me, not against me.* That had been her motto forever. Besides, it would test her fitness to reach the top. With her usual determination, Melanie latched the gate behind her and set off at a run.

There must be a right-of-way across the fields; at least there were no fences to keep her out and no crops to trample. The ground was covered in springy grass, and the wind whipped her short fair hair about her face. She quickened her pace as she neared the hill, enjoying the stretch of her body, knowing she was fit and strong and up to the challenge.

Melanie believed she was up to any challenge. Her current goals were to upgrade her apartment, upgrade her job, and invest her next raise in the more secure end of the stock market. The thought of losing everything, as her parents had done, terrified her so much that she used to wake up at night, damp with sweat. Now it only happened if she'd been visiting Suzie, and nowadays she and her sister were too busy with their own lives for more than the occasional phone call. There were times when Melanie felt guilty about that, but her relief usually outweighed her guilt. Suzie lived in a state of perpetual chaos that she called "being at one with the universe," and Melanie wanted no part of it. The most disturbing thing was, Suzie appeared to be happy with her life.

As Melanie ran, she began to make a mental checklist of all the things she had to do before she could leave Cornwall and go home to London. And what about Eddie, who paid him? Then there was the house itself. She was glad it wasn't her job to sell it. Maybe it could be transformed into a nursing home, or a hotel, or one of those places where rich people came to cleanse the poisons from their systems—in other words, a celebrity drug-rehabilitation clinic. No one these days would have the money or the inclination to take it on as a private residence, surely?

Still, the admission came grudgingly, as if deep down she was finding it hard to accept the inevitable. Ravenswood must have been beautiful, once.

There was a sound behind her. Panting, like a dog.

Melanie gave a quick glance over her shoulder . . .

And stumbled, letting out a gasping shriek.

The black hound was behind her, and it was broad daylight. Even as shock zinged through her, Melanie's analytical mind was telling her that "black" wasn't quite the right word because the hound was a darkish grey. As grey as Nathaniel Raven had been last night. Ghostly grey.

"Oh God!"

She picked up speed, forgetting the ache in her legs, but so did the hound. Its ears were flopping, large paws pounding the soft grassy ground, tongue flapping from loosened jaws. If it wasn't a ghost, she would have laughed to see it having such a wonderful time. Instead, Melanie ran even faster, her breathing short and choppy, her heart pounding. Then she realized what she should have known a moment ago, that she was climbing, the slight incline growing increasingly difficult as she headed toward the top of the tor. Behind her—she dared another look—Ravenswood was getting smaller, and she knew the sensible option would be to turn around and go back for help. But there was nothing sensible about what was following her.

Chasing her.

Gasping, her feet like lead weights, she struggled to the top.

The old standing stone was both broad and tall, and lichen was growing rampant on it. There was a large hole punched through the middle. Melanie, thinking she might be able to climb up on the very top of the stone, to escape the reach of the hound, forced her flagging body across the flat summit of the hill.

The hound was still loping along, following her at a steady pace. It didn't seem interested in attacking her or overtaking her, but how could she be sure . . . Melanie scanned the bare hillside. And how did she know the Raven wasn't around here somewhere on his ghostly horse, just waiting to spring out at her?

She had almost reached the stone, her chest on fire, her legs burning, when she realized she would never climb it. Behind her came panting breath, the thump of paws, but as she turned with a whimper finally to face her foe, the hound ran right by her and sprang gracefully through the hole in the middle of the old stone.

And vanished.

Melanie stood, chest heaving, staring openmouthed at . . . thin air.

She took a step back, looking one way and then the other. Nothing but open ground. On the western side of the tor there were views of Ravenswood and its extensive estate, and if she turned to the east, a cluster of houses down in the valley and the spire of the village church. To the north the sea was a flat sheet of steel beyond the edge of the cliffs, and to the south the stone . . . It seemed to mock her. But one thing was for certain, the hound really had vanished, and Melanie was alone.

Gradually, her heartbeat began to slow, the burning ache in her chest to fade, and her mind to clear. She rested her hand against the stone. The rough surface had captured what warmth there was in the day and she felt it now against her skin. She peered through the hole in the middle.

It wasn't a recent act of vandalism; that hole had been there for a long time. The edges were worn smooth, and when she looked more closely at the surface she could see carvings beneath the lichen. Celtic carvings. Symbols, a language, that only a few scholars could understand.

Melanie was now more curious than frightened. The hound hadn't hurt her, and it had jumped right through the middle of the stone.

In fact the hole was large enough to crawl through, but she wasn't quite brave enough for that, not just yet. Instead, she stuck her hand through, wriggling her fingers, a gesture of bravado, really.

Come and get me.

Something grabbed her, and Melanie shrieked. Another hand, so strong and cold. It closed on her flesh with a fierce determination. The hand tugged violently, catching her off-balance, and she fell forward, clutching at the stone for support, her hands slipping through. Her feet went up, her hip bruised on the inner circle, and then she was falling.

Tumbling through the middle.

There was no time to scream again. Before her the top of the hill had opened up, and there was darkness, going down deep into the earth. Like a great black mouth.

And Melanie was swallowed whole.

Four

It was beyond her comprehension, beyond belief, beyond horror. Above her the light faded, and she cried out, her nose full of the smell of damp soil and rotting vegetation. She was tumbling over and over through a long dark shaft, with nothing to stop her, nothing to hold on to.

And then she landed in a heap at the bottom, her head ringing, her stomach heaving.

It was all wrong!

She was inside the hill. It had opened up and taken her inside, and that was just plain impossible. It was a dream, that was it. She'd open her eyes, and it would be a dream.

But when she peered through her eyelashes Melanie found she was lying in a narrow tunnel that seemed to have no beginning and no end, while above her was only darkness.

Before the shock could ease, and she could begin screaming, *this isn't true,* a soft voice spoke.

"Welcome to the between-worlds, Melanie Jones."

Melanie promptly closed her eyes again, tightly.

"Are you hurt?" the voice added, closer now.

Melanie opened her eyes. All around her there was light, brilliant light of an indescribable color, and it was forcing back the darkness, and within it she could see a figure bending over her. The figure had long auburn hair that hung down in a curtain about her sweet young face.

"I can't be awake."

The sweet young face had blue eyes, neon blue, but as she gazed into them, mesmerized, Melanie realized they weren't young eyes at all but old. Ancient. They were like no eyes she had ever seen.

She shuddered and looked away, saying shakily, "The *between-worlds*? That's not right, there's only one world."

The young woman laughed, but the sound didn't make Melanie want to join in; instead, the hairs on the back of her neck stood straight up. She gave a sideways glance and realized that the figure was wearing a scarlet cloak, and beneath that a gossamer gown of iridescent silver rippled like liquid mercury as she moved. And her feet . . . weren't feet at all. They were talons.

Melanie stared, openmouthed.

"St. Anne's Hill is a door, and you have come through it. The door leads from your mortal world to the between-worlds, the realm that exists between life and death, and I am its ruler."

"Like a queen, do you mean?"

"That's right," the creature with talons said, with a little smile. "You can call me Your Majesty."

Your Majesty? Queen of the between-worlds? Melanie decided that was more information than she could process. She put her hands down on the ground— it was cold and damp—and pushed herself into a sitting position. Water was dripping, but thankfully not on her. The between-worlds? The realm between life and death? There must be another explanation, a more rational explanation . . .

With a start she realized that the brilliant light was receding. Anxiously she looked around for the queen.

"Where are you?"

"This way, mortal . . ."

The voice was behind her, moving away with the light.

Frantically, Melanie scrambled to her feet. "Don't leave me here!" she shouted, and promptly knocked her head on the ceiling of the tunnel. "Ouch!" She felt woozy, but now the light was getting very faint, and soon she'd be all on her own.

"Hurry, mortal." That melodious voice drifted back toward her.

"I want to go home," she answered, even as she was moving after the queen.

"It's too late for that, Melanie Jones."

Melanie stumbled along the tunnel, trying to remember to keep her head down. Something scuttled in the shadows, like claws on a blackboard, and she made a little whimpering noise. The light drew closer and then, just as she was beginning to think she'd catch up, slipped out of her reach again. It was as if the queen didn't want her getting too close.

"Where are we going?" Melanie's voice echoed around her, and set off more of the horrible scuttling. She quickened her pace.

". . . you'll see . . ."

"I don't want to see," she grumbled, "I want to *know*."

She walked on. She wanted to catch up so that she could argue and complain, scream and shout, and demand a proper answer. Instead, she was completely at the queen's mercy.

Of course she could turn back, but . . . A glance behind her showed pure darkness, the sense of things she couldn't see but were there, watching her. No, there was only one option, and that was to follow and see where the queen led her. And then, when the opportunity allowed, escape.

At least, she told herself, feeling light-headed, she'd have something to tell Suzie next time they spoke. Suzie seemed to think her sister's life was as dull as dishwater, every day the same. Well, her eyes would pop when Melanie told her about St. Anne's Hill, and the stone with the hole in the middle, and the between-worlds, the place that lay between life and death, and the queen with talons for feet . . .

"I must be crazy." It was the only explanation. "Or . . . dead?"

Maybe she'd had a stroke and now she was dead and this between-worlds place was really just another name for hell.

"Melanie Jones!"

Melanie blinked. Up ahead the light was different, the

color diluted, as though it were bleached, and . . . There was an opening! A door to the outside world! And—she took a deep breath—she could smell the sea.

Stumbling, gasping, Melanie ran toward it.

The queen must have exited this way because she was no longer anywhere in sight. Melanie burst through an arched doorway and out into the trees that lay between Ravenswood and the road.

She halted, confused.

It was nighttime. A huge moon hung in a cold sky. Melanie's breath came from her lips in puffs of white, and there was an icy stillness to the air that told her it wasn't late April anymore. This felt more like mid-winter.

She turned, wondering if she should wait here by the entrance to the tunnel . . . but the tunnel was gone. Instead there was a small summerhouse, the interior dark and empty, and some prickly bushes. She walked around, but there was no sign of the queen with the long red hair.

A chill breeze swirled about her, and Melanie folded her arms as she tried to orient herself. She was very near the beginning of the gardens. Lights blinked through the trees, and there were voices, the rise and fall of many voices, and suddenly, music. Not modern stuff but orchestral music, pleasant but certainly not highly professional. The violin scraped slightly off the note, but she recognized the old, familiar Christmas carol: "God Rest Ye Merry Gentlemen."

Melanie left the trees behind her and walked toward the house on grass that was no longer wild and unkempt. In front of her Ravenswood shone, but as she drew closer she realized the lights weren't quite right. They were strangely muted, more like natural flame than electricity. Candles in colored glass lanterns hung throughout the garden, which was no longer a wilderness but a wonderland of trimmed hedges and shrubs and bare winter roses. There were walkways sprinkled with gravel, the edges ruler straight. Couples in costume were strolling, huddled in cloaks because of the cold but obviously enjoying themselves. *It must be a fancy-dress ball,* Melanie told herself. The same orchestra she had heard before struck up again, but this time it was something more lively. Looking up, Melanie could see into the big upper room where she been standing such a short time ago, looking out at St. Anne's Hill. Now they were dancing up there—women in long gowns, with their hair up, and men in formal jackets with starched white neckcloths.

For a moment she simply stood and stared. It was beautiful, and it looked just like a movie set, a costume drama, or one of those reality shows where members of the public were placed in a period situation and told to act like their ancestors.

Suddenly a young girl in a long pale dress ran past her, her slippers tapping on the path, her fair ringlets bouncing. A boy was chasing her, and they were laughing. Neither of them glanced at Melanie, neither of them noticed her although she was standing in plain sight in her old jeans and sweatshirt and trainers.

Maybe they were just ignoring her, but Melanie didn't think so. She had a nasty feeling it was because she wasn't really here at all—not in the proper physical sense, anyway.

To test it she stepped forward just as another couple wandered by arm in arm, their cheeks rosy from the cold.

"Excuse me? Hello there!"

But they didn't look either. They couldn't hear her. They couldn't see her. Neither of them glanced her way, not even for a moment. She was invisible, and it was terrifying. What was she supposed to do? What was her reason for being here? The queen of the between-worlds hadn't handed her a book of instructions.

She found herself drifting closer to the house, drawn by the light and the noise. Besides, she was freezing, and the front door was open, beckoning her.

Inside Ravenswood it was surprisingly warm, although nothing like she remembered it. The marble floor was buffed, and the wood paneling and furnishings shone as if they were polished lovingly every day. Candles were everywhere, while great bunches of flowers stood in huge vases, their perfume stiflingly sweet. A door banged, and suddenly she was surrounded by a river of servants carrying covered platters. They surged by her, and for a moment the smell of food was overpowering.

"Did ye see him?" one of the young girls was saying in a loud whisper, her hair the color of curly cheddar. "How can a man be so pretty! I don' blame the mistress for wantin' him. I wouldn' say no m'self."

"From what we've 'eard, you've already said yes more 'an once!"

More giggling, a flurry of activity, and in another moment the servants were gone, and she was alone again.

Curious, Melanie peered into some of the downstairs rooms, but apart from a foursome playing some sort of card game and the supper table being laid, there wasn't much to see.

She turned to the stairs, resting her hand on the newel post, and looked up.

And froze.

There was a man up there on the landing, a dark shape against a branch of candles. He stood so still and silent, so watchful. As if, like her, he didn't belong. Melanie's heart began to speed up.

He can't see you, she reminded herself. *Don't be stupid, he can't see you.*

The man began to descend the stairs, slowly, his hand trailing on the banister as if he had all the time in the world. Her gaze was caught by a silvery gleam on his finger, a broad ring with some sort of heraldic design on it.

She recognized it. Recognized him.

Nathaniel Raven.

The many candles flared in the draft from the door, distorting his face, and then settling again. Strong jaw and high cheekbones, long, thin nose, his brown hair with its gold overtones tied back at his nape, his hazel eyes looking down at her.

Looking at her.

Melanie turned her head, hoping that she'd see whoever it was he was really looking at, but there was no one. Just the door standing ajar, and beyond that the winter garden dotted with colorful lanterns.

Reluctantly she turned back. He had halted only a couple of steps above her, and she could no longer pretend he couldn't see her. He was looking straight at her.

How can a man be so pretty?

Had the servant girl been talking about Nathaniel Raven? Melanie didn't think he was pretty at all, but he was handsome, oh yes, and there was something dangerous in his eyes. An attractive recklessness in his smile. She had known as soon as she saw the portrait that this man could break hearts, that he was exactly the type she should avoid. She just hadn't realized he'd ever be a problem for her, being dead and all . . .

He came down the final steps, his eyes still on hers, and she backed away to make room for him. Afraid that if he actually *touched* her, she might go up in flames.

"Welcome, Melanie Jones." There was a possessive note in his voice and a flare of excitement in his eyes. "Welcome to Ravenswood."

Five

She was afraid of him. She was trying to hide it, but it was easy enough to recognize. The fine sheen on her skin, the darkening of her eyes, the quickened breathing. It was either fear or lust, and although he'd like to believe she desired him that much on first sight, Nathaniel was more inclined toward fear.

He didn't want her to be afraid of him. He needed to win her confidence and her trust. It wasn't something he'd ever had to worry about before, but then he'd never been in this situation before, either.

If he hadn't needed her so desperately, he'd have shrugged his shoulders and walked away. But he *did* need her. She had to agree to help him, that was the first command the queen had given him, after she woke him and explained what needed to be done.

"When the mortal woman comes to you, you must gain her trust. She must agree to help you. Use your charm and powers of persuasion, but only after she agrees can you proceed on to the next step."

"Simple," he said and smiled. "Women find me irresistible, Your Majesty."

"Perhaps this time it won't be as simple as you believe."

He only laughed, expecting to sail safely through any storms the queen might whip up in front of him.

"Show her your enemy . . . what he's capable of. Let her see, but you must not interfere with the past. If you try and change the outcome of what has already happened, I will return you to the between-worlds. Do you understand me, my Raven?"

He made an impatient gesture. "I understand what you're saying but I don't know why it must be so. Let me at him now, Your Majesty. Let me—"

"No! That would do more damage than good. First you must understand what it is you are facing, and to understand you must have the help of the mortal woman. Gain her support. You will need her."

While he was distracted, Melanie had stepped farther away, clearly uncomfortable with being this close to him. Nathaniel reminded himself that despite her ugly clothing—strange coarse trousers and a tight overshirt with odd words on it and shoes like half loaves—she was probably the future equivalent of a gentlewoman. He must treat her with respect and care.

With deliberate patience, Nathaniel held out his hand.

Melanie glared at his fingers as if they were snakes.

"Come, I want to show you something, Miss Jones."

"Show me what? And back off."

Well, not a gentlewoman, perhaps, after all. He eyed

her doubtfully, wondering again how to proceed. With her short fair hair and slanting blue eyes she looked half-elf. The thought amused him, and he covered his mouth to hide the smile, then pretended to smooth his expertly arranged neckcloth.

"Show me what?" she repeated impatiently.

"I want you to see my family. I want you to see what my enemy has done to them."

"I don't—"

"Understand? No, but you will. I need your help."

"You need my help?" she repeated slowly, her eyes slanting even more as she looked up at him.

"You've come all this way, Miss Jones," he said engagingly. "You may as well look. You can't go home until you do."

That caught her attention. "I can go home afterward?" she asked him carefully.

"Of course."

He could see her wavering. He cast her clothing another glance, puzzling over the writing emblazed across her bosom: *I fought a bull and won.* She would look rather beautiful in the fashions of the day, the flimsy dresses designed to uncover more than they covered. She had the same appealing gamine qualities as Lady Caroline Lamb, but without the histrionics, and without Byron.

She'd caught him staring at her shoes.

"I suppose jogging isn't big in this century," she said, giving him one of her direct looks. Then, with a shrug, she took hold of his hand. Her fingers felt cold, and they trembled in his until she stilled them, giving him another glare, as if daring him to mention her momentary weakness.

He smiled. She wasn't as tough as she pretended.

"What?" she demanded, and attempted to snatch her fingers back.

He held on. "I don't think you understand what is happening to us. We don't have a choice in the matter, Miss Jones."

"It's Melanie. And who says I don't have a choice?" she added sharply.

And she was a shrew. Nathaniel gave an inner sigh. She probably believed women should vote. Maybe she was even a man-hater, an adherent of Sappho, the poet from the Isle of Lesbos? How could he win over such a woman?

"What?" She met his look.

But he shook his head. There was nothing for it. He'd just have to go ahead and try his best.

"This is Christmas Eve in the year 1813, and at Ravenswood we are celebrating our traditional Yuletide Ball," said Nathaniel. "The British army have been fighting the Peninsular War for five years, trying to preserve Portugal's independence against the invading French forces, who have already overtaken Spain. We are worried that, if France invades and subjugates Portugal, then it is only a short step across the Channel to our own shores. So we fight.

"Last year, things looked grim. Napoleon Bonaparte controlled a large swath of Europe—Italy, Germany, Spain among them. But he was greedy, he wanted more, he wanted Russia. The Russian weather defeated him, his troops dropping dead on the long retreat back to Paris. Consequently he has been weakened, over-stretched. This year things are looking brighter. Wellington has the French on the run. Just last month he crossed the frontier into France. We believe that very soon Napoleon will be captured, and the war will finally be over. It is time for us to celebrate."

"Christmas Eve, 1813," she said, with an edge of hysteria. "Right."

"At Ravenswood the Yuletide Ball is a long-held tradition. This year the son of the house"—he gave her a little introductory bow—"is back from the war, alive, although recovering from injuries. But with the good news comes the bad. Mr. Raven Senior fell from his horse in the park not long since, and died of a broken neck, plunging the household into mourning. Despite that, it was decided to go forward with the Yuletide Ball."

Melanie cocked her head, and he could see her listening to the laughter and music upstairs, thinking that Ravenswood didn't sound much like a house in mourning.

"Major Pengorren is here, too. He was my commanding officer in the army, and has been a pillar of strength in my family's time of need."

"Pengorren? As in Miss Pengorren? Then—"

She didn't finish because Sophie, in a pale blue dress, her dark hair elaborately styled on top of her head, came out of the ballroom and down the stairs. Nathaniel found himself looking at his sister through a stranger's eyes, seeing how young she still was although she'd deliberately dressed to appear older. The neckline of the high-waisted dress showed off a surprising amount of bosom, and he wondered how his mother could allow it. But, then, his mother was occupied elsewhere these days.

"Nathaniel," Sophie said, and smiled her sweet smile.

He felt a painful stab in his heart, seeing her like this after so long. Although she could not know he had been dead for nearly two hundred years, that he had only returned for the purpose of showing an invisible stranger his family, he felt the moment weigh heavily upon him.

"Sophie, my dear sister." He set aside his confused feelings, gathered up his wits. "You're blooming tonight, a rose in the dead of winter."

She giggled, pleased with the compliment, and all of a sudden she was his little sister again, following him about with her constant chatter and gazing up at him adoringly.

"You look very handsome yourself, sir," she teased, and stretched up to kiss his cheek. "Although Mama will say you smell of the stable. Why haven't you changed into your evening wear, brother? Or at least your uniform. A man looks very dashing in a uniform." He wanted to capture her, hold her, warn her . . . But he wasn't allowed to, and she was already moving away, her eyes shining.

"Speaking of uniforms, the major has promised me a dance, which makes me very special for, as you know, he never dances. Oh, and Sir Arthur Tregilly has drunk too much claret and is ogling the ladies' ankles, and Miss Trewin is asking where you've got to for the fourth, no, the *fifth* time."

"I can't help breaking hearts."

Sophie giggled again, but perhaps not quite so innocently as before. "I know you can't, Nathaniel."

He hesitated. He was breaking the queen's rules, but he couldn't help it. He had to speak. "Is everything all right with you, Soph? You would tell me, if it wasn't? I'm always here."

Except he wasn't, not when she needed him.

Sophie looked at him strangely, and then she shook her head. "Silly," she said, and continued on her way, probably to pass some message from his mother on to the cook.

Well, so much for brotherly concern. Nothing was going as planned.

Melanie had pressed herself back against the wall so as not to touch Sophie, and was looking dazed. He took her hand in his again, and this time she didn't argue.

"Come on," he said with quiet desperation, "let's get this over with, and then you can go home."

Six

They were standing outside the room where the guests were dancing. Melanie had always imagined dancing in the nineteenth century to be elegant and restrained, but there was little restraint here. Couples galloped around the room whooping and laughing, and the air was strong with the smells of alcohol, scent, and sweat.

It brought home to her that these were real people, not cardboard cutouts in a television drama.

A short while ago she had stood in this room, staring out of the windows at St. Anne's Hill, and there had been nothing but empty, dusty silence. Now the windows were framed by bunches of green ivy and mistletoe with white berries, and dozens of candles were reflected in the glass. She wanted to cover her eyes with her hands and hide, like a child.

The guests could see Nathaniel, just as his sister had seen him, and he bowed his way elegantly through the crowd gathered around the space that had been cleared for the dancers. Melanie eyed him curiously, taking in his dark blue jacket, white waistcoat, and tight beige trousers. Several women, who—in Melanie's opinion—should have known better, giggled and fluttered their lashes, saying things like, "Oh, Mr. Raven, you are looking much better, I was so sorry to hear of your injuries," and, "Oh, Mr. Raven, I hope you will call upon us soon, I do so want to hear all about your adventures in Spain," and, "Oh, Mr. Raven, Major Pengorren has been telling us how brave you were."

"Mr. Raven, Mr. Raven, Mr. Raven," Melanie muttered, as she trailed in his wake, growing increasingly irritated. No one looked at her; no one saw her. She was like a shadow. She didn't realize she was dragging her feet until a sharp tug on her hand brought her up hard against his back.

"Oomph!" her breath huffed out.

Despite his lean elegance, he was all hard muscle.

"Do you mind?" she hissed, pulling away, and becoming entangled in a some swaths of ribbons by the windows.

He frowned at her and laid one long finger carefully against her lips. "You must listen," he told her, staring intently into her eyes. His voice deep and smooth, like warm, melted chocolate.

Melanie didn't trust him or the way he drew that finger away, turning it into a caress.

But there wasn't time to take him up on it.

The dancers had stopped dancing. Everyone was looking toward the dais, where a man and a woman stood at the front of the small orchestra. The man was tall and fair and very handsome. Melanie blinked. More than just handsome—he was the handsomest man she had ever seen—and instinctively she understood that *this* was the man the curly-haired servant girl had been speaking of earlier.

It was strange, but the longer Melanie stared at him, the more his presence affected her. Almost as if she were being dazzled by the sight of him—dazzled in a way that was unnerving and definitely unwelcome.

She shivered. "Who is *that*?"

"Major Hew Pengorren," Nathaniel Raven spoke quietly at her side. He didn't need to ask whom she meant.

Her client's ancestor, the progenitor of the Pengorren line, and Nathaniel's commanding officer. The blond god was wearing a red uniform jacket and white trousers, with a dress sword strapped to his side. Irresistibly, her eyes were drawn back to his face, the golden beauty of it. She felt a little light-headed, starstruck in a way she'd never felt before, not even in her teenage years, when she and Suzie had gone to rock concerts and screamed themselves hoarse.

"It was bliss," Suzie used to say, eyes closed, lying on her bed with a silly grin on her face.

This wasn't bliss. This wasn't a nice feeling at all. There was something horrible and squirmy about Major Pengorren.

With a supreme effort, she reached up and rubbed her eyes, and almost immediately the feeling was gone. If she couldn't *see* him, then she was okay.

Again Nathaniel's voice murmured in her ear, and she tried to pay attention, glad of the distraction. "Pengorren tells everyone I am a hero and plays down his own actions, but everyone knows it is he who is the real hero. He's a gallant and brave officer, and he is at Ravenswood because I invited him. Miss Jones, he is my friend."

There was emotion in his voice, but what was it? Something out of place. Something that jarred in the context of the words he had spoken. She didn't have time to figure it out, because Major Pengorren began to speak, and Melanie made the mistake of looking at him.

Again the bedazzlement swept over her, but now that she was aware of it, she was able to hold back a little, observe her feelings more coolly and scientifically. She glanced at the faces of the crowd and realized they were feeling just as spellbound as she. Pengorren was having that effect on everybody in the room.

"Friends!" he boomed, his voice deep and hearty and sincere, like a politician on election day. "Tonight is the most marvelous night of my life, and I wish to share it with you all. Felicity and I . . ." And he turned fondly to the woman at his side. She was in her late forties, slight, with a face that was pretty but tired—the shadows under her eyes matched her high-waisted black dress. She also wore a besotted smile.

"*Dearest* Felicity and I are to be wed!"

There was a hush, as if the audience didn't quite know how to respond, and then everyone hurried to cover the gaff with extraloud congratulations and applause.

Melanie leaned toward Nathaniel, and whispered, "Isn't she a bit old? She must have at least fifteen years on him. A man like that could have anyone, couldn't he?"

Nathaniel leaned back toward her, and the warmth of his breath against her ear made her want to shiver. "You're talking about my mother, Miss Jones."

"Your mother?"

"Felicity Raven is my mother."

"Oh . . . you said your father was . . . ?"

"Dead. A tragic riding accident eight weeks ago."

That explained the black dress then. But eight weeks . . . it was surely too soon to fall in love with another man? Although the look on Felicity's face seemed to suggest that this was exactly what she had done.

There was a rustle of clothing, a murmur of voices, and the crowd gave way as Sophie, Nathaniel's sister, rushed into the room, pushing her way toward the dais. Melanie recognized the dark head upon the long, elegant neck, and the pale blue dress made of a cloth so thin it was a wonder she didn't freeze to death.

"You are marrying *her*?" Sophie's voice was shrill, and she was looking at the major. She turned to her mother. "What does this mean?"

Felicity's face had blanched. "Sophie," she said, helplessly, with a beseeching glance at her handsome companion. "I know your father hasn't been gone for very long—"

"Eight weeks!"

"—But the major has been so very good to us, and he is Nathaniel's dear friend, *our* dear friend . . ."

Sophie burst into noisy tears.

Melanie could hear the whispers, the shuffling, as

the guests bobbed and strained to see what was going on. There was an air of shock, but also a feeling of unwholesome anticipation.

Pengorren was patting Felicity's arm and at the same time murmuring compassionately into Sophie's ear. Her sobs quietened and she nodded. Relieved, Felicity sighed and drew her daughter into her embrace.

"I miss your father, too," she said, her eyes sparkling with tears, "but life must go on."

It sounded like a line someone had fed her, but Melanie was willing to give her the benefit of the doubt. And Sophie was obviously upset . . . Just then Sophie peeped over Felicity's shoulder at the major, and Melanie saw the expression on her face. No grief there, none at all, just pure, undiluted lust. Sophie wanted Pengorren for herself. That was the real reason she was crying.

And Pengorren knew it.

Even as he made the right noises and pulled the right faces, there was an answering gleam in his eyes as he looked at Sophie. Melanie's heart gave a sickening jolt. He was enjoying himself, playing the two women off against each other. It was a turn-on for him.

"What an egomaniac," Melanie said in disgust.

Nathaniel gave a startled crack of laughter.

The major looked up.

The dais was high enough so that he could see over the heads of the guests to the back of the room, where Melanie stood. As his gaze swept past her, she stepped back, instinctively, pressing herself against the window. His eyes narrowed. His brow wrinkled. Slowly, his gaze slid back toward her.

Cold fear trickled through her. "I thought you said I was invisible?" she hissed.

"You are," Nathaniel said slowly, thoughtfully.

"It doesn't feel like it." Melanie didn't want to take her own eyes off Pengorren, in case . . . well, just in case. She moved a step closer to Nathaniel.

"Nathaniel!" Pengorren was beckoning him. "What are you doing over there? Come and congratulate your mother and me!"

"Congratulations," Nathaniel said under his breath, but he didn't move.

Someone must have instructed the orchestra to begin playing again, for they struck up a slightly desperate jig, and the guests resumed their dancing. Major Pengorren was still staring in Melanie's direction; but Felicity was urging him to join in, and a moment later he climbed down from the dais, and the crowd surged in.

Nathaniel reached for her hand and his fingers were a lot more comforting than she'd admit. "Come with me," he said, but it was more like a command than a request.

Outside the room, the landing and the stairs were empty, and the entrance hall below was deserted. Everyone was in the ballroom where the action was, as Nathaniel led the way down. Melanie felt dazed, as if she'd been drinking. The floor tipped and shimmied beneath her feet, and she clung to the only thing that seemed solid and real: Nathaniel Raven.

The notion was so ironic that she actually giggled.

The Raven gave her his charming smile. Nothing appeared to bother him, apart from . . .

The humor drained out of her.

"How did Major Pengorren know I was there? He did know, didn't he?"

Nathaniel looked up at her—they were near the bottom of the staircase, and she'd stopped a couple of steps above him. "I have no idea," he admitted.

"He was so good-looking and yet . . ."

"And yet," Nathaniel agreed, and that strange undercurrent was in his voice again.

"Why did you bring me here to see that? Why did you make me listen?"

"So that you could know my enemy." He wasn't smiling now.

"Pengorren? *Why* do I need to know him, Nathaniel? What is it to do with me?"

His eyes were more gold than hazel, and there was something very compelling about them. About him.

He leaned closer, further impressing his presence upon her. It was quite amazing, really—whereas Major Pengorren had made her feel cold and squirmy, Nathaniel Raven made her hot and squirmy. Although both, she told herself primly, were equally unwelcome.

"This is my last Yuletide Ball at Ravenswood. Soon it will be my turn to be laid in the ground, although the manner of my death means I won't be allowed to join my family in the Raven crypt. My grave will lie outside the church boundary."

"That's all very sad, but I—"

"I have been given a chance to change history. To save myself and my family. To save Ravenswood."

"That's not possible!"

"It is. But to make it happen I have to find a way to

defeat Major Pengorren," he went on. "You saw what he's like. Such evil can't be allowed to triumph."

Melanie blinked. What he was saying was so bizarre she wanted to reject it out of hand, but she couldn't. She'd seen for herself. That was why, she realized, she'd been forced to come, so that she had no choice but to believe.

"You must help me. The queen says you're the only one who can."

But Melanie knew her limitations. She was a solicitor. She made lists. She didn't battle evil.

"I'm sorry," she said, gently but firmly. "It's out of the question."

What did he have to do to convince her? Nathaniel had never felt so frustrated with a woman. There was only one thing for it. The "better man" speech. It had always worked in the past. He assumed his most sincere face.

"Are you all right?" she said unhelpfully. "You look like you have a stomachache."

"Melanie, I need your help to succeed. Perhaps I'm not worthy of that help, yet, but I am trying. I want you to teach me to be a better man. Must I beg?" he finished, letting his voice drop into a heart-wrenching whisper.

Ah, he had her now! She was gazing up at him with her big blue eyes, no doubt dreaming of turning him into her tame pussycat. He should have remembered before that women liked to believe they alone had the power to change men. And the more badly behaved the man, the more the challenge, and the better they liked it.

Melanie took a breath and let it out slowly. "If you

want to be a better man, then I suggest you go and join the Red Cross, or Amnesty International, or the Lost Dogs' Home. Don't ask me to do it; believe me, we'd both end up in tears."

Nathaniel narrowed his eyes. He'd been too optimistic. Melanie Jones was not like other women, so none of the usual tactics would work on her. What in God's name was he meant to do?

"We *have* to work together," he cried in frustration. "We have no choice."

"No," she said baldly. And then, jabbing her finger into his chest, "Under no circumstances whatsoever."

She spun around and walked away.

Seven

Melanie chanced a glance behind her. He was still following, his tall dark figure just a few paces back. She knew she should be frightened, but the tingling running through her wasn't just fear. The Raven was obviously a man of action, with a great deal of brawn and very little brain. A hero in battle, but a danger to himself and others in peacetime. Which was probably why he came to such a tragic end.

But *that* wasn't making her tingle. It was the way he'd been watching her; as if he wanted to pounce but was holding himself back. As if he was in control of the situation, no matter what she thought. With his smooth charm and knowing eyes, with his easy grace and his long, lean body, he was exactly the type of man who frightened her the most. Because she knew she was vulnerable to him. How could she trust him? How could she trust herself? Work together! She'd found it difficult to be in the same room with him.

Even if it means making him a better man?

She was tempted . . . what was it about the female need to turn a bad boy around? But Nathaniel Raven was well beyond her experience, and she'd be a fool to believe otherwise.

Melanie looked up. There it was, silhouetted against the moon.

St. Anne's Hill.

The place where this nightmare began. Now it seemed as good a place as any if she wanted to find her way back home.

Once outside the grounds of Ravenswood, Melanie started to run, and once she'd started running, she couldn't seem to stop. The ground was hard and frosty beneath her feet as she crossed the fields, and it annoyed her when Nathaniel Raven didn't seem to have any trouble keeping up. She felt like a madwoman, everything spinning out of control, when being *in* control was what she desperately craved.

Why me? Why is this happening to me? Why did the queen of the between-worlds choose me?

"Will you stop running!" Nathaniel Raven sounded as if he was losing control, too. "I am not going to hurt you, Miss Jones. Whatever you may think of me, I am a gentleman."

"You mean the sort of gentleman who robs people at gunpoint and wears a mask?"

As if on cue the moonlight dimmed, and Melanie looked up to see large clouds gliding in. Snow clouds. Soon it would be too cold to stroll in the gardens, and the guests would retreat to the house. Felicity, the merry widow, and pretty Sophie, who was so upset that her mother was marrying Major Pengorren, and Nathaniel, who would soon be shot dead and wanted her to help him become a better man . . .

There was a sound at her back, one she remembered all too well. With a whimper she turned and saw it bounding along behind her, ears flopping, tongue flapping from the big jaws. The black hound.

"Teth!" Nathaniel Raven was calling it to heel, but the hound ignored him. It ran right up to her and then did a circle around her.

Melanie tried to avoid bumping into it by side-stepping, and ended up slipping on the steep slope. She fell to her knees, and the hound promptly pounced on her, his hairy face pushed up against hers, his tongue wet and hot and rough as it laved her skin.

"Is he real, too?" Melanie said breathlessly, trying to push the hound away.

Teth's tail was wagging furiously.

"I don't know what he is. He comes from the between-worlds. Some sort of demon, probably," he added darkly, as Teth made another lunge for Melanie. She shrieked, shielding her face from the slobbering tongue.

"Heel!" Nathaniel grabbed the hound around the body, struggling to drag him away from Melanie. She collapsed on the hillside and watched him trying to sub-due the overexcited animal. His fine clothes were rum-pled and muddied, his neckcloth was array, and his hair was coming loose from the ribbon at his nape.

Suddenly, Nathaniel Raven looked very vulnerable.

Eventually, he wrestled Teth into submission and sank down on the ground beside her with a groan. After a moment, the ridiculousness of the situation seemed to strike him, his mouth quirked up, and he rolled his eyes. "Sorry. Teth has a mind of his own."

"It's not funny."

"He likes you," Nathaniel said, puzzled, as if the reason for this escaped him. Teth stirred again, and he fixed him with a steely eye. "Behave. Sit." The hound decided to obey him and sat quietly, panting. Satisfied, Nathaniel climbed to his feet and reached out his hand to Melanie. It was done in such a confident, companionable manner that Melanie found she had given her own hand without even thinking about it. He helped her back onto her feet with the same easy grace with which he did everything.

"Is it true? What you said?" Melanie asked, looking up at him, her breath a white mist in the cold darkness. "About changing history?"

"Yes."

"You mean you can actually go back and rearrange it to suit yourself?"

"Not exactly," he said dryly. "The theory is that if I discover how to stop Pengorren, the queen of the between-worlds will allow me to return to the past, save my family and myself, and we can all live happily ever after." He sounded faintly amused, but she couldn't see what he was really feeling because he was looking away from her, and she couldn't read the expression in his eyes.

"Are you telling me the truth?"

That made him look. "Yes, I am." His hazel eyes were full of frank honesty, his dark lashes as long as any girl's. "I have this one chance, Melanie, to do what's right." He no longer sounded like an actor in a bad play. He sounded like a desperate man on a quest who genuinely needed her help.

"It's more than most people get."

"I know this must seem very strange to you—"

She gave a choking half laugh at the understatement. He squeezed her fingers in sympathy, and she realized he was still holding her hand.

"Help me," he said, looking straight at her, nothing in his face but honest need. "Please."

Melanie felt something inside her shift and open up. Something warm and tender, and completely outside her control. She knew then that she was going to say yes. No matter how insane and irrational and frightening it was, she was going to agree.

"I'll help you."

Nathaniel gave her a slow, satisfied smile and, lifting her hand to his mouth, kissed it. Just like in her dream, Melanie felt his touch right down to the tips of her toes. Embarrassed at her own reaction, she shook off his grip and resumed her climb to the top of St. Anne's Hill. He fell into step beside her, Teth trotting behind them. Melanie hid a smile at the picture they must make.

Just an ordinary family outing.

The standing stone loomed up in front of her.

The thought of going back through it, of those dark, damp tunnels of the between-worlds and the scuttling things that lived down there . . . Maybe she whimpered again, because he reached out and brushed her cheek lightly with the backs of his fingers.

"It won't be as bad this time. You'll go straight through the stone and arrive back in your own century."

"No between-worlds?" she asked quietly, feeling the urge to cling to him and resisting.

"No between-worlds." He gave her his confident smile. But Melanie wasn't so easily persuaded, and she had serious doubts about Nathaniel Raven's ability to tell the truth.

"But why not? I don't understand."

His smile didn't waver. "Because I have arranged it so."

There was something he wasn't telling her. Melanie tried to read his face, but this time it was expressionless. She turned to the stone, tall and dark and ominous, and took a step forward. Her shoe was loose, and she stopped and bent down to tie the lace, doing the other one at the same time, just to put off the awful moment when she'd have to make that leap into God-knew-what.

When she straightened, Nathaniel was watching her. He was standing with his hands in his pockets, looking as if he were a scientist observing some curious alien life-form.

"That's not very flattering," Melanie said.

"What's not very flattering?"

"The way you're staring."

He grinned. "I was trying to decide what your clothing signifies." He took a hand from his pocket and brushed the *I fought a bull and won* with one long finger. The words just happened to lie on the part of the sweatshirt that covered the upper curve of her breast, and Melanie felt his touch like an electric jolt.

"You're not wearing a corset," he said, loud enough to make Teth bark. He looked so surprised she almost laughed.

"No, corsets aren't in anymore."

"In?"

"Fashionable. We burned our corsets years ago. Us modern women prefer our comfort."

"Then what *do* you wear?" There was a sudden gleam in his eye that made her very nervous.

"I don't think that's any of your business."

"I'm a connoisseur of women's undergarments," he offered, but he was flirting. At a time like this.

"Not mine, you're not," Melanie said, and turned her attention, and his, back to the stone. "Should I say something?" She waved her hand at the hole through the middle.

"There's no need. Just crawl through."

But still she hesitated. There was a shudder inside her, and probably a scream or two, but she refused to let them out. He knew, though.

"Don't worry," he said, in that deep and persuasive voice that made her begin to tingle all over. "I promise I won't let anything happen to you. You have my word, Melanie. The word of a Raven."

The word of a Raven?

"I want to believe you," she murmured. "I really do."

But you're such a liar.

Melanie took a deep breath and plunged her arm through the hole. As that awful dizzy blackness flapped at the edges of her mind, something occurred to her. She turned her head and tried to find him.

"How will we work together if you're here and I'm there?" What she really wanted to ask was: *Will I ever see you again?*

"Trust me."

She laughed, but something like grief weighed heavy on her heart. She began her crawl through the middle of the stone, the pounding in her head too loud for any last good-byes. Anyway, she told herself miserably, it was for the best. How would she have explained Nathaniel to her friends and relatives? And he would have been bad for her, very very bad . . . But as she fell sickeningly through to the other side, she felt someone's hands fasten on to her ankles.

Startled, frightened, she tried to kick him off—she knew who it was. But he held on to her. And then it was too late, and she was tumbling down into darkness, into nothing. Waiting for the jolt that never happened.

A moment later she opened her eyes and found the sky bright with morning sun.

Far overhead a jet droned.

Melanie laughed, because it was the most wonderful sight she had ever seen.

And then a face blotted out the jet.

"See, I promised you I wouldn't let anything happen to you," said Nathaniel Raven.

Eight

Her upside-down position made her dizzy, or maybe it was Nathaniel Raven who made her feel that way.

"Are you feeling faint?" he asked, and there was that smile lurking in his eyes, on his lips, as if life was just one big joke to him. "You look rather pale, Melanie."

"*Word of a Raven?* Crap! You lied to me," she said, and her voice sounded as if she'd been shouting for hours, husky and throaty and very sexy. "You used me to get through the stone."

"It was the only way I could come through to your time as a mortal. You said you would help me, Melanie—"

"But not like that! You should have told me what you were going to do."

"I didn't tell you because, well, to be frank, Melanie, you wouldn't have been very happy with me, would you, if you knew I was coming back with you?"

"Of course not!"

He smiled as if he'd made his point. She was still lying on her back on the ground, so he squatted on his haunches at her side. The muscles in his thighs bunched beneath the tight trousers, and Melanie couldn't say for sure whether or not he was wearing any underwear but . . . Her gaze lifted abruptly to his.

"Go on, say what you have to say. Clear the air. I promise not to interrupt." He was speaking in an infuriatingly patient voice.

"You're dead. You died in 1814. You can't be here. It's impossible. It's not logical."

"I've already explained that. I *was* dead, but now the queen of the between-worlds has given me a second chance. To change history, to change my past. To save myself and my family."

"But why *you*? Out of all the men in all of history, why should *you* get a second chance?"

He thought for a moment. "Why not?"

Melanie groaned in frustration.

He reached out and hauled her unceremoniously to her feet. "I accept that this must be a terrible shock to you. Are you sure you're not going to faint?"

"You'd like that, wouldn't you? No, I'm not going to faint! Definitely not." But her head was spinning, and her stomach was heaving, and she took one breath, and then another, and closed her eyes.

His fingertip was against her skin, following the curve of her cheekbone, then veering toward the corner of her mouth. "You said you'd help me," he said, and he was so close she could feel the warmth of his breath on her skin. Dead men didn't breathe. Dead men didn't smell of clean laundry and leather boot polish, and something else that was warm and male and spicy. Still she kept her eyes shut, as though by doing so she was removing herself from an impossible situation.

"Melanie," he whispered, "I need you," and his lips brushed lightly against hers.

Electric. Every nerve ending in her body sat up. She knew she should tell him to stop, but just now she didn't have the energy—or perhaps she was waiting to see exactly how far he would go to get his own way.

His mouth came down again, this time more forcefully, and he cupped the back of her head with the palm of his hand. Holding her in position for his warm, confident, and very experienced kisses. It was just like the dream except that this time she wasn't going to wake up.

"Help me," he whispered, lifting his head a fraction, and then he went in for the coup de grâce. Lips, mouth, tongue, even teeth, nipping gently at her swollen lower lip.

Oh, God. Melanie knew she had never been kissed like this before. She'd never lost herself in any kiss so totally, so completely, to the point where her inner voice was silenced. Well, almost. It was still there, a tiny murmur, reminding her that he was manipulating her and that she mustn't trust him, but it was so hard to push him away when she was enjoying herself so much. He'd made every inch of her come alive. He was a sensual gourmet, and she was the feast . . .

I can't. I don't want to.

But even as her libido was protesting, Melanie gave

him a hard shove in the chest. He stumbled back. She glared at him, her skin flushed from something more than anger. There was an expression in his eyes . . . He looked confused, as if for a moment he'd been as lost in the kiss as she. But then he blinked, and he was smiling that smile again, that nothing-ever-bothers-me smile, and she dismissed any doubts she might have had.

"Curiosity," he answered her unspoken question. "I wanted to know if women still taste the same in your time."

"Well now you know that they do, don't do it again."

"What, never?" he asked, in mock innocence. "Don't men kiss women in your time? Maybe that's unfashionable, too."

Melanie'd had enough. She stepped around him and proceeded down the hill.

The house was visible across the fields, but it was very different from the Ravenswood of the Yuletide Ball of 1813. Now neglect reigned supreme.

"What happened?" Nathaniel Raven was right behind her. "I saw Ravenswood when I was a ghost, but I couldn't make myself heard or understood. I couldn't ask anyone for help," he added, with a meaningful sideways glance at her. "The place looks as if no one's lived in it for years."

"Miss Pengorren was old; she let things go."

"Even so . . ."

"It's been a long time since you lived here," Melanie reminded him, hurrying along. "You can't expect it to be the same as—"

"This is my fault," he cut her off.

"How can it be your fault? You're dead." *God, did she really say that?*

"Exactly."

"What you did in the past couldn't possibly have any bearing on the here and now." She sounded like her old self again, in charge, in control. It was a tremendous relief to be back in her own time again, even if she was still in Cornwall and not at home in London.

"Of course what we do in the past has a bearing on the here and now," he was saying. "Don't be naïve, Melanie."

The wall with the gate in it was getting closer. Maybe she could shut him out and phone for help? And tell them what . . . ? *Save me, I'm being stalked by the infamous Raven?*

"My death changed history."

"Now who's being naïve?" she said irritably. "In a minor way, perhaps, yes, but you must have known what would happen if you became a highwayman? It's not a respectable profession, is it? You were breaking the law, and you were bound to be punished eventually."

"Whose law?" His voice was getting fainter, but she was too busy arguing to take much notice.

"Whose law? Good old English law. The stuff I had to pass countless exams on. What other law"—she glanced back—"do you mean?"

Nathaniel Raven was gone. Melanie stumbled, coming to an abrupt halt with her hand against the rough wood of the gate. A splinter dug deep into her palm and she yelped and pulled away.

"Where are you?"

There was no answer. She looked carefully all around her. The fields were empty, a chill morning breeze stirring the grass, and away to her right she could hear the sea pounding against the cliffs. Other than that, nothing. He really had vanished.

Maybe he had never *been* in the first place.

Was it all a dream after all? But she'd touched him, spoken to him, experienced the full force of his charm. He had kissed her, for God's sake! Could she really have dreamed all that?

Not possible.

"Nathaniel, where are you?" Only this time she whispered the words, as if she was afraid of the answer.

Still nothing.

With shaking hands, she unlatched the gate. A voice hailed her as she closed it behind her, but it wasn't Nathaniel's voice. Eddie was coming toward her through the overgrown gardens, wearing a jacket that made him look like a refugee from an eighties disco party. He cupped his hands and blew into them, rubbing them together energetically.

"Chilly morning. Have you been out already? You're a keen one."

He looked younger in the morning light, in his thirties rather than his forties, his hair hardly grey at all, and his brown eyes were smiling and friendly.

"I went for a run," she said, knowing she was beaming back at him and unable to help it. He was just so *normal* that Melanie wanted to throw her arms about him.

"What, up there?" Eddie jerked his head toward St.

Anne's Hill. "They say there are piskies inside that hill."

"Piskies?"

"It's the Cornish way of saying pixies. You know, faeries. According to folklore they come out at night and dance and get up to mischief, steal your children and put their own little miserable creatures in the cradles instead. That's what people used to say in the old days, anyway."

Melanie knew there were worse things than faeries in St. Anne's Hill. For a moment she was tempted to tell Eddie everything, as she had last night, but some inner sense of caution and self-preservation stopped her—he'd think she was a nut. Anyway, she wanted to think it over somewhere quiet.

"You don't believe in faeries, do you, Eddie?"

"I fluctuate." Eddie dug his hands in his pockets, shoulders hunched as he walked along beside her. "I keep an open mind. Lot of superstition still around down here. What about you?"

Melanie shrugged. It was the best she could do.

"You haven't seen him again then?" Eddie said. "The Raven?"

Melanie eyed him uneasily, but he didn't wait for an answer.

"He's become quite famous, our Raven. The local tourist office has a guide brochure on him, and his grave gets quite a few visitors. Most of them teenage girls with a crush on him."

"I can't imagine it." But she could, that was the trouble.

"There's a book in the house, in the library—all about the family, if you're interested."

"The library?"

"Miss Pengorren used to call it that. It's the room where she did her paperwork."

"Oh, the ballroom."

He gave her a curious look, but thankfully he didn't take her up on it. His mind was on other matters. "It was strange, how she went to that place in London at the end. She'd always said she'd die at Ravenswood. Everyone expected her to stay."

"She was ill, Eddie—"

"There's a nursing home near Truro, private hospital. She had her sights set on a bed there, if worse came to the worst and she had to leave the house. But London . . . it makes no sense." He shook his head.

"She wanted to come to London," Melanie spoke gently. "She rang and asked Mr. Foyle to make the arrangements for her. I was there at the time. I wouldn't worry about it, really, Eddie. Sometimes when people get sick they get frightened. They change their minds. Maybe she didn't want to be by herself in such a big house."

"She wasn't alone. She had me."

"I'm sorry, Eddie. She wanted it that way."

He pulled a face, but he didn't seem convinced. "Do you need me to be around this morning? To go over the house or anything? It's just that I planned to go into the village, get a few things from the shop there . . . post some letters . . . I shouldn't be long."

"I'll be fine." They had arrived outside the house, and Melanie climbed the steps to the door. She reached out her hand to open it, but the contact caused a sharp pain in her palm, where the splinter had lodged.

"Are you all right?"

"It's nothing. A splinter."

He looked genuinely concerned. "Do you want me to get it out for you? I have a first-aid kit in my cottage."

"No, I can manage." His mention of the cottage reminded her of something she'd meant to ask next time she saw him. "Eddie, is your caretaking job full-time?"

His wry glance told her he knew what was in her mind. "Cushy job, eh? No, it's not full-time, and it doesn't pay much. I'm writing a book, you see. This gives me somewhere to live and a bit of money until I make my first million."

"Oh." It was difficult to tell whether or not Eddie was serious.

"I'll see you later then. Give me a hoi if you want anything." He waved as he turned away.

Alone outside the door, Melanie found herself reluctant to go inside. She was anxious, unsettled, and despite his sudden disappearance, she had the very uneasy feeling that her adventure with the Raven was far from over.

Nathaniel had climbed over a stock gate farther down the garden wall. He'd enjoyed listening to Melanie calling for him and letting her think he could vanish at will. As soon as they were back in her own time, she'd begun to get far too bossy, and he wanted to regain some of the upper hand. He'd every intention of rejoining her inside the grounds, but a man had come up to her, and they'd begun to talk. So Nathaniel had taken himself off, an intruder in his own home.

Now he wandered disconsolately through the park, kicking at fallen branches and piles of rotting undergrowth. It was a mess, and he was frustrated that everything he had loved and valued had come to this. Surely there was an easier way to change history than persuading Melanie Jones to help him?

"No, there isn't. It's the only way."

The voice came from above him. Nathaniel halted and looked up cautiously. A large eagle sat on the branch of a tree, gazing down at him with strange blue predatory eyes above a curved yellow beak.

"Your Majesty?"

The bird flapped its wings, and there was a flash of red. "You tricked her into letting you through the stone, my Raven. That wasn't very fair. She's not a fool, you know. She'll be wary of you next time you ask for her help."

"I had no choice. I don't have enough time for subtleties, as you well know. Besides, I knew I could bring her around later."

"I hope so, for your sake."

There was silence; the park had gone quiet. Maybe the queen had that effect on all creatures, great and small.

"Is all of this my fault?" he asked, and she seemed to understand that he meant the extinction of his family name as well as the deterioration of Ravenswood.

"Everything that happens is linked," the eagle said.

"You said that Melanie will help me understand my

enemy and defeat him," Nathaniel reminded her. "When we were watching the dancing, Pengorren knew she was there. He sensed her. How could that be, Your Majesty?"

"So many questions!"

"I wouldn't feel comfortable if I was bringing Melanie into danger."

The eagle sighed. "Very commendable."

"Not really, I am merely preserving my manhood. Melanie Jones seems well able to take care of herself, and if she knew I was using her as some sort of bait"— he glanced inquiringly at the eagle—"she would remove my balls."

The bird chuckled in a most disturbing way. "What a pair you make, you as smooth as crème brûlée and she as prickly as a thistle."

"Hmm, a French dessert and a Scottish weed. You see, we're completely incompatible." But he smiled. "I have an idea, Your Majesty. Perhaps you could find me another woman, one who isn't quite as difficult to get along with."

The eagle spread its wings. "Don't try and cozen me, Nathaniel!" it shrieked. "Do as you are told or suffer the consequences."

"But—"

"I must go. Remember this, you do not have long, Nathaniel. Don't waste too much time being charming."

"But, Your Majesty!" he shouted, as she flew away.

She was gone.

He was filled with unaccustomed gloom. Despite what he'd said to the queen, he didn't believe Melanie was capable of saving herself from Pengorren. The last thing he wanted was someone else to rescue in the limited time he had to succeed. And what, pray, was her contribution to his redemption going to be? A good telling off? He might as well go back to the between-worlds right now and await his fate.

That's right, Nathaniel, you'd like to give up and die, that's your way out, isn't it, when things get tricky? Except that I need you. You're my pathway to a new life.

Startled, he turned around, but there was nothing and no one, only the dappled shadows thrown by the trees. The voice was inside his head, a memory from those confused and pain-ridden days in Spain after he was wounded. Now it triggered inside him a slow, angry longing for vengeance.

"You won't get away with it," Nathaniel told the voice. "Not this time. This time I'm going to stop you."

Nine

Melanie had found antiseptic and tweezers in the antiquated bathroom. Now she stood by the mullioned windows in the big upstairs room, head bent over her throbbing palm, trying to decide on the best way to extract the splinter. It was deep, but it looked as if it was all in one piece. She leaned closer, adjusting her grip on the tweezers. If she could just get hold of the end and ease it—

"Can I help, Melanie?"

His voice directly behind her startled her so much that the tweezers jerked violently, driving the splinter farther into her flesh. "Ow!" She spun around, heart thumping wildly, furious that he'd crept up on her.

Nathaniel Raven, with his hazel eyes gleaming wickedly and his mouth quirked up into an equally wicked smile, stared at Melanie.

"My apologies," he said politely. "I didn't mean to startle you." His gaze dropped to her hand. Before she could begin to tell him what she thought of him, he'd taken her palm in a gentle but firm grip. "How did this happen?" he asked, brushing one finger lightly over the injury.

She should stop him, but his presence, his touch paralyzed her. "The wooden gate into the garden," she said, watching him closely.

He held her eyes a moment longer, and then returned to his examination.

"You are real then?" she blurted.

He gave a deep chuckle, lifting her hand to the light.

"Where did you go?" she asked, as much to distract herself from the unreality of the situation, and his warm touch, as because she wanted an answer.

"There's another way into the grounds, a little farther along the wall—a gate for livestock. I went that way. I would have told you where I was going, but you were too busy talking to yourself. Then I saw you with a man." He raised a dark eyebrow, waiting.

"That was Eddie," she said. Her faculties seemed to be returning to normal—at least her heart had stopped racing—although with him standing so close it was difficult to breathe evenly. Ridiculous schoolgirl stuff. She'd have to get control of it before he noticed, if he hadn't already. "Eddie's the caretaker."

"He looked more like a play actor."

"You mean the jacket?" Melanie smiled. "You're not exactly dressed inconspicuously yourself."

"Oh?"

"Well . . . you look like Mr. Darcy."

"I am dressed like a gentleman, Melanie."

"Is that what you—oh!"

Nathaniel had bent his head over her palm again and suddenly raised it to his mouth. His tongue found the splinter. Startled, she tried to pull away, but he was gripping her too tightly. White teeth closed on the protruding end of the splinter and pulled. It came out smoothly, and although Melanie hissed, the pain was minimal, and she was more surprised than hurt. Well, to be honest, she was shocked.

What he had just done seemed so . . . *primitive*.

Melanie couldn't imagine any of the men she knew doing that; they'd be either too squeamish or too diffident.

Nathaniel Raven was holding her palm to the light, a frown between his brows as he checked to see whether or not there was any of the splinter remaining, and then, with a satisfied grunt, he released her.

Melanie automatically reached for the antiseptic and applied it. "Thank you. I-I was beginning to think I'd imagined you," she said, screwing the lid back onto the bottle. She laughed nervously, in a girly way she hadn't done for years. Oh *God* . . . She resurrected her nononsense look and fixed him with it. "Perhaps in a minute I'll wake up at home in bed in London. What do you think?"

He had been watching her apply the antiseptic with interest, and now he took the small bottle from her, turning it over in his hands, examining the label. "No, you didn't dream me," he said, twisting the lid for himself and sniffing the contents with a twitch of his long, aristocratic nose. "I'm real enough." He looked up and gave her a warm glance. "Do you want to feel me, Miss Jones?"

He was still flirting with her. Unbelievable.

Melanie had enough. "The situation is ridiculous, you must see that?"

"Well—"

"As I reminded you before you disappeared, you were a highwayman, a thief who died during a robbery. Your victim was protecting his property. Sad, yes, but not much of a surprise, surely? How can you deserve a second chance?"

Melanie thought she'd gone too far. The atmosphere became charged, tense, and he was using his superior height to look down at her with a glint in his eyes that was no longer humorous. No, he wasn't laughing.

"I was murdered," he said. "At least, I think so. If Pengorren didn't kill me himself, then he arranged for it to be done. That's one of the things I'm here to find out, and to prove, if I can. That's why I have the unenviable task of asking for your help, Melanie."

I was murdered.

The words hung between them. Melanie's blue eyes widened in her pale face, and he wondered whether she was finally going to faint. He wouldn't blame her—in his experience it was something women did when faced with any matter they found too overpowering. He would almost prefer it if she did faint because then he would have known how to handle her.

But Melanie wasn't like the women he was used to.

She was already straightening her shoulders and gathering her thoughts. And then she said, in a tone of voice that made him think she would be just as good as his old company sergeant when it came to getting to the heart of a difficult situation, "Tell me exactly what happened the night you died?"

Nathaniel set the antiseptic bottle down carefully on the windowsill. For a moment he gazed out at the park, seeing it not as it was now, shockingly overgrown and neglected, but as it had been. His park, where he had played as a child; his house, where he had grown up; his family, whom he had left to go into the army and expected always to be the same. He knew now he'd been naïve, but at the time he'd been like any other young gentleman seeking adventure, seeing only what lay before him and not what he'd left behind.

"I need to go back farther," he said.

"All right, as far as you like."

Nathaniel bowed his head and smiled, as if to thank her for her permission, but there was no humor in his voice when he spoke again. "Major Pengorren was my commanding officer. We were leading a small group of soldiers on a patrol into enemy territory in Spain when we were ambushed. The men were killed. I survived because Major Pengorren managed to drag me to shelter while the enemy were distracted, thieving from the bodies. I was wounded, and for days we hid. I don't remember much of it—apart from the heat and the thirst. I was delirious, and I used to ramble about Ravenswood, thinking I was back here. Evidently I made it sound like a heaven on earth.

"When it was safe, we made our way back to camp. At least Pengorren did; I wasn't much use. I believe he carried me most of the way, although he always laughed and refused to take credit. But Pengorren saved my life, plain and simple. When I'd recovered enough I was shipped home. I invited Major Pengorren to visit me at Ravenswood, when he himself was able to return to England. I wanted to thank him in some way—I knew I owed my life to him. But I didn't really expect him to take me up on it. And then one day he turned up, and that was that."

"You mean he never left?"

"You make it sound as if we wanted him to go. We didn't. He was the perfect guest, everyone loved and admired him. When my father died, it was a terrific shock, and perhaps it was selfish of me, but I was grateful Pengorren was there to help comfort my mother and sister, to share some of the burden. He was wonderful during those dark days. When he married my mother . . ."

He shrugged, as if trying to shake off something unpleasant.

"I didn't feel resentful or pained on my father's behalf. I knew it was very soon for my mother to remarry, but he was our friend; he had been so kind to us. He made it all seem . . ."

"Perfectly normal," Melanie murmured. "What is it about some people? They can persuade you that black is white and vice versa, and sell you a car you know is totally unsuitable, but because they're doing the talking, you believe them. Is that the sort of man Pengorren was? A nineteenth-century used-car salesman?"

He frowned at her, trying to decipher her strange words, and then gave up and looked away again, out over the grounds. "When I was with him, I couldn't see any-thing wrong in what was happening. I still don't know whether or not there was something I should have done before it was too late."

"But you had your suspicions, yes?"

She was a good listener. So attentive as she took in what he was telling her. Her eyes were the color of forget-me-nots. With a start he remembered that Pengorren was able to do something similar; focus his formidable self entirely on you. Make you feel as if you were the most important thing in his world. It was very flattering. People were drawn to him, they loved him, because they thought he loved them back.

Nathaniel, you know I will look after you and your family. I accept I can never take the place of your dear father, but I will try to be his second-in-command.

Pengorren's voice sounded in his head as if he were here in the room. Nathaniel shook his head to get it out.

"The thing is," he said, "I find it hard to believe it of him, even now. Major Pengorren was my friend; he saved my life. He was a bloody hero, for God's sake!"

"Come on, Nathaniel, there must be more to it. Why else would you bring his name up? There's something you're not telling me, and I need to know the full story if I'm ever to help you."

He gave an irritable flick of his fingers. "It didn't make sense, that's why I'm finding it difficult to explain to you what I felt."

"Try."

He turned his head and met her eyes. He knew he wanted to tell her. He needed to unburden himself at last, after nearly two hundred years, and she was the one who had been chosen to listen.

"Whenever I was away from Pengorren . . . everything seemed to change. I was no longer sure of him. His words, comments that made perfect sense when I was in his company, began to appear in a different light. I started to think him capable of things . . . unspeakable things. I would make myself half-mad thinking them, knowing in my heart what a fine man he was, and yet I didn't seem able to help myself."

"What unspeakable things?" Melanie asked quietly, as if she had caught his own disquiet.

Even now, in some part of his being, he didn't want to say them aloud. It seemed like a betrayal of Pengorren, a disloyalty to the man who had probably been more of a father to him that his own father.

"Come on, Nathaniel, tell me."

"I couldn't get it out of my head." He rubbed a hand over his eyes. "That there was something wrong. Although I was certain I was imagining it, and at the time I was still recovering from my time in Spain. I had headaches, you see, unbearable headaches from the wound to my head . . ."

"Just stop mucking around and say whatever it is that's worrying you."

He laughed. "Do you talk to everyone like this?"

"Yes."

He gave in. "After Pengorren married my mother, he stepped into my father's shoes in other ways, becoming the district magistrate. He was scrupulously fair, everybody said so, but I couldn't shake off my doubts. There were times when he seemed to favor those who could be of most use to him whether they were innocent or not. I found myself arguing the point with him for no particular reason. He was always so calm, so controlled; he never seemed to get upset or angry. I wanted to irritate him, and I began to believe that if I could find a way to upset him, shake him into losing his equilibrium, then I would finally know what really lay underneath Pengorren's amiable surface."

"And did you?"

He smiled mockingly. "There were moments when I thought I did, but no, not with any certainty.

"But you didn't stop?"

"No. And then my mother died. She fell down the stairs and broke her neck."

"Oh." Melanie seemed genuinely shocked. "I'm sorry . . ."

"So the next night I held up Pengorren's coach and made him stand at gunpoint while I rifled his pockets and stole his purse. I wanted to humiliate him. The look on his face . . ." Even now Nathaniel could not describe that look, but it had chilled him to the bone.

"But why did you want to humiliate him? I don't understand. Nathaniel?"

The words burst out of him like a pistol shot. "Pengorren was with my sister."

She blinked at him, puzzled, and he knew he'd have to explain. Say the words that even now sickened him to his soul.

"The night my mother died he was in my sister's room, in her bed. She was seventeen."

Melanie sat down abruptly on a chair, her hurt palm cradled in her other hand. "You don't think your mother—"

"Killed herself? It's a possibility, but not one that was ever spoken aloud in Ravenswood. My sister . . . she didn't seem to have any shame. At my mother's funeral she hung on Pengorren's arm, gazing at him as if he was the only star in her sky. People said it was kind of him to take the time to comfort her, but *he was in her bed*! I saw them. And I wished to God I hadn't. There's something to be said for blissful ignorance, Melanie."

"Did you tell Pengorren that you'd seen him with your sister? Did you confront him?" Melanie had regained her wits, and her blue eyes had that intensity he was coming to know well.

"Yes, I confronted him with it. He gave me a look—as if I'd let him down—and said I'd had a terrible shock—a double shock, with both my parents now dead—and I must be aware how hurtful and unfair I was being to him to make such accusations."

Even now the memory made him feel nauseous, a greasy sick feeling in his stomach and a foul taste in his mouth. "But do you know what was even worse than his lies? The fact that I tried to persuade myself I believed him. Telling myself that I must have imagined it, even though I had *seen* it with my very own eyes." He squeezed his hands into fists, feeling his anger roaring through him.

"You didn't want to believe it," Melanie said, but she

was watching him warily. "What happened after that?"

"I took to highway robbery with a vengeance. I began holding up more and more coaches, and although at first I managed to keep my identity a secret, I knew it would leak out eventually—I was too well-known. After a month Pengorren took me aside and gave me a warning. He said he understood I was just indulging in 'high spirits,' but even a man in his position could not protect me forever from the full force of the law. I needed to stop, to consider himself and my sister. It was a very generous warning, considering the embarrassment I must have been causing him."

"So despite his lying to you about your sister, he must have cared enough about you to try to keep you out of trouble until you came to your senses."

He laughed savagely. "I held him up again straight after that warning, just to see what he'd do. I didn't care what happened to me. I was half-crazy with grief and guilt, and there was a fear twisting inside me, telling me that this was all my fault, that I should have done something earlier to stop him, and I didn't."

Melanie hardly dared ask. "And then?"

"Within a week I was dead. And my head tells me that Pengorren was the one behind my death, although my heart still can't believe it of him."

She was unconvinced. "I heard you were shot robbing a coach. Was it Pengorren's coach?"

"No."

"Then how can you say he had a hand in your murder?" Melanie seemed determined to be devil's advocate. "It's a tragic story, yes, but is Pengorren really the

villain of the piece? He might have been promiscuous—
I sensed that when I saw him on the dais with your . . . the
two women—but that doesn't make him a murderer.
Surely someone would have noticed if he was a homi-
cidal manic? Someone other than you, that is, because
you're hardly the most reliable witness. Your own lawless conduct makes your testimony less credible. Where's
your proof?"

"So now you want proof." He sounded bitter; he'd
thought she'd believe him. But then why should she? No
one else had.

"You're saying that Pengorren decided you were
causing too much trouble for him, and he set about getting you bumped off?"

"Bumped off?"

"Done in. Killed."

"I was causing him trouble, yes. I had seen him with
Sophie, and he didn't like that. He tried to lie his way
out of it—I think if he'd told the truth, begged my for-
giveness, then I might have been inclined to think better
of him for it. Instead, his lying made me wonder what
else he was capable of, what else he might have done
that he was concealing from me."

"You mean was Pengorren responsible for the deaths
of your mother and your father?"

Trust Melanie Jones to say the unspeakable aloud.

"Yes," he answered, grimly. "Yes, Melanie, that is
exactly what I am thinking."

Just then Melanie's cell phone began to ring.

Ten

Her mind was still off with Nathaniel, lying cold and dead on the road, Pengorren standing over him with the smoking gun. Fumbling the cell phone out of her pocket, Melanie took the call without checking the number—it was probably the office in London. She should have contacted them hours ago.

"Mr. Foyle, I'm so sorry, I—"

"Mr. who?" Suzie's chirpy voice brought her wide-awake. "It's me. Suzie. Your sister," she added, when Melanie still didn't reply. "Just wondering how you are down there in the depths of Cornwall."

Nathaniel was staring at the phone in her hand as if he couldn't believe his eyes. Melanie turned away, hunching her shoulder and not allowing him distract to her.

"I'm fine, Suzie. Why shouldn't I be?"

"Aren't I allowed to ask?" Suzie sounded oddly defensive for a woman who had once declared she never felt the urge to apologize for her actions. "I just wondered, that's all. Had a feeling, if you must know."

One of Suzie's feelings. They always made Melanie feel uneasy, just as anything paranormal did. Though, scarily, they were often spot on.

"What sort of feeling?" she forced herself to ask. At least it gave her time to pull herself together. She stood up, stretched, and walked toward Miss Pengorren's desk. Something pinged in her memory. Running her finger along the leather-bound spines, she found the diary she'd been reading earlier that morning and slid it out.

"Just a feeling. You're not in some sort of trouble, are you? I was shivering when I woke up. Cold, damp, dark. Been in any places like that recently?"

She had, but she wasn't going to tell her sister about it. "No. I'm fine, Suzie. There's plenty to do down here. I've barely started yet. How are you?"

"Fine. Kids are with their father, so I'm all alone at the moment." There was another pause, and Melanie realized to her horror that she was meant to fill that pause with an invitation. *Come on down here, Suzie, and stay with me.*

"You know I'm working," she said sharply. "This isn't my house."

"All right. You don't have to sound quite so gleeful about it. It was just a thought."

Now Melanie felt guilty, but not enough to change her mind. "Look, maybe we can meet up when I get home? Have lunch?"

"Oooh, lunch, lovely." Suzie sighed and brushed off her sarcasm. "Whatever. Just look after yourself, all right? See ya."

The call ended, and Melanie looked at her phone. It

was unusual for Suzie to call her like this, and she felt unsettled. There were just too many strange things happening today . . .

Nathaniel was staring out of the window again, so she made her check-in call to the firm. Mr. Foyle was out of the office, but she left a message to say everything was fine, then ended the call and slipped her phone back into her pocket. She brought the diary over to the window and held it out. Nathaniel glanced down at it and then back at her, doing that single eyebrow lifting thing again.

"This is the final diary of Miss Pengorren, the last owner of Ravenswood, the last of the Pengorren family. She died without heirs in a nursing home in London—that's why I'm here, to sell the place."

If that information hurt him, he didn't let it show.

Melanie wiggled the book in front of him. "Read the last entry."

He took the book and opened it, flicking to the back.

A monstrous injustice. I wish I could restore Ravenswood to its rightful owner.

After a moment he looked up at her, an expression in his eyes that might have been hope.

"What does she mean, 'a monstrous injustice'?"

Melanie shook her head. "I don't know. Maybe it doesn't mean anything. She was going a bit gaga, judging by some of the other things I read in there." Then, at his blank stare, "Senile, losing her mind."

She held out her hand for the diary, but he didn't give it back. Instead, he smiled, managing to appear devastatingly attractive despite having been dead since 1814. He'd said that Pengorren was good at manipulating people, but Nathaniel was pretty damn good at it himself.

"Do you mind if I hold on to this? I would like to read the rest of it."

"If you like. There are more of her diaries over there, on the shelf above the desk."

He didn't glance in the direction she pointed; his gaze was fixed on her. He was measuring her, deciding what to tell her, how much more she could take.

"I need to find out what happened here *after* I died. I need to know if I was the only one who saw something unwholesome in Pengorren. I need to know if it was my failure to act decisively," he added bleakly, "that led to the destruction of my family and my own death, or whether it would have happened anyway."

"How will that—"

"I tried to send Sophie away, after I saw her and Pengorren together, but it was too late. She refused to go. She wouldn't listen to me. She looked at me as if she hated me for even suggesting it."

"Nathaniel—"

"I was never the perfect son or brother, Melanie, but now it's time to rise to the occasion. I'm twenty-seven years old and I have to grow up and be a man."

Melanie would have said he was already a man, but her heart was thudding, she felt light-headed, and her hands were sweaty. He had that effect on her. Not that she liked what he made her feel, the way she seemed to spiral out of control when she was around him. She had her own life, and now it was being hijacked by a man who wasn't even alive, someone who had literally attached himself to her and followed her home. It seemed incredible. Beyond belief. One moment she was here doing her job, and the next . . . Her job.

"I'm in line for a partnership with my firm," she heard herself say. "I'm twenty-nine, and it's something I've been working steadily toward ever since I joined the firm. You might not think it's much compared to what you've been through; but it's my goal, my future, and it's important to me."

"I'm not asking you to give up your future, Melanie."

"No? I thought that was exactly what you were doing. You want me to dash off with you instead of acting responsibly. I'm here to do a job. Call me shallow, but I dream about an office with my name on the door, clients who respect and trust me, a smart apartment on Canary Wharf with the Thames flowing past my front door."

Nathaniel's stomach rumbled, loudly. She glared at him, and he shrugged, the corner of his mouth quirking up, and his eyes gleaming with wicked amusement.

"My apologies," he said, "but even dead highwaymen get hungry."

"You're hungry?" She couldn't help but be surprised.

"Yes."

"But . . . do you eat?"

"Do you?"

"It's not the same, I'm not a-a . . ." Melanie eyed him suspiciously. "What *are* you, anyway?"

"I'm a man. I'm not sure for how long, but for now I

am a mortal with a mortal's needs and wants and desires."

There was something almost suggestive in the way he said it, dropping his tone like that. Melanie ignored the innuendo, concentrating on him as a man who needed feeding.

"Come on then," she said, and led him down the stairs and into the kitchen.

Nathaniel followed her, enjoying the sway of her hips in the strange trousers she wore. He'd thought for a moment there that he'd lost her, that maybe he'd laid it on too thick. *I have to grow up and be a man.* Nathaniel grimaced. A bit emotive for him. Not that he didn't mean what he'd said, but he usually preferred to keep those sorts of inner feelings private.

What was it about Melanie that made him blurt it out? Open himself up to a woman who was very much a stranger? The need to gain her help so that he could save his family and himself might have something to do with it, he thought wryly. Simply put, he was desperate.

But in his heart he knew he was undervaluing himself. And her. This wasn't just about desperation; there was more going on between the two of them than either of them would admit.

After his awakening by the queen, she had led him to the door that crossed from the between-worlds to the mortal world. But he had been little more than a shadow. A ghost. He'd tried to make himself known to people, appearing before them, but he'd only ended up scaring them. They didn't understand, and what they didn't understand frightened the wits out of them.

That was when the queen had told him what he must do. He must wait until Melanie Jones came to him in the past, and then ask her to help, and she must agree. Most importantly, he must gain her trust.

Except that Nathaniel couldn't wait that long—the old recklessness coming out in him again. So he'd come to her in his ghostly form and raced her along the lane. He grinned now, remembering it. He hadn't felt so good for a long time, and whatever she might believe to the contrary, he knew Melanie had enjoyed it, too.

Now, thanks to Melanie, he was once again a living, breathing, warm-blooded man. And at the moment Melanie's curves were warming his blood more than usual.

"I don't suppose you spent much time in the kitchen when you were here the last time," Melanie said, with a glance over her shoulder.

Was she trying to annoy him, make him bite? Nathaniel knew his easygoing manner irritated her, but she was like a permanently overwound watch.

"You'd have servants to see to mundane things like cooking and cleaning," she went on, casting him another little glance to see how he was reacting.

"Of course," Nathaniel said in a bored voice, "doesn't everyone?"

Would she be like that in bed? Overcautious, precise, warily watching every move he made? Or would she lose all her inhibitions completely? He'd seen a glimpse of what she could be when she raced his ghost. Nathaniel let himself fantasize. Melanie Jones, skin flushed, slanting eyes shining, her mouth swollen from his kisses. She'd probably never allowed herself to unwind long enough to really enjoy a man.

Nathaniel knew he'd like to be that man.

They reached the kitchen, and he stopped, looking about him at the big echoing room with its myriad shelves, long, solid table, and enormous wood-burning stove. Things hadn't changed since he was a boy, well, not much. There were a few modern additions, but not many. If he closed his eyes he could see the servants hurrying about preparing food, or giggling over some silly joke. Dorrie and Tamlyn and the rest, and Mrs. Vercoe, the cook, like Wellington, ordering her troops into battle.

"Well?"

He blinked, focused. Melanie was standing by the table holding a jar in each hand.

She seemed to understand his dislocation. "I said do you want peanut butter or marmite?"

"Peanut butter? Marmite?"

"Marmite's a popular English spread, dark and yeasty. Salty. You either like it or you don't. Peanut butter is peanuts and . . . butter. It's your choice. Eddie doesn't run to haute cuisine, so we're left with just the two basic food groups."

"Eddie?"

"The caretaker. Remember? You saw me talking to him in the garden. He lives in a cottage in the grounds." She set down the jars and began to open the lids. "I'll have to think up some story for him if you're going to be around here for a while. Or maybe you could hide whenever you see him? No, that wouldn't work. He'd probably think you were a burglar. Or a ghost." She smiled wryly.

"I can claim to be a distant relative of the Raven family."

"Wrong side of the blanket." She said it like it was a private joke. Melanie finished spreading the contents from the jars onto buttered slices of bread and held one out to him. When he took it, cautiously, she licked her fingers.

The sight of her delicate pink tongue made him hot. Like the burst of heated air after a cannon was fired, it took him by surprise, momentarily stopping all thought. He felt disoriented, confused, adrift.

"What?" Melanie said. She frowned and tucked her hands into the pockets of her trousers, suddenly self-conscious.

He realized then that he was staring at her as if she were one of those strange sea creatures that were washed up after a storm on the little half-moon beach below Ravenswood. He used to examine them when he was a boy, spending hours dreaming about where they'd come from and what wonders they had seen before they came to his isolated Cornish shore.

Melanie was a bit like that. She was strange and exotic, and he wanted to examine her, find out what made her the woman she was.

Nathaniel bit into the bread. The dark marmite spread was very salty, catching him by surprise, and he pulled a face.

She laughed at his expression. "Marmite not to your

liking then? Here, try the peanut butter." She handed him another slice, and he sampled this one more cautiously. Still salty, only this time crunchy as well.

He swallowed with difficulty. "Mrs. Vercoe, our cook, always had food put away in the pantry. Saffron cake or some pasties, even star-gazy pie, if she felt so inclined." He gave her a hopeful look, but he could see she was unmoved.

"I'm sorry, but cook doesn't live here anymore. You could ask Eddie, if you don't frighten the wits out of him first. And that reminds me—he's seen your portrait, so he'll notice the resemblance."

She folded over one of the slices of bread and began to work her way through it.

"Who's Suzie?" he asked, laying his own slice down.

Her eyes assessed him. "My sister," she said, when her mouth was empty. "My older sister. She lives in a flat in Shepherd's Bush—the better part. Divorced, two kids."

"Divorced? You say it as if it means nothing. In 1814 the only way for a couple to be granted a divorce was by Parliament."

She thought about that, starting on another slice of bread. "Bummer."

He choked. "Are you divorced?"

"Uh-uh. Never married. I'm a career girl." Then, seeing his blank look, "I live for my job."

She knew the concept, where a woman was concerned, was alien to him. The women of his day were supported by their families until they married, and then they were supported by their husbands. What a terrifying thought, women doing as they pleased!

"Have you any family? Other than Suzie?"

"My parents, but I don't see them all that often. They divorced when I was young, after we lost everything. My father played the stock market," she added, and there was tension in her shoulders, in the line of her mouth. "We went from being relatively well-off middle class to poverty-stricken and on-the-streets . . . or near enough. Everything I am now, everything I have, I've worked bloody hard for."

Melanie sounded proud of her achievements, and why shouldn't she be? It was true, all her hard work had paid off, or it would soon, when she became a partner. She might be driven, she might even be a control freak, but Melanie would never allow herself to be placed in such a vulnerable situation again.

"No man at the moment then?"

"Man?"

"Lover."

The question threw her. She stared at him, trying to think of a flip answer when she was tempted to tell him to mind his own business. Maybe she just wouldn't answer. But he wasn't going to let her get away with that.

"I'll keep your secret, I promise. Word of a Raven."

She laughed.

Nathaniel folded his arms and leaned back against the counter, watching her. There was the hint of a smile on his mouth, and a lock of hair had fallen over his brow. He'd crossed his legs at the ankles, and his tight-fitting trousers showed up every muscle in his long legs.

Her gaze slid up, over the waistcoat and the blue jacket, clinging to his chest and shoulders. The neckcloth was looking grubbier than it had, and not quite as neatly fastened, and there was golden stubble on his jaw, but that only made him look more sexy.

She met his eyes. They were gleaming through the fringe of his lashes. He was returning her perusal with interest and a double dose of smoldering sexual desire.

"I told you, there's no one. I'm not interested in men at the moment. I'm a career girl."

Abruptly Melanie looked away and took a quick bite of her peanut butter sandwich. She tried very hard to swallow. Nathaniel Raven wasn't a man you could easily ignore, but for her own sake she had to try. She was almost certain that if she gave him the slightest reason to do so, he'd reach out now and pull her into a hot and heavy embrace. He'd probably have her up on the counter in no time. *I am a connoisseur of women's undergarments.* Yeah, right.

Her fingers twitched as if she could feel him already, and she curled them into tight fists. *No,* she thought. *No, no, no!* But deny it all she might, the sparks were still flying between them. Making her feel wildly, vibrantly, wonderfully . . .

. . . alive!

Eleven

It was late afternoon, and Melanie sat at Miss Pengorren's desk in the torn leather chair, trying to ignore her headache while sorting through the old woman's papers. Nathaniel was browsing his way along the bookshelves that covered part of one wall. That was why, she supposed, the room was called the library, even though it was a fairly modest one.

After they'd eaten—well, Melanie had eaten, and Nathaniel had made faces and reminisced about his cook—she'd decided it was time she did some work. What she really wanted to do was to get as far away from him as possible. This attraction between them was like a ticking time bomb, just waiting to go off. But after he'd listened to her excuses, he'd smiled and promptly followed after her.

Melanie glanced across at him. He had taken out one of the books and was flicking through the pages, pausing now and again to read. He seemed completely focused on what he was doing, but Melanie knew that, despite his air of relaxed ease, he was one of those men who seemed to know exactly what was going on in the room around him. He was probably aware of her right now . . .

"Here's something," he said, and turned, catching her staring.

Melanie jumped and began fumbling with her piles of bills, knocking some of them to the floor in her haste to pretend she wasn't doing what she so obviously was. Watching him.

"What is it?"

He didn't answer, and when she found the nerve to glance up at him again he was leaning against the bookshelves, one eyebrow quirked inquiringly. He knew she was attracted to him, of course he did. It was all a game to him, but it wasn't a game to her. Melanie had sworn long ago that, after her father destroyed her life, she'd never let another man close enough to do it again. She'd had lovers, but she hadn't been in love, and one of the reasons for that had been her determination to stay clear of the sort of men she knew would hurt her. The sort of men she craved.

I'm like a junkie, she thought, *but my weakness is for Nathaniel Raven. I can't afford to take even one bite, or I'll be hooked.*

"Well, what have you found?" She sounded irritable, as she re-sorted her papers.

"I've found a book called *The Raven's Curse*— delightful title, by the way. I have an entire chapter to myself," he said, as if it didn't really bother him at all.

"I'm not surprised you have an entire chapter to yourself," Melanie replied.

He laughed and walked over to a leather armchair, throwing himself down into it with careless grace. "You disapprove of me, don't you, Melanie?"

"I don't approve or disapprove of you," Melanie said levelly, turning back to her work. "I don't have an opinion, Nathaniel. I'm not interested."

"I don't believe you." His voice was low, teasing.

"Believe what you like."

Melanie picked up her pen and began to make lists. She made a list of the phone calls she needed to make, and another list of the ones that could wait, and then a third list of those calls she'd need to discuss with Mr. Foyle. By the time she had finished to her satisfaction—lists always made her feel better—Nathaniel was once more deep in his book.

He was frowning, stroking his strong chin with one long finger as he pinned the book on his thigh with his other hand. *If only he wasn't so distracting,* Melanie thought in frustration. *If only he wasn't here.*

Before she knew it, she was watching him again, and it wasn't until his deep voice made her start that she realized it.

He was reading aloud: *"Nathaniel Raven was a complex character, angelic one moment and demonic the next."* He shook his head in disbelief. "That sounds a little extreme," he said. "I was never angelic."

Melanie, who had taken a sip of her coffee, coughed. He observed her catch her breath and mop at her streaming eyes, his expression outwardly sympathetic, but his eyes were full of laughter.

"Should I read on?" he asked her innocently, and then proceeded to do so without waiting for an answer. *"The Ravens were comfortable rather than rich. Unfortunate investments by an ancestor during the eighteenth century South Seas bubble had seen them lose an estate in Derbyshire and with that went much of their wealth, but they continued to be well thought of in Cornwall. The elder Nathaniel Raven was a scholar, a gentlemanly man, more used to the pen than the sword, but when his son showed himself to be a far more restless character, the father wasted no time in purchasing him a captaincy in an army regiment."*

Nathaniel Raven looked up. "Restless," he murmured. "Is that where I went wrong? Should I have been a bookworm like my father? And yet I don't think I had it in me. Cornwall seemed so far away from all that was important in the world, and I wanted to fight Napoleon. I wanted to be a part of history."

"You were young and adventurous," said Melanie.

"To put it mildly." He turned again to the book.

"After distinguishing himself in battle and proving himself to be a brave and gallant soldier, Nathaniel was sent on a reconnoitering mission behind enemy lines. During an ambush he was wounded, and, although he got himself to safety, Nathaniel was no longer fit for service. He returned home, to Ravenswood, to take up the life of the country gentleman to which he had been born. Unfortunately for all concerned, the excitement of the army had spoiled him for country life.

It soon became apparent Ravenswood was far too tame for his liking."

Irritably, Nathaniel flicked at the page with his fingertip. "What rot! It wasn't tedious, it was never tedious. I was fully prepared to be the squire of Ravenswood— I knew I was lucky to be alive." Then he gave her a sheepish glance, "Well, maybe I was a little bored, but wouldn't anyone be who'd just returned from fighting Napoleon? I needed time to adjust, to interest myself in local affairs, to find a wife! In time I would have settled down, I know it."

Melanie wondered whether he was trying to convince her or himself, but she was feeling charitable. "It's a well-known fact that men take longer to grow up and shoulder their responsibilities than women. You were probably a late starter."

He smiled as if she amused him. "I wouldn't say that."

So much for her being kind. Now he was flirting with her. "You've ruined my concentration, so you might as well keep reading."

"Your wish is my command." He sketched a bow without getting out of his chair. *"To pass the time Nathaniel Raven took up a hobby; robbing coaches on the Truro Road. He would lie in wait for the vehicles and then ride out, brandishing his pistol, and demanding—"* Nathaniel stopped, and looked up at her again. "Are you certain you want to hear this?"

Melanie widened her eyes and said, breathlessly, "Of course I want to hear it. Read on, Mr. Raven."

Nathaniel shook his head at her performance. "I

suppose I deserve that . . . *Major Pengorren, who had been Nathaniel's commanding officer and was now his stepfather, was another man like the elder Raven. Fine and upstanding, he sought to protect Nathaniel as best he could from his own recklessness, but it was too late. The local families were already tired of his rascally behavior and decided to take the law into their own hands. Finally, in the very act of one of his daring highway robberies, Nathaniel was shot dead by Sir Arthur Tregilly's coachman. A lucky shot and although tragic in its consequences, perhaps a blessing in disguise.*

"One can speculate as to why Nathaniel Raven went bad. Perhaps the head wounds he received during his time in Spain had something to do with his dangerous behavior. There were rumors at the time that those head wounds had never healed; indeed, that they had sent him insane."

Nathaniel threw the book violently and then jumped up, pursued it, and kicked it to the other side of the room. It landed in a tangled mess of pages against the far wall.

Melanie held her breath, watching him warily.

He turned and glared at her. His chest was rising and falling quickly, there was a flush along his cheekbones, and his hands were clenched into fists.

She hadn't seen him lose his temper like this, and she no longer wondered whether or not he was capable of the things he was supposed to have done. "That's a shame," she said cautiously. "I was waiting to hear if there was a chapter on Major Pengorren."

"That *was* a chapter on Pengorren. I read it first. To myself."

"Well, what did it say?"

The anger was gone as quickly as it came. But still Melanie kept a watchful eye on him as he sat down on the arm of his chair.

"A month after I was shot to death Pengorren married Sophie. The writer of that heap of rubbish wants us to know that the wedding was a 'ray of sunshine in a household heavy with sorrow and gloom.' Pengorren could do no wrong in his eyes, it seems."

"Ah." Melanie could understand his feelings; maybe the author deserved to be kicked across the room. "Did . . . I don't quite know how to phrase this . . . Did Sophie fall down the stairs, too?"

"According to the dates on the family tree in the back of the book, Sophie must already have been with child by him when they married. The baby, a son, was born only four months later, in October of 1814. She didn't bear Pengorren any more children, but she lived a good few years after 1814. And no"—he cast her a humorless smile—"it doesn't say *how* she died."

This was his sister they were speaking about, not just a name from the distant past. Sophie was real, and Melanie had seen her in the flesh. A pretty girl, her smile as wickedly charming as Nathaniel's, on the verge of womanhood.

"I'm sorry."

He showed his teeth. "It's Pengorren who should be sorry."

"Maybe you're right, maybe he was a lecherous

bastard who preyed on a vulnerable young girl, but that doesn't make him a murderer. For all you know they might have been deliriously happy together."

He didn't answer; he was looking out into the park. Lost in his own thoughts.

His new vulnerability made Melanie uncomfortable. She preferred his cockiness; at least she knew how to keep him at a distance when he was like that. But now . . . she was fighting the urge to go over to him and pat his shoulder. Or give him a hug.

"Did Pengorren marry again after Sophie?" she asked quickly.

"Not according to the book . . . if the author can be believed."

"Well, there you are then! He was heartbroken."

But her words sounded hollow. She could not imagine the man she had seen at the Yuletide Ball heartbroken. He was far too self-obsessed.

"Do you know what happened to Pengorren after Sophie died?"

"He lived on here at Ravenswood, and then one day he went down to the sea and never returned. He was supposed to have walked into the water and drowned, accidentally or on purpose, no one knows. Ravenswood was passed on to his son . . . Sophie's son. I suppose that's some consolation for me—there was Raven blood mixed in with the Pengorren."

"And then, eventually, everything came down to Miss Pengorren, the last of them all." It was sad that such an old family had dwindled to one. "Was there a body?

I mean, after he walked into the sea, did they ever recover his body?"

Nathaniel shrugged impatiently. "I don't know, the book doesn't say, or the author doesn't know. What does it matter after all these years? If he wasn't dead, then he certainly is now."

"Unless the queen of the between-worlds wants to give him a chance to change history, too."

As soon as she said it she wished she hadn't. The idea of Pengorren alive and well in her world gave her the same squirmy feeling she'd had when she first saw him. Nathaniel was one thing—she didn't trust him, and he made her uncomfortable—but she wasn't scared of him. Pengorren was different; he definitely gave her the creeps.

"You ask a great many questions," Nathaniel said softly.

"Maybe you should have asked more."

His eyes narrowed. "And you're very free with your opinions, Miss Jones."

"These days we don't have to wait until we're spoken to, or curtsy to our betters," Melanie retorted, and couldn't seem to help herself. She just couldn't shut up; he had that effect on her.

And now she had a headache, and it was getting worse. It had been a long day, and her journey into the between-worlds hadn't helped. She wiggled her shoulders, moving her neck from side to side to try and ease the kinks. At home she visited a masseuse, but she hadn't had time to make an appointment before she left for

Cornwall. Now, with everything that had happened, tension was causing all sorts of problems. She wondered if her headache was going to turn into a migraine. They'd been the scourge of her teenage years, waves of pounding agony that had incapacitated her for days on end.

Suzie always said she was strung too tightly and needed to relax, but it wasn't just that. There had been other reasons for the migraines, reasons she never spoke of these days . . .

"You have the headache."

His warm hands rested firmly on her shoulders, making Melanie jump. But he was already working with his thumbs on the little knots of pain clustered near her shoulder blades.

"Ouch!"

"Be still." He was right behind her, and she could feel the solid warmth of his body. The confident touch of his hands was like being branded—there was no escaping it. "You're like a bitch I once had, Melanie. Always jumping and whining, never relaxing into just being. Sometimes being in the moment is more important than thinking about what has passed, or what is to come."

"A bitch!"

She tried to wriggle free, but he held her, and bending closer, murmured in her ear, "*Be still*. Please, let me help you."

Melanie had a choice. She could scream and run from the room, or she could sit and let him do his thing. Her head was throbbing—he couldn't make it any worse . . .

He hadn't waited for an answer, seeking the painful

spots with his strong fingers and working on them until the pain eased, and then moving on to the next ones. He knew what he was doing, Melanie decided with relief. Her doubts melted before the pleasure he was giving her, and Melanie moaned softly and let her eyes drift shut and her head sink forward onto her chest. His fingers crept upward, into the taut muscles of her neck, circling, pressing, caressing in a way that was truly amazing.

Sinfully so.

"How did you learn to do this?" she asked, her voice barely audible. In a moment she'd be panting, her tongue lolling.

His chuckle was soft and seductive. "There was a Moorish woman. After I was wounded I had appalling headaches. I would lie for days in a darkened room in agony, or turn to opium to dull the pain. Her fingers saved me from that. I asked her to teach me the technique."

Lethargy was claiming her. Soon she'd be beyond speech, beyond anything but putting her head down on the desk and closing her eyes.

"Was that the only technique she taught you?" She was fighting to get just the right note of sarcasm in her voice, fighting not to surrender herself to his skill.

His fingertip brushed over her collarbone beneath her sweatshirt. "I didn't need lessons in pleasing a woman. I can show you my 'technique' in that, too, if you wish. Are you brave enough, Melanie?"

He was laughing at her. Her lethargy vanished. Melanie straightened and pushed his hands away, turning to glare up at him. A spiky layer of her fair hair fell into her eyes, and she shoved it back impatiently. He was close, his eyes only inches from hers, and despite his teasing, there was a challenge in them.

He was daring her.

But Melanie knew she was frightened of him and what he made her feel, and she had no intention of relaxing her guard when he was around. The massage had been a mistake, one she wouldn't repeat. It was much safer to take a couple of ibuprofen tablets.

"I appreciate you trying to ease my headache," she said levelly, "but it's better now."

"I don't believe you, Melanie."

He waited a beat, to see if she'd answer him or change her mind, and then he gave her that mocking bow and moved toward the door.

"Where are you going?" Melanie fought to keep the anxiety from her voice.

"For a walk," he said levelly, and kept going. "I want to think, and I find nature conducive to thought."

"Will you be staying here at Ravenswood tonight?"

At the door he turned and gave her his full attention. "Where else would I stay, Melanie? Ravenswood is my home."

"*Was* your home," she reminded him. "My room is the one overlooking the cliffs."

He smiled, and she realized how that must have sounded. Her cheeks felt warm, and she cursed her own clumsiness. "*I mean,* the other rooms are free for you to choose from. Just not that one."

"I understand you perfectly. Don't concern yourself." He gave her his devilish smile, and then he was gone.

Melanie bit her lip. She had been ungracious, but she couldn't help it. Nathaniel threatened her carefully regulated world, the world she had created to keep herself safe. No matter how she fought to stop him he seemed to be dismantling it, with a smile, a word, a touch . . . bit by bit.

I didn't ask him to come here, I don't want him here.

Then why, deep inside, was she purring like her Aston Martin? As if Nathaniel Raven had just turned the key.

Twelve

*Nathaniel kicked at a dandelion head, watch-*ing the white fluff float off in the warm air. Early-evening shadows lay long across the landscape and the light was mellow and gold. His favorite time of day. It was a shame he had to spoil it by thinking about Melanie Jones. She was an infuriating woman. How could he possibly work with her? The queen was wrong; this woman would never be able to help him. They'd end up killing each other . . .

Or making the most wonderful love.

Nathaniel was a simple man. At least his life appeared simple to him, so he never thought too hard about what might or might not happen. He just reacted when it did. Now he was meant to pore over the past for clues.

The old lady, Miss Pengorren, had believed something was amiss. He hadn't read her diary, yet, but the final entry was tantalizing. Had he been right all along? Was there something very wrong with Pengorren?

Then again, Pengorren might be exactly what he seemed, and it was Nathaniel who was at fault. Nathaniel, who caused his own death, lying on the road and bleeding his life away for nothing more than an insane delusion. The head injuries . . . much as he was reluctant to admit it, it made a sort of sense.

So what was he to believe? He stood in a patch of bluebells, looked up at the sky, and reached down deep into his heart and soul.

Pengorren was a monster.

The words sounded in his head, measured, solemn, and absolutely certain. He felt the resolve growing inside him. He'd complete the task the queen of the between-worlds had set him, and this time he'd get it right.

A long, damp nose butted his hand. With a grimace, Nathaniel looked down into Teth's grinning face.

"What do you want, you demon?" he demanded, catching Teth's muzzle and shaking it.

In reply the hound pulled away and caught the tail of his jacket in his teeth and began to tug, growling playfully.

"You'll tear it," Nathaniel warned, then, "Heel!" But Teth wouldn't let go and wouldn't stop tugging. "What is it?" Nathaniel asked, allowing himself to be led along. "What is it you want from me this time, you hellhound?"

Teth released him and bounded off through the trees.

Glad for an excuse to stop cogitating over his former

life and get back to what he did best—physical action—
Nathaniel set off after him.

The bluebells reminded him of Melanie's eyes, although forget-me-nots better described her color. He
hadn't meant to touch her, but when she began to wriggle
her neck and shoulders and her eyes clouded with pain,
he'd recognized the signs of the headache. Of course she
wouldn't admit it; she didn't want him to see her weakness. He already sensed that she was the sort who would
walk a mile with a broken leg rather than limp and admit there was something wrong. So Nathaniel took the
initiative, and as he rubbed the painful knots out of her
muscles, feeling her slowly giving herself into his hands,
he'd been aware of her skin beneath his fingers, as exqui-
site as any he'd ever known.

She was strong and stubborn, but beneath the prickles
there was a sweetness, a sensuality, that a man like him
found irresistible. Because he wanted her.

Nathaniel gave a self-satisfied smile as he remembered how he won her over with his fingers, took control
of her senses. She'd all but given in to his superiority,
until he tried to push her too far, too fast, and she'd
wrested control back from him. Just as well, he told
himself, kicking another dandelion. She was here to
help him, not to make matters more complicated than
they already were.

But Nathaniel knew in his secret heart what he wanted
to do—have her and the consequences be damned. He
was a man who took risks, who enjoyed taking risks,
and Melanie Jones was certainly a risk.

Teth led him to St. Anne's Hill and around to the

other side. Across the patchwork of fields and stone walls lay the village, a sprawl of the old and the new. Cottages, the shop, the pub, the grey snub-towered church sitting prominently on its own small hill. Everything was so familiar, he felt as if he had slipped into the past again.

Teth was panting by his side as Nathaniel sat down on the grassy slope in the shadow of St. Anne's Hill. "Yes, I know," he told the hound. "You want to get going. But we have to wait until it's dark. We don't want people to see us, do we, Teth? We don't want to frighten them again."

Obediently the hound lay down, placing his head on his paws and watching Nathaniel with liquid eyes. Apart from the occasional drone of a car engine, everything was peaceful.

Nathaniel stretched out beside Teth to wait.

Mr. Trewartha was dozing, as he did most of the time nowadays, seated in his recliner, neither awake nor asleep, just lost in the past. It was a preparation for death, he knew that, and although he once fought against it, now he accepted it. His long life was coming to an end . . .

The shrill ring of the telephone barely disturbed his thoughts, but some part of him was aware of the answering machine picking up.

I am currently unavailable. Please leave a message or ring back during business hours, 9 to 4.

"Mr. Trewartha. I'm sorry to disturb you. It's, eh, 5:00 P.M. I've been ringing around some of the better-known antique businesses in the area, and your name came up several times. I realize you're semiretired these days, but you come very highly recommended by your peers."

The sound of *her* voice.

He sat up, blinking, instantly awake.

"My name is Melanie Jones, I'm from a London firm of solicitors, and we're undertaking the sale of an old family home. Fully furnished and untouched. Everything will need to be cataloged and valued. I know it will be an enormous job but, well, from what I've heard, you'd be perfect for the task. I hope you'll consider it."

Ravenswood? Dear God, she meant Ravenswood.

He was shivering with excitement. The sort of excitement he had not felt in a very long time.

"Please, get back to me," the voice went on, and then she gave her number with professional efficiency. There was a pause, before she added, "I'd appreciate it," and her tone was no longer quite so confident.

Mr. Trewartha heaved himself out of his chair, forgetting his aches and pains, and shuffled over to the answering machine to replay the message. Again the husky female voice washed over him like a warm sea, teasing him, soothing him.

But it wasn't just the voice. There was something else, and he recognized it as clearly as a fingerprint.

Mr. Trewartha smiled.

The "old family home" was Ravenswood, it must be, and Ms. Melanie Jones needed his help. Good manners decreed he must do what he could to assist her.

His smile turned into a chuckle. Mr. Trewartha had always been known for his good manners.

* * *

Nathaniel waited until day finally tipped into night, and then he waited again. When everything was quiet and the village was asleep—even the small pub had closed its doors and the last patron gone home—he and Teth made their way through the streets.

The church rose above them. They paused a moment, staring at the long, solid shape of it against the stars, before continuing up the narrow lane. Someone had grown some roses against the fence, and there was a painted board, noting the times for the services, but apart from that nothing had changed in two hundred years. The ground in the graveyard was still lumpy and uneven, and some of the old headstones leaned sideways.

He found the Raven family crypt, with its iron gate securely locked across the entrance, and when he peered through the rusting bars, he could see steep stone steps leading down into the vault. When he was a child he'd given himself shivers by imagining his ancestors climbing out. Now he wondered if Pengorren was inside, sleeping peacefully between his two wives, until he remembered that Pengorren had drowned himself in the sea.

A guilty conscience?

It seemed unlikely.

Nathaniel stepped back and looked up at the place above the door where the name RAVEN had once been chiseled into the stone. Now it said PENGORREN. Even here, Pengorren had supplanted him. Even among the dead.

Sickened, he turned away.

A line of flowering hawthorns grew along the boundary of the churchyard and there was a signpost, pointing, with the words: *Grave of the infamous highwayman Nathaniel Raven.* Nathaniel smiled wryly. He *was* remembered, just not in the way he wanted to be, and not for the reasons he believed he should be.

He followed the mowed track, and there it was. The hedge around it was neatly clipped, the stone was upright, and the inscription freshly painted. There were even some bunches of cut flowers, their perfume still detectable.

Nathaniel stood and looked down at his own grave.

NATHANIEL RAVEN
HERE LIES THE INFAMOUS RAVEN
WHO PUT FEAR INTO THE HEARTS
OF ALL WHO TRAVELED
THE HIGHWAYS OF CORNWALL,
AND WHO WAS SHOT DEAD,
IN THE YEAR OF OUR LORD 1814

Teth licked his fingers. He had forgotten the hound was there, and it was comforting now to rest his hand upon the big smooth head.

Why would Pengorren, who seemed to have everything, murder and lie and steal his way into Nathaniel's life, and then take over it completely? What had he done to attract the attention of the monster?

That's how he felt. As if his life had been stolen from him.

Where was mention of his part in the fighting in

Spain, his captaincy in the army? What about his qualities as a son and brother? All that people remembered now were his lawless escapades as a highwayman, the manner of his death, and, according to the author of the book, *The Raven's Curse,* his possible insanity.

Nathaniel knew his life amounted to far more than that.

Leave me . . . let me die.

He froze. The voice was his.

That's right, Nathaniel, you'd like to give up and die, that's your way out, isn't it, when things get tricky? Except that I need you. You're my pathway to a new life.

This time it was Pengorren's voice. Nathaniel swayed, reaching out to steady himself against his own headstone. He felt the Spanish heat, the burning sun on the dry ground and tumbled rocks, the unforgiving landscape he had believed he would die in. The cries of his men echoed in his aching head, with the smell of death.

"Please. Leave me. Save yourself."

And again Pengorren's voice, whispering in his ear, drawing him back into the past.

"Hush, Nathaniel. That's very noble of you, but you don't want them to hear you. Remember, we are hiding from the enemy. You will remember that, won't you? They'll be finished with the bodies soon—we'll give them the benefit of the doubt, shall we, and say they're poor and starving? English powder or a pinch of snuff is probably like gold to them."

"Let me—" He was slurring his words and his head was thudding from the blows he'd received during the ambush.

Pengorren placed a hand over his mouth. "Sshh, Captain Raven, I mean to save you despite yourself and send you back to your home and family. Oh yes, my fine hero, I'll see you survive this. Not for your sake, mind you. I want to save you for my own."

"Ravenswood."

"Aye, Ravenswood. You've led me to believe it's the most wonderful place on earth. A grand house set upon the Cornish cliffs with the blue sea beneath and the blue sky above. A perfect little piece of England that belongs to you and yours." His voice deepened, grew dreamy. "It's a very long time since I was in England."

The pain was suddenly unbearable, and Nathaniel lost several moments as he struggled to remain conscious. When the pounding in his head had dulled, and Pengorren had moistened his lips with the precious water from the canteen, he could listen again.

"I like the sound of your Ravenswood, Nathaniel. I've liked it from the first moment you mentioned it. You should be grateful for that, because otherwise I would have let you die with the rest of the men, or maybe I would have left you here in the rocks, to bake. Now when I arrive at Ravenswood I can be hailed as your savior rather than the bearer of sad tidings. So you see, keeping you alive will be so much better for me."

The sun was burning against his eyeballs, and he closed them.

"You're delirious, Nathaniel," Pengorren was still whispering in his ear. "You won't remember any of this, and if you do . . . well, it was just part of the nightmare."

"Major?" he managed, his voice a harsh croak.

"Yes, it's me," Pengorren answered jovially. "Rest now, dear boy, that's the way. I have work to do."

But Nathaniel forced open his eyes, just a crack, as Pengorren stood up in full view of the enemy. They would see him and come for them, he thought, without any great terror. He was half-dead anyway, so it would be quick.

But the enemy didn't attack. Nathaniel managed to lift his head slightly, so that he had a clearer view from his hiding place up in the rocks. There appeared to be only one of the guerillas remaining. He came forward to meet Pengorren, all the time glancing behind him nervously.

Pengorren spoke, but they were too far away for Nathaniel to follow the quick Spanish. Then Pengorren tossed a small leather bag at the other man, the sort of pouch that coins are kept in, and the guerilla caught it. A few more words were exchanged, and then the man hurried away, soon vanishing into the landscape.

Pengorren strolled back up the hill toward Nathaniel, passing by the dead bodies of his men. He paused, glancing down at them. "Ah well," he said, "they probably would have died anyway. I just got it over with sooner. But you see, I had to have you, Nathaniel. Just you. I need to be a hero, welcomed to Ravenswood with open arms." He looked up, and his eyes were dazzlingly bright. "I need to be loved."

Teth was whining. Nathaniel shook his head, clearing it. The air was chill and damp, the salty smell of the sea ridding him of the stink of death.

This was the first time he'd been able to remember those desperate days in Spain so clearly. If he'd remembered before then, he would have been able to warn his family . . .

"By the way, Mother, Major Pengorren, your husband, is a murderer who wants to steal Ravenswood from me and sire children on my sister."

Would they have believed him? No one wanted to believe ill of the person they loved, and everyone had loved Pengorren—the major's wish was granted in that.

He had to discover how to stop Pengorren.

How to put things right.

Thirteen

There's going to be a storm and the old oak tree in the park is going to fall over.

The words were already in her head when she woke. A premonition, just like the ones she used to have when she was young, before she learned to shut off that part of herself. Before the headaches started coming. There was an throbbing pain in her head now, but the ibuprofen had helped. Why was this happening to her again? Why had it come back now after all these years?

And then she heard the noise. There was something scratching on her bedroom door. Melanie's eyes opened. Her bedroom was very dark. She could hear the soft patter of rain on the casement window, but it didn't sound soothing. It sounded sinister, like an ominous sound track to a spooky movie.

The scratching came again, louder this time.

Mice, probably, she told herself. *Or rats.*

She shivered as she sat up, reaching for her robe. The flashlight was on the table by the bed, and she fumbled to turn it on. The light was too bright, momentarily blinding her. As her eyes grew accustomed, she swung the beam around the bedroom. A chair there, the fireplace here, her suitcase against the wall by the door. Nothing to be afraid of.

Ravenswood was empty.

Even its namesake had deserted her. When she went to bed Nathaniel still hadn't returned, and she was beginning to wonder if he ever would. Not that she missed him, of course. That was ridiculous. How could you miss a man you'd only just met and who wasn't a "man" anyway, not in the normal meaning of the word.

"It'll be a relief when he's gone," she said aloud, and then wished she hadn't when her voice sank without trace into the silence.

Robe wrapped around her, flashlight in hand, she made her way to the door. She was pleased to note that when she reached for the doorknob her fingers were perfectly steady. She pushed the door open and stepped out into the corridor, quickly sweeping the torch in an arc, hoping to catch whatever was doing the scratching.

Again, nothing.

Melanie held her breath and listened to the stillness. It was almost as if the house were listening, too. To her? Or whatever was lurking in the shadows?

Lurking! What kind of a word is that? Get a grip, Melanie.

Melanie drew her robe closer around her, as if the soft fleecy cloth in lemon yellow was designed to keep her safe. She didn't like this. She had never felt so far out of her comfort zone. Give her a nice neat office and clients asking questions she was qualified to answer and she was perfectly all right. Instead, she had a dead man and a stone that led to another world and a black hound from hell and a red-haired woman with talons for feet who terrified her.

"Where *is* he?" she whispered.

Maybe Nathaniel really wasn't coming back this time.

Melanie admitted she'd be very disappointed if that was the case. Unnervingly, an image of his handsome face popped into her mind, with that charming, teasing smile playing on his mouth. Just thinking about him made her feel as if she had lowered her emotional barriers. Made herself vulnerable.

She felt guilty, too.

As if she were indulging in something that went against her personal code of conduct. Like eating two slices of chocolate cake instead of one, or drinking the whole bottle of wine, or reading erotica and then feeling all hot and bothered, and so lonely . . .

Nathaniel Raven could definitely be classified as erotica. He was hot. Suzie always said life was too short not to enjoy it, she'd think Melanie was crazy not to have asked him up to her room already; it wasn't as if they hadn't connected. The sexual tension had been sizzling between them from the moment she saw him. But Melanie wasn't Suzie. Even though it was nearly two years since her last lover, she was happy with her life the way it was—she didn't need complications— and she certainly didn't thrive on them in the way Suzie did.

And why was she even thinking about Nathaniel Raven right now?

Melanie turned to face her bedroom and peered back through the doorway, training the flashlight on the four-poster bed. Empty, of course. The Raven wasn't lying there wearing nothing but a smoldering look. She tried to smile, but the room felt so cold and lonely, and she wasn't tired anymore. Maybe she could read some more of Miss Pengorren's diary? It didn't seem as if Nathaniel was going to do it, and she *had* promised to help him although they didn't seem to be doing much "working together."

But it was as good an excuse as any not to go back to bed.

Melanie had finally accepted that the electricity wasn't going to work tonight, no matter how often she swore as she flicked the switches. A search of the kitchen cupboards produced a lamp and some candles, and she set them up around the library, hoping the soft light would rid her of the sense of dread that seemed to have lodged deep inside her.

Instead, the mullioned windows reflected back an eerie glow, reminding Melanie uncomfortably of her recent trip into the past, and the shadows in the corners made her think of ghosts and ghoulies and things that went bump in the night.

"Or, in this case, scratch in the night."

Her voice sounded small, but Melanie was determined not to let her imagination take over.

"This is an old house," she reminded herself, like an

adult talking to a child, "and it would be very easy to begin thinking . . . thinking too much about what has happened here."

She might be retracing Nathaniel's steps in time, but there was no way she was going to start seeing ghosts or any other scary shit like that. She'd been there once, and she wasn't going back. The thought of meeting Felicity Raven on the stairs with a broken neck, or Major Pengorren leering at her from the landing, made her feel queasy.

Melanie looked around the room. Her throat was tight, and she kept needing to swallow, but she knew it was all in her head. "Overactive imagination," the family doctor had said when they took her to see him when she was a child. After that, they called anything she saw or heard or felt that no one else did her "imagination."

Melanie knew there was no place for imagination here, now. The candles were burning steadily, the room was empty, and everything was quiet. Time to get on with what she came to do.

With a determined breath Melanie turned to the contents of Miss Pengorren's desk.

Despite coming here with the sole purpose of reading through the diaries, at first she resisted them. She sorted through a wooden box full of photographs she'd found in a bottom drawer, inspecting the sepia faces and trying to decipher the shaky writing on the backs. The names were not ones she recognized, but they must have meant something to the old woman who lived most of her life in this house.

One small photograph, probably taken on an old box

Brownie camera, showed a young and smiling Miss Pengorren arm in arm with a handsome young man in uniform. According to the date on the back, it was 1943, during World War II. Melanie examined the faces. They looked so fresh and vibrant, so full of life and determined to enjoy every moment. War did that to people, she supposed, made them value the time they had. Perhaps Miss Pengorren had a lover who died during the war? Perhaps that was why she had ended up alone here at Ravenswood, a crotchety old spinster.

Melanie shook herself. Usually she didn't let those sorts of thoughts into her head—she was not prone to melancholy or flights of romantic fancy. Miss Pengorren was a formidable old lady with a sharp tongue, not someone to be pitied.

She tipped the photographs back into the box and pushed it to the back of the drawer she'd found it in. And then she reached for the final diary in the set and, going to the very first page, dated halfway through last year, began to read.

Miss Pengorren was complaining about the weather. It wasn't until Melanie was a third of the way through the diary—and by then she was getting quite expert at deciphering Miss Pengorren's writing—that something out of the ordinary caught her attention.

I saw him. He stood by my bed and stared down at me. I closed my eyes and when I opened them again he was gone.

Melanie felt a chill that was nothing to do with the lack of a fire. Was this an intruder? Or was Miss Pengorren dreaming, or worse, beginning to show symptoms of mental deterioration? Or—the thought came out of nowhere—was the "he" Nathaniel Raven? Miss Pengorren believed that the house belonged to Nathaniel and replaced his portrait. Did he frighten her into doing that? The first time Melanie saw Nathaniel, he was a ghost, and Eddie told her that others saw him "walking." Miss Pengorren had more reason to see him than most—she was living in his house, she was related to him through his sister.

The hairs on the back of her neck bristled.

Melanie's head came up, and she stared around the room. Shadows danced beyond the glow of the candles and the steady light of the lamp. It was very quiet. The earlier rain was gone, and even the constant wash of the sea against the cliffs was barely audible. Everything was hushed, waiting.

Again Melanie told herself to ignore her unease. After what she'd been through recently, surely nothing could ever frighten her again? The trouble was it didn't seem to work that way. If anything, the realization that there were worse things in heaven and hell than she ever imagined only made her more anxious.

It was as if a little voice in her head was whispering, *I told you so.*

And there was the sense of something inside her, stirring, opening up, and she didn't like it. She tried to tell herself she didn't know what that "something" was, but she did. On some other level, she did know what lay inside her, had always known that her so-called imagination was genuine, and the knowledge terrified her.

There's going to be a storm and—

"No!" she cut off the thought before it could properly form and forced her attention back to the diary.

There were pages and pages of Miss Pengorren rambling on about her neighbors and the wanderings of their sheep, and a series of disputes about a fence that kept falling down. She meticulously noted the quotes she'd received from the various fencing contractors and then, abruptly, in the middle of it all, another strange entry.

He came again last night. He stood over my bed, and he seemed to glow, like the moon at its brightest. I closed my eyes. I wasn't myself, a giddy excitement gripped me, as if I was a young girl. My heart was pounding. When he left I felt so weary. Too much excitement. Even so, I cannot help myself. I know it is wrong, but I long for him to come to me again.

Miss Pengorren was an old lady. What was happening to her? Who was "he" and what did he want? Melanie's eyes slid over the following page and found another, more terse entry, which told her that Miss Pengorren didn't understand her predicament any more than Melanie.

He came again. God help me. He must be a devil. I begged him to go, to leave me in peace, but he laughed. He torments me. What does he want?

Something creaked in the room. Melanie looked up, but there was nothing to see, only the shadows in the corners, and although she held her breath and listened hard, there was nothing further to hear beyond the silence.

She flicked once more through the pages.

I long for him, although I fear him. I know who he is and the awful thing is . . . I don't care . . . I want him back . . .

"That's enough."

Her own voice was loud and startling. She didn't even know who she was speaking to. Herself? Whatever was inside her, stirring? Or Miss Pengorren's midnight visitor?

Abruptly she stood up and shoved the diary into its spot on the shelf. She felt as taut as a violin string and didn't want to continue with this tonight. She couldn't. She was tired, and her hands were shaking. She turned around quickly, to blow out the candles, and that was when she saw him.

It.

Not Nathaniel. This wasn't tall, handsome Nathaniel. This was something smaller, shrunken, and even though it was in the corner, she knew it wasn't a shadow. The shape of it looked more or less human, but hunched over on itself, almost as if it lacked the strength to stand upright. She couldn't see the face; it, too, was bent over between gaunt, bony shoulders, and the skin of its skull gleamed through the sparse clumps of white hair.

Old. Ancient. But it wasn't just the age of the creature that made her heart hammer like thunder in her ears. It was the awful sense of malevolence that drifted from it. A dark, dreadful evil. Melanie had never experienced true evil before, she didn't realize it had a smell, a taste, a heavy and oppressive ambience. She felt dizzy and sick. With one hand covering her mouth, she clutched at the back of the chair with the other, holding herself up on jelly legs.

The chair creaked, and the thing turned slightly toward her. It was wearing a robe, the cloth dark and coarse, with sleeves that dangled down over its hands, and boots of cloth tied to its feet. A monk, maybe, or . . . or . . . But her shocked brain wouldn't give her answers. There was nothing in her world that looked like this.

Melanie began to ease away from the desk toward the door, her eyes fixed on the crouched figure. It didn't move again, but she knew it was aware of her. She knew that in a moment it would begin to approach her and that skull would begin to lift, and she would see . . .

Melanie lost it completely.

With a choking cry, she turned and ran.

A sound behind her, and she knew it was dragging itself across the floor in her wake. She flung herself at the door, fumbling with the doorknob. Time seemed to slow so that it took ages to open, and when it did, she burst out onto the landing.

A wedge of candlelight spilled from the room behind her, but the stairs were dark. Melanie didn't see the fold in the carpet runner. Not until her toe caught it and she tumbled forward, just like Felicity Raven.

Into space.

Fourteen

"*Melanie?*"

Hands, smoothing her hair, the brush of gentle fingers against her cheek. Melanie felt the sofa beneath her and realized she was back in the very same room she had just run from, except that this time Nathaniel Raven was kneeling on the floor beside her.

She tried to order her thoughts. She'd been lying on the stairs when he found her. She'd managed to catch the banister as she fell, swinging herself around and saving herself from a headlong dive. He'd carried her in here despite her protests.

"You're shaking," he said, as if such a thing was incredible to him.

Did he think she was made of concrete? Melanie wanted to take offense, to start an argument, to launch into a fight. There was a slow, angry burn inside her, and she wanted to let it out. Because it wasn't fair that this should be happening to her, now, after all these years.

After all the hard work she had done to make herself safe. To make herself *normal*.

"Melanie?"

"Of course I'm shaking. I tripped on the carpet and nearly fell!"

"What were you doing running down the stairs in the dark?"

"There was something in the room." She forced the words out, her voice huskier than usual. But she didn't get up.

"What sort of *something*? Where?" His hazel eyes were very serious as they looked into hers, but there was a wariness about him, too. As if he knew secrets he had no intention of sharing with her.

So that was how it was going to be.

Melanie caught herself before she said too much. "I-I don't know. A rat?"

He didn't believe her. "Where?" he asked again.

"Over there, in the corner," she said, waving her hand. She was starting to pull herself together; the light-headed feeling was wearing off, although she was still very tired. It wasn't as if seeing things was new to her, after all. It was just a long time since she'd had to deal with it. But she was an adult now, not a hysterical girl. She would cope.

"What was it doing?" He was peering into the shadows as if he expected it to wave back.

"Playing the fiddle," she muttered, "what do you think? It was just *there,* sort of bent over, wearing a robe. I thought you'd gone for good," she added, and despite her effort to be indifferent, she sounded accusatory.

"I haven't found what I came for yet." He was watching her closely, trying to read her, too.

"Remind me, what was that again?"

"The truth. I want the truth."

"Don't we all."

"The truth about Pengorren," he retorted.

She took a determined breath and sat up. The room was spinning. Melanie didn't remember feeling like this when it happened before. She closed her eyes but it only made things worse, so she forced them open. The candles were beginning to burn down to waxy stumps and the lamp was flickering, almost out of oil. It must be nearly dawn—the sky outside the mullioned windows wasn't quite as dark.

His hand closed on her arm, and she could tell he was being careful not to exert his strength. "You could have broken your neck," he said grimly. "Just like my mother."

Melanie shuddered. She remembered lying in the darkness, her heart pounding from her almost-fall, and she'd heard it behind her. Breathing. Shuffling closer. A dark, nightmare shape. And then she felt it touch her hand, a brief burning sensation, just as Nathaniel came in the front door.

The next instant it was gone.

She glanced down at her hand. There was a plum-colored mark on it, as though she'd brushed against something hot. Not enough to blister the skin or cause serious damage. It hardly even hurt.

When Melanie looked up, Nathaniel was still watching her with unnerving intensity. "Shall I call a physician, Melanie? I imagine you have such men in this strange time."

She shook her head, then nodded instead. His mouth quirked up reluctantly. "Yes, we do have physicians, and no, I don't need one," she clarified.

"Do you have the headache?" he asked, his voice dropping an octave.

She shivered again, but this time it wasn't from fear. The thought of his hands on her skin, his breath warm in her ear as he murmured her name. At no time in her life had she ever felt this tempted to throw caution to the winds and give in to her primal instincts. She wanted him, even if it was only for one night. One hour.

Melanie wished, with a sudden aching longing, that she didn't have to worry about tomorrow.

"No, I . . . I'm tired." From somewhere she found the strength to say it. "I need to go to bed. Alone," she added, as he opened his mouth.

He smiled, still watching her. "You don't trust me, do you, Melanie?"

"Because I won't fall swooning into your arms like every other woman you've probably ever known? What do you want me to say?" She made her voice low and throaty, like a B-grade actress in a B-grade melodrama. *"Oh Nathaniel, kiss me with your manly lips, caress me with your manly hands."*

He threw back his head and laughed.

For a moment Melanie was too surprised to do anything. She'd been taunting him, but instead of taking offense or carrying on the argument, he was enjoying himself. He was enjoying her. And oddly enough, that pleased her.

"Believe me, you're not like any other woman," he said at last, still smiling, watching her in that way that made her distinctly nervous.

"I need to go to bed," she said again, plaintatively. "I need to sleep. My body feels like lead. I've been up most of the night."

His smile changed. "So have I."

"Why—"

But he was straightening up in that graceful way, and instead of helping her to her feet as she expected, he slid his arms under her shoulders and knees and lifted her up against his chest.

Melanie was astonished. Although she wasn't a big woman, she was fit and strong, and she didn't considered herself a lightweight, but he didn't appear to be staggering or gasping for air. He was walking with her in his arms, carrying her easily. In a moment they were out on the landing, and he was moving with his usual catlike surefootedness toward the bedroom.

She let her head fall back as she gazed up at his face; he still had that little smile on his mouth. "I can walk," she said.

"I'm sure you can."

"Put me down."

"Be quiet."

Melanie opened her mouth, but he looked at her—a stern look—and surprisingly she closed it again. She should be furious with his macho arrogance, but she wasn't. She was excited, as if he'd tapped into one of her deepest fantasies. For someone who usually flared up at the slightest sign that her authority was being undermined, Melanie was enjoying being mastered. Perhaps it came from reading too many gothic romances when she was young.

Was this how the heroine in *Rebecca* felt when Max de Winter took her in his arms? Or the willful Dona, in *Frenchman's Creek,* when she encountered the French privateer? Or Mary Yellan, when she came up against Jem Merlyn? Although when it came to *Jamaica Inn,* Melanie had always preferred the crazed Vicar of Altarnun. To her mind there was something very sexy about him, and the way he wanted Mary as his mate for now and eternity, whereas Jem's vague promises of life on the road only made Melanie depressed. She was sure the Vicar would have set Mary up in style.

Melanie blinked. What was she doing, daydreaming at a time like this? She needed her wits about her, every single one.

Nathaniel had reached her bedroom and a comforting dawnlight was creeping in through the windowpanes. She felt as though the supernatural experience had taken all her energy, and she didn't even protest when Nathaniel Raven laid her gently down onto the bed. He drew the covers over her, adjusting them to his satisfaction. It was very nice, and as Melanie stared dreamily up at him, she found her eyes drifting shut.

"Good night, Melanie," he murmured, and bent close.

His lips touched her temple, lingering, caressing. She could smell him, the soap and the clean clothes and whatever it was he put in his hair. There was a male scent about him that appealed to her. She told herself it was probably better to pretend she was already asleep, rather than have to acknowledge that zing of sexual attraction when her resistance was so low. She told herself that even if that thing came back again, she could handle it. She'd always handled these episodes before.

Once, when she was young and her imagination was strong—before she'd learned to block it out—she'd seen an old woman at the end of her bed. Frightening, but insubstantial. She'd also seen a boy in her classroom in old-fashioned clothing, and he'd watched her all through her English lesson. Sometimes her dog—run over in the street years before—would follow her about.

But Melanie knew she'd never felt anything like this; she'd never seen something so solid and real and intent on doing her harm.

"Please, stay," she heard herself speak the words, although she didn't remember forming them. "Just until I'm asleep."

His steps were receding, but now they stopped. She thought she heard him sigh, and then he was coming back. The other side of the bed shifted and when she glanced over he was lying on top of the covers by her side, lying on his back with his head cradled in his arms, staring at the ceiling.

He turned to look at her, and despite his face being

shadowy she could tell his expression was uncharacteristically serious.

"Thank you for staying."

He smiled, but there were weary smudges under his eyes and lines near his mouth. His neckcloth was more rumpled than ever, and the stubble on his jaw was darker.

"I need to get you some proper clothes," Melanie said dreamily. "And a razor."

"There might be some clothes in the attic," Nathaniel replied, still watching her.

"Not an Armani suit, I'll bet," she murmured, and began to drift away into exhausted sleep. At least she was safe for now, until the creature came back. And it would. She had felt it reaching out to her, probing in her mind, searching for that place inside that she'd kept locked down for so long.

Just when she needed to be at her most calm and clearheaded, her imagination was breaking free, and her mind was running amok. And it wasn't just her mind, either.

She peeped through her lashes. Nathaniel was still there, but his eyes were closed, and his chest was rising and falling steadily. Melanie smiled. She'd known it was only be a matter of time before she and Nathaniel found themselves here.

In bed.

Nathaniel watched the light against his closed eyelids turn to gold. He should go back to the room, to see whether it really was empty, but Melanie needed him. Besides, he'd already felt that lingering sense of a presence. Of evil. He'd felt it like a vibration deep in his bones, just as he was able to feel the power exuded by the queen of the between-worlds.

He knew that Melanie wasn't imagining whatever it was she'd seen in there, whatever had sent her running for her life. She obviously believed the creature meant her harm. But there was something she wasn't telling him. There were things he wasn't telling her. They had been brought together to collaborate, and yet there were barriers between them, holding them apart.

Work together, the queen's voice echoed in his head.

If only it were that simple.

Nathaniel felt time pressing on him, or rather his lack of it. How could he save himself and his family by discovering the truth about his death, about Pengorren, and at the same time keep Melanie safe, and make her his?

Keeping her safe and making her his depended upon his gaining her trust. She was physically attracted to him, but with Melanie that didn't seem to be enough. She needed more than that. The good things in life had always come to him easily, too easily, up until his father died and everything began to go wrong.

Until his father died . . .

A chill passed through him. His father fell from his horse in the park, and his neck snapped when he hit the ground. He was out alone, and it was only when the horse returned riderless that they realized what had happened.

Everyone thought it was just an accident, and at the time Nathaniel never contemplated it might be otherwise, but now he knew that nothing was as it seemed.

Maybe Ravenswood held some clue? This morning he would search it from top to bottom, and if anything remained of Pengorren's guilt, Nathaniel would find it.

Fifteen

Melanie was dreaming. She knew it was a dream, and yet she didn't seem able to stop it or escape it. And the worst thing was it didn't feel like a dream. Like the creature in the corner, it felt real.

Once more Ravenswood was aglow, and colored lanterns hung throughout the garden. Melanie was walking among them, but now she wore an ankle-length dress, her fair hair was feathered about her face, and jewelry glittered at her throat. These were sapphires, to match her eyes.

Up the steps to the front door of the house, and the staircase was in front of her, candelabra burning at intervals, the flames making the faces of the portraits smile. The chatter of the guests and the dancing were beckoning her upward. Melanie allowed herself to be drawn, trailing her hand along the banister rail.

She felt light, as if her feet weren't quite touching the ground, and yet she wasn't dizzy; she was strong in her mind and spirit. Her skin tingled as if she'd had one of those ultraexpensive body scrubs, and her vision was clear and sharp, perfect twenty-twenty. It was like every part of her was running on full power, as if she was completely at one with herself, utterly focused.

She peeked into the library. It was just the same as it had been, cheery with decorations of green ivy and red holly berries, the people dancing, the candles flaring in the mirrors. Nathaniel was there, dancing with his sister. He looked gorgeous, so handsome and happy, no wonder the women were ogling him.

In her dream Melanie smiled, because she knew that back in her own time Nathaniel was lying beside her on her bed.

She lingered a moment longer and then she continued on. There was a door and when she opened it there was another corridor, leading to the servants' bedchambers.

She realized then that her wanderings had a purpose. She was looking for someone, and she knew that this was where she would find him. Melanie floated—walked was too mundane a word for what she was doing—down the long, bare corridor. No need to make servants' quarters pretty.

She could hear it now, getting louder. The sound was rhythmic and familiar, and she knew exactly what it was. She instructed her dream feet to stop, to turn back, but they wouldn't listen to her. It was like swimming too near to a riptide and then not being able to get out again. She was being drawn closer and closer in.

A door stood ajar, a wedge of pale candlelight spilling out. Melanie could hear voices now, the man's low and rumbling, and the woman's softer and gasping. They were making love. She watched her hand reach out and press open the door another inch, just enough so that she could see into the room without having to enter it.

Pengorren's broad naked shoulders all but hid his partner. His breeches were unbuttoned and pulled down over his muscular buttocks. The girl was smaller, slighter, her head thrown back, her face slack with ecstasy, her fair hair a tangled mass of curls covering the pillow. Her white thighs were open, cradling him, but her arms were bent above her head, her hands clasped about the brass rods at the head of her bed.

Melanie remembered her. It was one of the servants she had seen on her first visit into the past, one of the giggling, whispering girls carrying the food to the supper room and wishing Major Pengorren was hers. Well, it looked as if she had got her wish.

"Doan' stop," the girl whimpered. Because Pengorren had stopped moving and was observing her flushed face.

"Then ask me nicely," he said.

"I asked you already, sir."

"Not nicely enough, it seems. Come on. Or have you had enough . . . ?"

"No," she cried. Melanie saw her throat move as she swallowed, seeking for the words that would please him, while he watched her with a cold attention at odds with their situation. "Please, sir, I do love ye. I want ye more than . . . more than . . ."

"More than what, Dorrie?" he mocked, and twisted a corkscrew curl of blond hair about his finger, giving it a cruel tug.

"More than my ma or pa or my brothers and sisters."

"Hmm, not enough."

"Oh, sir, ye know I love ye!"

Pengorren chuckled. "I know that."

"I love ye more than life itself."

Evidently that was what he was waiting for, because Dorrie squeaked as he began to ride her again. And it wasn't gentle, there was a brutality to his movements that made Melanie, who wasn't easily shocked, feel queasy. But there was also something about the way Pengorren had made her beg, as if he wasn't making love to her at all or even having mutually pleasurable sex.

He was exerting his power over her.

Melanie began to back away as silently as she had come.

Pengorren raised his head. He looked surprised, and then his teeth flashed white as he smiled, like a lion about to make a kill. Here was the ruddy handsome face and piercing blue eyes she remembered so well; the feeling of being sucked into a dazzling vortex.

"Melanie?" he whispered. "You're stronger than I thought."

She spun around and began to run, back down the corridor. *He knows my name,* she thought. *He knows who I am.*

And then, fear pounding in her chest: *Is this really a dream? It doesn't feel like a dream.*

She reached the stairs, but they were gone.

Ravenswood was gone, and it was no longer 1813.

Melanie was alone on a beach, that same beach where

Suzie's clumsy boyfriend had smashed her sand castle and made her cry. Cautiously Melanie looked down at herself and saw those skinny goose-bump-covered legs and the hideous pink bathing suit. She was a child again, and it was that summer in Cornwall, after their parents had lost everything. Her mother and father had spent the whole time arguing bitterly over her father's poor investments, and a short time later had divorced. Her mother had gone to France to "find herself" and her father had rarely been home. Just Suzie and Melanie, really.

Melanie looked around her now, at the stretch of sand and the blue water, and tried to breathe calmly.

"I can stop this dream anytime I want to," she told herself. "I can wake up. I can." But her voice was small and weak, like a child's.

There was a shadow by the cliffs where the sand ended. Melanie peered across at it, holding her hand up to her eyes to cut out the glare. As she looked, the shadow moved and turned into a man. Unknown to her, he'd been standing by the rocks all this time, watching her.

Melanie had been told often enough to keep a lookout for strangers, so she kept a wary eye on him as he approached, muscles tensed and ready to run if he showed the least sign of trying anything nasty. But he was smiling, and there was a beauty to his smile, a dazzling beauty, like the sun in the morning, all golden and new. She found herself gaping up at him, everything else forgotten.

"What's your name, child?" he asked, in deep voice that seemed to vibrate through her skinny body.

"Melanie Jones," she said, pleased it was *her* name he wanted and not any of the other girls on the beach. That it was *her* he had singled out.

"Jones." He thought a moment, and then sighed. "So many. I can't remember them all. I am getting old."

"You're not old!" she retorted, because that was what adults always wanted you to say. But he was. There were lines in his face, and his eyes were tired-looking, as though he'd seen lots.

He laughed at her attempt at flattery, then his face grew serious, his gaze intent. "Melanie." He bent down on one knee and put his hands on her skinny shoulders. Immediately, she began to tremble, and her legs went all wobbly, as if the strength were being pulled out of her. Those blue eyes were boring into hers, filling her world.

"You're mine, Melanie Jones," he said, and his voice was booming in her head. "All mine."

She felt frightened, but she also felt as if what he was saying was right. She *was* his. And to be his, she must be special and wonderful. It was nice to be special for a change, instead of being the one no one wanted to be bothered with.

And then Suzie spoiled it all.

"Get away from her, you dirty bastard!" she screeched, as she came down on them, a fifteen-year-old fury.

The beautiful man fell over in the sand.

"Dirty old bastard," Suzie said again, spitting at him, and then she snatched up Melanie's hand and began to drag her away.

"Let me go! I want to stay! Let me go!"

But Suzie didn't let her go. "Don't you know any better than that?" she shrieked, panting, her eyes wild.

"I hate you," Melanie said. And she did, but she loved her, too, because special and wonderful as the man on the beach had made her feel, he had also frightened her. She had felt, when he touched her and looked into her eyes, as if he was taking something from her. Something very important to her.

That night she crept into Suzie's bed and cuddled up against her for comfort, and for once Suzie didn't tell her not to be a baby.

"He didn't hurt you, did he?" Suzie asked sleepily. "I'll kill him if he did."

Melanie made a sound that meant "no."

"Well, we'll be going home in the morning anyway, so you don't have to worry. He won't find you again, Melanie, I promise."

And Melanie believed her. Suzie was her big sister, and big sisters had the power to make everything all right.

Only this time Suzie was wrong, he *had* found her again.

Because the man on the beach all those years ago had been Major Pengorren.

For a moment after she woke, Melanie didn't know where she was. The incident on the beach was so long ago, she hadn't thought of it since, maybe because it was so strange and creepy. Suzie had been her hero in those days. No matter how deserted she'd felt by her mother or her father, she had believed that Suzie would always be there for her.

Melanie felt a twinge of guilt. It was a long time since she'd thought of her sister as more than an irritation, or a blood-is-thicker-than-water responsibility she would rather avoid.

The guilt turned into a hollow sensation in her stomach as the face of the man on the beach rushed back to her.

Instinctively, she turned to look beside her, but Nathaniel was long gone, leaving only the hollow in the pillow to tell her where he'd lain.

When her cell phone rang, it was almost a relief to suspend her thoughts and answer it.

"Hello?"

There was a pause, a heartbeat.

"Miss Jones?" the croaky old voice was faintly familiar, although she couldn't place it until he spoke again. "This is Mr. Trewartha. You rang me yesterday evening. About Ravenswood? It is about Ravenswood, is it not? Naturally, I had heard the sad news about Miss Pengorren's passing."

Melanie relaxed back against her pillows; it was the antique dealer who lived in Launceston. "Oh yes . . . I'm sorry, I . . ." *Slept in?* She peered at the window and saw that the sun was high.

"Nothing to be sorry about. You're probably enjoying the weather." His voice dropped to little more than a whisper, and Melanie wondered if there was something wrong with his throat. "I'm afraid I'm semiretired these days, but I do know of Ravenswood. If it would suit you,

I could come around and take a look. If that helps you at all? No strings attached. As I said, I am semiretired, but in this case I admit that I'm curious. It isn't very often that one of our oldest and grandest houses comes up for sale."

"I suppose not."

"Will you be staying long in Cornwall?"

"Only a week, although I'll probably need to come back again later to oversee things, when the arrangements for the auction have been made. Thank you for offering to take a look at the place, I'm very grateful, and naturally we'll pay you for your time and expertise."

"If you insist, Miss Jones. I assure you, though, I don't need your money. Coming to Ravenswood will be enough of a treat for me."

He was a bit of an old sweetheart, thought Melanie with a smile. "I'll look forward to meeting you."

"I'll make my arrangements and let you know when to expect me. Good-bye, Miss Jones."

Well, at least she'd managed to do something related to her job. She should have been up hours ago, eaten, dressed, gone for her run. What was happening to her routine? Hard to believe that all these years she had worked so hard at making herself safe, and after just two days it was all beginning to unravel.

Sixteen

When Melanie got down to the kitchen she found the cavernous room empty, although there were signs that someone had been here earlier. Whoever it was—and she had a good idea—had eaten most of the toast and marmalade. She made do with a crust with marmite and a cup of instant coffee, and wandered outside. The sky was hazy; the air still and humid.

Her dreams left her feeling strangely distant from her surroundings, although she had recovered from her almost-fall down the stairs and that nasty moment with that . . . well, whatever it was. She wanted to believe that was part of the dream, too, but even before she glanced at the fading mark on her hand she knew it wasn't. It was real, just as Nathaniel Raven was real.

Maybe they had brought it with them from the between-worlds? Maybe it latched on to them like a burr, and now it was here, inside Ravenswood? But even if that was so, what did it want? Her soul? Or just to send her out of her mind?

"Too late," she murmured.

Melanie squinted at the sky again.

There's going to be a storm, and the old oak tree in the park is going to fall over.

The vision of the tree, blackened and broken on the ground, was so clear she could have reached out and touched it. But the next moment she was backing away from it, denying it, telling herself she had enough problems and to stop this right now.

She was so busy refusing to listen to her own inner voice that it wasn't until she looked down at her feet that she realized she was walking. She was on the weed-strewn path that meandered past the house, in the direction of the cliffs. Melanie hadn't been near the cliffs yet, although looking out of the windows she'd noticed the shaky-looking railing and steep stairs that led down to the small half-moon beach just below Ravenswood. The tide was out at the moment, leaving the pale sand uncovered, glistening and virgin, and very tempting.

"I should be working," she said aloud to herself. "I have so much to do."

But Melanie didn't feel like working; she didn't feel like being responsible and serious. In fact she didn't feel like being Melanie Jones, from Foyle, Haddock and Williams. She wanted to sit on the sand and breathe in the smell of the sea. She might even roll up the legs of her navy blue cotton pants and wade in.

You'll have to think about Pengorren soon.

But Melanie didn't want to think about Pengorren, or the weird dream she'd had of him and the servant girl, Dorrie. *You are more powerful than I thought.* And then there was the dream/memory from her childhood holiday here in Cornwall, the man on the beach who asked her name and put his hands on her shoulders and made her feel as if she was special. Her practical side was telling her it couldn't possibly be the same man—Major Pengorren died in the nineteenth century, drowned in the sea, probably from this very beach. Her subconscious must have twisted the real memory into a false memory, using the face of the man she saw at the Yuletide Ball. Just as she dreamed about him and the servant girl, building on what she already knew and guessed, and making something completely imaginary from it.

Oh yes, she could rationalize it all. And if walking on the sand helped her to put all this craziness behind her, then maybe she shouldn't fight against it. Ravenswood would still be here in an hour or so; it wasn't going anywhere, and neither was she.

Cautiously, meticulously testing each footstep, Melanie began her descent to the beach.

Nathaniel had gone over the entire house, from cellars to attics. Apart from there being a great many more bits and pieces than he remembered—there were plenty of trunks of musty old clothes, and he helped himself—he could find nothing that shouldn't have been there. No thick dusty book with, *What Really Happened!* written in his father's handwriting. No letters pointing the finger at Major Pengorren.

How was this going to help him? Nathaniel thought in sudden despair. On the surface his father's death was nothing more than a tragic accident, and then his mother's death had compounded it. Pengorren had been nothing if not kind and generous. That's what everyone thought at the time, and what they still thought, if one believed *The Raven's Curse*. Nathaniel's memories of Spain, his suspicions about Pengorren, were unproven, and now there were hints that he was insane.

Maybe what he'd actually come back to learn was that Pengorren had won.

That's right, Nathaniel, you'd like to give up and die, that's your way out, isn't it, when things get tricky?

"No, that's not true, I won't give in."

Angrily, he brushed the dust off his new black trousers and stood up as best he could beneath the low attic ceiling. Teth had left pawprints in the dust on the floor, but the hound was gone now. After patiently following Nathaniel about for hours he'd suddenly lifted his head, as if someone—or something—was calling him, and then bounded off. He hadn't returned.

Nathaniel looked through the warped and cracked glass of the attic windows, toward the sea, and saw that at least that hadn't changed. There was a movement below, and he dropped his gaze down to the edge of the cliff. Melanie was standing there, her hand on the railing, staring anxiously at the old steps that led down to the beach. The railing looked as if it had been replaced many times since Nathaniel was a boy, but the stairs were cut into the stone cliff, worn down by the tread of countless feet.

They needed to talk about last night. He had to know what was happening here at Ravenswood and what part

Melanie was playing in it. She hadn't told him the whole story, and he meant to convince her to do so.

When he'd found her on the stairs, she'd been terrified. Whatever it was she'd seen in the room, he felt it, too, or the essence it left behind. He'd seen many horrors in the between-worlds, and he knew that terrible things happened to good people, but the thought of something attacking Melanie . . .

He had his suspicions. The sense that Pengorren was aware of Melanie at the Yuletide Ball bothered him. Would the queen of the between-worlds really use Melanie as bait? He wouldn't put anything past her, not really. Was there more going on than either Nathaniel or Melanie realized?

Despite being a soldier who had fought Napoleon, who many a time had taken aim with his pistol and sent his enemies into oblivion, this time he had no current plan of action. And it was driving him mad with frustration.

Then again, perhaps the frustration came from another source.

Why had he resisted climbing into bed with her last night? He'd wanted to, she'd been receptive, and once he would have taken advantage of her without a second thought. But he'd stopped himself. He'd lain chastely on top of the covers while she slept, all warm and soft and desirable underneath them. He'd pretended to fall asleep himself, but he hadn't been able to stop thinking about her or imagining what he'd like to be doing to her.

Why did he do that? Why was he wasting time? They could enjoy themselves now, live for the moment, just as he'd always done.

Except that Nathaniel no longer wanted to live like that.

Melanie began to step down the cliff, slowly and carefully, one hand on the railing. He was surprised she would attempt it at all. She was stubborn and strong, yes, but she resisted anything risky. He found himself tensing, fingers gripping the sill, and praying that the cliff steps were dry and the railing sound.

He should go after her, just to be sure.

Nathaniel left the attic without a second glance.

Melanie was sitting on the sand, arms looped about her bent knees, staring out to sea. The salty breeze had helped clear her head, but she still felt woozy. Not herself. Maybe she was coming down with something. It would almost be a relief if that was all that was wrong with her. She'd choose the flu over a malevolent manifestation any day.

"This place isn't any different from the last time I was here."

Melanie turned her head. Nathaniel was standing a few feet away and he'd changed his clothing. She blinked. He wore black trousers and boots that came to his knees, a white cotton shirt, open at the throat, with ruffles down the front and on the cuffs. He looked like a cross between a highwayman and a pirate. The effect was devastating.

Melanie felt something flip over inside her. "Where did you find the new clothes?"

"In the attic." He raised his arm and sniffed his cuff. "I smell like lavender . . . they must have used it for the moths."

You look like heaven.

"I found a cutlass, too, but I thought I'd better leave it up there."

"Yes. People don't walk around waving cutlasses these days. Unless, of course, they're pirates."

Nathaniel was observing her curiously, as if he wanted to read her mind. "What is it?" he asked in a deep, quiet voice. "You look different."

"Different?"

"Yes." He was frowning, and abruptly Melanie turned away and pretended to count the seagulls.

He sat down on the sand beside her, mirroring her pose, with knees bent, his arms draped over them, staring out to sea. She risked a glance at him, but his profile told her nothing other than that he'd used a razor.

"There's going to be a storm," he said.

"I know." Melanie bit her lip as soon as the words slipped out. "I dreamed about Ravenswood last night," she said quickly, before she could change her mind. "I went back into the past, only this time it was just me. It was the night of the Yuletide Ball, and you were there, dancing with Sophie. You looked . . . happy."

Nathaniel was intent on her now; she had certainly captured his attention.

"I didn't stay for the ball, I just looked in the door, and

then I went to the servants' bedrooms. Major Pengorren was there with someone called Dorrie. They were having sex . . ." She stopped, wondering how it was possible to convey the sheer awfulness of that scene to someone who hadn't been there.

"I remember Dorrie," he said softly. "Curly fair hair, sweet-natured. Her father drowned, leaving a wife and several young children, and Dorrie came to work for us when she was quite young herself."

Melanie shot him a look.

"No," he said dryly, "I didn't take Dorrie to my bed. She was *too* sweet for me."

"Right," she shrugged as if she didn't care. "That's what made it so horrible. She was so sweet and he was so skanky."

He frowned. "Skanky?"

"Squirmy, horrible, nasty."

"Ah. I see." He thought a moment. "And yet Hew Pengorren was loved by everyone."

"They believed they loved him. I think he made them believe it."

"How, Melanie?" He sounded as if he was really interested in her opinion.

She waved a hand. "A magic spell?" she said, making a joke of it, but it fell flat.

He gave it his full consideration, and she wasn't sure whether that pleased her or just embarrassed her more.

I've seen him before. The words were on the tip of her tongue, but she couldn't speak them aloud. It was as if by not saying them she could go on pretending. Because if she *had* seen him when she was a child, then what did that say about Pengorren and the danger she was in?

"You told me that before she left Ravenswood, Miss Pengorren replaced Major Pengorren's portrait with my own," he said quietly. "I was up in the attic a moment ago, but Pengorren's portrait isn't there. Do you know where it is?"

"No. Why?" she asked, puzzled by the connection between her dream and the portrait.

"I thought it might be significant."

"Eddie would know where it is." She dug her fingers into the sand beside her and let it trickle out again. "Remember, if you come face-to-face with him, then you're a distant relative from the wrong side of the blanket. I don't think you should try and tell him the truth. He'd get you locked up."

His eyes narrowed. "I remember, although why I should have to explain who I am to a caretaker—"

"You're very arrogant," she cut him short. "The days of the lesser classes being seen and not heard are over. Most of us believe we're all equal."

"You sound like a French revolutionary," he said. "Liberty, equality, fraternity!"

"Maybe the revolution wasn't so bad."

He snorted.

She watched him carefully, thinking he might be terminally insulted by what she'd said—after all, he was an English gentleman from the early nineteenth century, with all the hang-ups and prejudices of his time. But he wasn't. He was smiling at her and shaking his head, and she realized that she hadn't dented either his pride or his self-esteem. Nathaniel Raven was confident enough to be impervious to her criticism. Well, that wasn't a bad thing, was it? Melanie accepted that she was touchy enough for both of them.

Which made her the exact opposite to Nathaniel.

Seventeen

Magic.

Melanie had reacted as if he'd laugh at her suggestion, but Nathaniel had learned not to dismiss anything, no matter how far-fetched it might seem. Pengorren definitely used something to blind people to his true nature, and his true purpose, so why not a magic spell? And as for Melanie's dream—if that was what it was—Nathaniel accepted the picture she drew of Pengorren seducing Dorrie. The man he had come to know would have had no compunction in using sweet Dorrie, just as he used Sophie and Felicity.

His gaze slid back to Melanie, and lingered. She *was* different. After her experience last night he would have expected her to be white-faced and ravaged, but instead her skin glowed, and even though the sun wasn't shining, her hair was. When she turned her head, strands of it drifted out, gleaming like liquid gold.

His heart began to beat in a slow and sensual rhythm, as if in response to some invisible siren's call.

Did she feel it, too? She was staring out to sea. They were sitting close together, so near they were almost touching, and yet a chasm lay between them. *Work together,* the queen said. Nathaniel had resisted her demands but now he was getting desperate. His time was running out, and soon it would be too late.

"The thought of your seeing Pengorren in your sleep makes me extremely uncomfortable," he said, trying for the honest approach. It had worked before.

She laughed without humor. "Here's something that will make you even more uncomfortable. In my dream last night he called me by my name."

Unfamiliar cold anger built inside him. "It's almost as if he's set his sights on you, Melanie. As if, for reasons we still don't understand, he is calling to you from the past."

"But that's impossible, surely? The idea of Pengorren's sending messages through time . . ." She shivered, and a breeze hissed in from the water, stirring her hair. She pushed it back. "Last night in my dream, it was as if he was playing a role. He was there with Dorrie, doing what he did in 1813, and at the same time he was fully aware of me and who I was. Just like you, Nathaniel, when I went back through time. You were there, being Nathaniel Raven in 1813, and yet you knew you were taking part in a scene that was nearly two hundred years in the past." She took a deep, uneven breath. "There's something else. I should have told you this first, but I didn't want to believe it . . ." She frowned. "It's about Pengorren. I've met him. Not at the Yuletide Ball. It was when I was a child, here on the beach in

Cornwall. He came up to me and asked my name, and when he touched me I felt as if he was drawing out my strength, my being, my . . . my soul, for want of a better word. I only remembered this after my dream last night, and at first I thought my brain was confusing the faces, that I was making it up. But I'm not. It was definitely him. I must have blocked it out, or pushed it to the back of my mind, but last night I remembered everything. It was Pengorren, and that's why he knows me," she finished bleakly.

"You think that's why you're here now? Because of your connection with Pengorren?"

"Yes."

"You think he's able to move back and forth through time?"

She glanced away, out to sea again. "Yes, I do." Her mouth was set in a line, her hands clasped tightly between her knees.

"We have to face this, whatever it is. We need to be prepared." He wrapped his fingers around her arm and found she was rigid with tension beneath the sleeve of her top.

"It's my imagination," her voice trembled.

"Melanie, your imagination can't hurt you."

She gave a disbelieving laugh as she turned to him. "Then what's happening to me? I'm seeing things, hearing things. It can't be right."

Nathaniel took her face between his hands. "I don't know what's happening to you, Melanie, but whatever it is we're in it together."

"Are we?" Her voice was husky with suppressed emotion.

"Yes. You and me. Together we'll get to the bottom of this mystery, and defeat Pengorren."

"So then you can regain what's rightfully yours," she said, as if reciting a fairy tale, "and we can all live happily ever after."

"You in your time, and me in mine."

She smiled, but he could see it was an effort—her lips trembled. Whether she admitted it or not, Melanie was terrified, and he'd always been drawn to beautiful women in distress.

"I want to kiss you," he said, and wondered why he was stupid enough to warn her. Now she'd tell him no.

She blinked, and then she reached out her hand and touched his mouth with her fingertips. "Go on then," she whispered.

Nathaniel bent his head and claimed her mouth in a hot, desperate kiss. Her lips responded, returning his pressure, her mouth opening to his. Her arms slid around his neck, and she clung to him. She tasted sweet, as sweet as he'd remembered, and for a moment the kiss overwhelmed him. He forgot everything but wanting to push her back onto the sand and be inside her.

"Melanie," he murmured, and kissed her cheeks, her eyelids.

"I don't understand any of this," she said, and now she was shaking. "I don't understand what's happening to me, or why. I'm afraid. I'm afraid of you and myself, and of Pengorren. That thing in the room—"

"We'll come through this," he said harshly, as if he really believed it. He held her away, feeling the siren pull of her and resisting it, and when he looked into her eyes he was impressing upon her his own confidence.

He believed in himself. And knowing it gave her courage. He might be the Raven, the reckless and daring highwayman, but he was also Captain Raven, the brave and gallant officer. And most important of all he was Nathaniel, who had come from the past to make everything right for those he loved.

He was a hero.

Why didn't she realize that before?

"We'll work together," she said, with hardly a tremor.

"Yes, we will."

Melanie looked into his eyes a moment more, and then she smiled. "Come on then," she said, getting to her feet, "I need to be doing something." She turned toward the steps, calling back over her shoulder, "I'll go and speak to Eddie about the portrait."

Nathaniel followed her up the cliff steps. "You'd think Miss Pengorren would have been proud of her namesake, so why take his portrait down in favor of an infamous highwayman's? What did she learn, and how?"

Melanie remembered then she hadn't told him about the entries in the diary, and updated him quickly.

"But we still don't know who or what was visiting her in the night?"

"Maybe she told Eddie?" Melanie said.

"She was probably too proud, or too frightened, to admit anything was wrong."

"If it was the thing I saw last night, then I could understand her being frightened. But she also seemed to be drawn to whatever it was that was visiting her. As if she was revolted and yet fascinated at the same time."

They reached the top of the cliff. Nathaniel moved closer, but this time he resisted kissing her. "Go and see Eddie."

"Okay."

"Melanie, there's something I should tell you." His eyes were very serious. "I don't know how long I have before I have to go back to the between-worlds. I don't think it will be infinite."

"But . . ." She shook her head. "God, Nathaniel, we haven't found out anything!"

"We have. We're making progress. I have hopes we will accomplish our task."

Melanie felt as if she'd been for a ride on a roller-coaster and left her stomach behind. "When? I mean, when is your time up? Does a gong sound or something? Do you get a warning, or do you just vanish?"

"I don't know. She didn't say."

"Fabulous," she muttered, so shaken she just wanted to get away from him.

"Are you all right?"

"No. No, I'm not."

"Melanie, I promise you, I will see you safe . . ."

But she left him there, walking quickly toward Eddie's cottage. She'd known he wouldn't be here forever, but she'd thought it would be months. Maybe even years. Now he was telling her it could be much sooner. She still felt the heat of his mouth on hers!

She didn't know whether to feel angry or frustrated, or just plain miserable.

Eddie's cottage was made of the same grey stone as the house. Smoke trickled from the chimney and the upper windows were curtained, but Eddie would be downstairs by now anyway. Melanie could hear the clack of his keyboard as she knocked, and then it stopped, and after a pause the door opened. Melanie blinked. Today he was wearing an Hawaiian shirt, complete with girls in grass skirts, and his hair was standing up as if he'd been running his hands through it. But his smile was friendly, and his eyes lit up at the sight of her.

Or maybe he just wanted to knock off work.

"How's the book going?"

He grimaced. "I'm too far into it to be able to tell." His eyes narrowed slightly as he took in her pallor. "You all right? You look as if you've seen a ghost," The irrepressible smile was back again. "Sorry, couldn't resist."

"There was a rat in my room last night. It kept me awake."

"Oh. Not much I can do about them, and I have tried. Miss Pengorren used to go on at me about vermin, but she stopped toward the end. Must have got used to them."

Or maybe she found something worse to worry about.

"Have you had anything published?" she asked politely, as he closed the door behind her.

Eddie shook his head. "I was close but then Dan Brown had the same idea as me." He winked, to show he was joking. "No, I'm afraid my stuff isn't on the bestseller lists yet. I'll live with it. How is it going with Ravenswood? I know there's a ton of stuff in there, and some of it must be worth something. Pity there were no heirs. She left everything to charity, didn't she?"

"Yes. I rang Mr. Trewartha in Launceston. I'm expecting him in the next few days. He's retired, but he's familiar with Ravenswood, so he's going to make an exception for us and take a look. I'm hoping he'll agree to list the contents and give us some evaluations—"

"Trewartha?" He thought for a moment and then shook his head. "Sounds familiar for some reason, but nothing to do with antiques. I don't know anything about antiques."

Melanie eyed his shirt but decided not to comment.

Eddie gave her a pensive look. "You realize that when Ravenswood's gone, I'll be out of a job."

"I know, and I am sorry. Have you anywhere else you can—"

"I have a sister in Scotland. It won't be like living here, though, with Miss Pengorren." He smiled. "She had a nasty tongue on her, tore strips off me sometimes, but you couldn't help but admire her spirit."

"You said you were born on the wrong side of the Pengorren blanket," she reminded him, hoping he'd elaborate.

Eddie was pleased to accommodate her. "That's right, I was. Long way back, though. Major Pengorren was my dubious ancestor. He impregnated half of Cornwall in his time. Right Don Juan he was."

She should have known; so much for the wedded bliss between Sophie and the major. Maybe it was Dorrie who was Eddie's great-great-whatever-grandmother, although looking at him she couldn't see much of Dorrie's sweet blond looks in Eddie's pleasant but plain features.

"Do you know very much about Major Pengorren?"

"I think he was well liked. Maybe he was one of those lovable rascals that no one can refuse. No woman, anyway," he ended wryly, as if he envied the major his skill.

"Maybe."

But that didn't seem right to her. Pengorren wasn't a lovable rascal, not from the snippets she had seen of him. He was an evil man, someone you would never turn your back on.

"You mentioned last night that there was a portrait of Pengorren that used to hang in the stairwell. You said that Miss Pengorren replaced it with the one of Nathaniel Raven."

"That's right."

"Well, I can't find it. It's not in the attic. I was wondering whether you'd seen it around."

Eddie's eyes widened, and then slowly his face turned red. "Oh bugger," he whispered. "I borrowed it before she went away. I have it here. I thought it might give me some inspiration. For my book, you know? You'll think I was going to steal it. You do, don't you?"

He was so genuinely mortified by his oversight that

Melanie did her best to make the right reassuring sounds. "Perhaps you could give it to me now," she suggested, after he'd apologized again. "I could take it back with me and—"

"God no, I'll dust it off and bring it over for you. I swear, I never meant to . . ." Eddie was clearly terribly embarrassed by the whole matter.

"Eddie, I believe you." She didn't feel like pushing it. She was tired, and her head was aching again. "Just tell me this. Did Miss Pengorren ever mention dreams? Unpleasant dreams? Did she ever see anyone in the house at night?"

He's genial face lost its humor and became almost serious. "You're talking about her diary," he said. "I read that, too."

"You *read* her diary?"

He gave her a guilty glance. "I probably shouldn't have, but I'm related, remember, and I was fond of her. I suppose I was curious, too, when she went to that nursing home in London after she'd always sworn to me she wouldn't. I was hoping there might be something in her diary to explain her change of heart."

"But there wasn't?"

"No. Unless whatever . . . whoever was coming to her in the night was reason enough for her to want to go."

"A ghost?"

"Why not? Ravenswood is an old house with a sad history. The Ravens weren't a happy family, and then the Pengorrens had their share of tragedy, too. Take a look at the genealogy chart in the back of that book in the library, *The Raven's Curse,* and you'll see what I mean."

"I will. Don't forget the portrait."

"I won't. Actually I'll be glad to get rid of Pengor-ren. Lately, he's been giving me the creeps."

Eighteen

Nathaniel ducked his head beneath the roof of the tunnel and squinted ahead. He hated the between-worlds just as much as Melanie did, which was why he hadn't told her what he was intending to do.

She would have wanted to come with him, and he preferred her to be safe and secure, inside Eddie's cottage.

Behind him the usual assortment of scuttling creatures crept from the shadows to watch him pass. But he wasn't concerned about them. All of a sudden he heard what he'd been listening for, the faint thud of approaching paws. Nathaniel smiled as Teth came loping out of the darkness, tongue lolling from his whiskery face. Reaching out, he clasped the hound's big head firmly between his palms and gave him a little shake. "There you are, hellhound." He peered intently into the hound's liquid dark eyes. "I want you to take me home, Teth. Back to Ravenswood."

The hound cocked his head to one side.

"Come on," Nathaniel whispered. "I could probably do it myself, but I'd be wandering in this bloody place for days, looking for the right door. You showed me the way before, Teth."

The hound stared back at him, and Nathaniel reined in his frustration. Teth could help him, he knew it . . . Maybe the hound could smell his way home? Nathaniel had changed his clothing, but not entirely. He reached up and pulled loose the black ribbon from his hair, and then held it toward Teth.

"Take me home," he murmured. "Home, Teth!"

Teth gave the ribbon a sniff, thumped his tail vigorously, and then launched himself forth into the tunnel. Hoping they were going in the right direction, Nathaniel set off at a run behind him.

He was acting against the queen's instructions, he knew that, and she would punish him. He was even acting against his own good sense, and the promises he'd made to himself to be less impulsive and hotheaded. But he couldn't sit still any longer, waiting for something to happen. It was driving him crazy. How many times was he going to search Ravenswood looking for clues? How many books was he going to scour for information? And while he waited, Melanie was under threat. When she had told him about Pengorren, he'd known then he couldn't wait any longer. The queen might be a powerful and awesome being, but he wasn't sure he entirely trusted her where Melanie was concerned. Besides, he was used to making his own decisions and striking hard and fast at his enemies.

Nathaniel was a man of action, and he was sick and

tired of trying to be patient. It was time he took control of the situation.

Ahead of him, the darkness of the tunnel began to lighten. He could see Teth, bounding along, silhouetted against an opening laced with branches and leaves. As the hound jumped through, Nathaniel followed, pushing aside the prickly curtain. He realized then where he was, on the far side of the garden, in the clump of bushes growing by the summerhouse.

He could smell roses and the warm sweet breath of summer.

It must be the summer of 1813, soon after his return from Spain. Pengorren hadn't arrived at Ravenswood until the autumn. He had time to go and speak to his father and mother and his sister, to somehow make them understand what was to come. He would defeat Pengorren before he even arrived, and bedamned to the queen of the between-worlds.

All would be well this time, he told himself, as he strolled toward the dark, sleeping house.

Melanie had taken a shortcut through the vast and overgrown vegetable garden that separated Eddie's cottage from Ravenswood. She had a strong urge to sit down on the rustic wooden seat, where the cabbages had gone to seed, and have a nap. But strange things were happening to her, and she was afraid to sleep. She was equally afraid to stay awake. The truth, unnerving as it was, was that she wanted Nathaniel. Only he understood what she was going through.

But Nathaniel was leaving her, he'd made that plain.

This was not the sort of story where they would be walking off into the sunset together.

And yet, she thought, weaving through some broken stakes with last year's wilted vines still attached, *I'm certain Nathaniel needs me as much as I need him. That's why the queen of the between-worlds has brought us together . . .*

A soft breath of wind stirred her hair and rattled the old flower heads at her feet. She looked up, suddenly tense. The sky was darkening. Something ominous approaching.

A storm, she told herself, nothing more. Surely she wasn't afraid of a storm? She was never one to hide under the bed when the thunder sounded. But it wasn't just the storm that was unnerving her. The feelings inside her were stirring, unfurling, and she knew that this time she'd be sensible to heed the warning.

Melanie quickened her steps toward the house.

A horse whickered. Nathaniel stood in the stable doorway, letting the familiar smells engulf him. This was always one of his favorite places, and after he returned home from Spain and recovered enough to ride again, he enjoyed nothing more than galloping away across the park. There was a sort of freedom in it, an escape.

He knew he shouldn't be here, he should have gone straight up to Ravenswood, but somehow his steps had deviated. Perhaps he just needed a moment to think, to collect his thoughts, to put aside his doubts, before he began the task of persuading his family to believe the impossible.

He admitted to himself that he was relying on father's quiet strength and intelligence to persuade his mother and sister to listen to what would seem a wild story. He trusted his father, and as a boy he'd wondered how he could ever replace him as lord and master in this little patch of England. Was that why he'd gone off to war? It was easier to charge the French or ambush some Spanish guerillas, than it was to set one's mind to the difficult tasks of rents and crops and money in the bank?

"You're straightforward. Honest," his father said to him upon his return. "You treat everyone as if you expect the best from them. That's a good thing, Nathaniel. You'll grow into your inheritance. One day, when I'm gone, you'll make a fine master."

His father was right. He was beginning to grow into the job he had been born for . . . and then Pengorren came. Usurped him, stole all that was his. Pengorren wasn't honest or straightforward, and Nathaniel was taken in. And by the time he realized it, it was too late.

The horse whickered again, this time more urgently. Nathaniel smiled when he recognized the dark face and erect ears above the door of the box. It was Neptune, *his* horse.

The horse he had raced alongside Melanie's car had been a ghost horse, some demon from the between-worlds he'd borrowed for the occasion, *and* received a memorable telling off from the queen. That creature hadn't been anything like the warm flesh-and-blood beast before him now, and he realized just how much he had missed the real Neptune.

There was a lantern hanging from a hook in the

ceiling, but it was turned down low. The boy must have forgotten to turn it out again, he thought, because the stable was empty. Nathaniel came forward to pat Neptune's nose, murmuring a greeting as the horse tossed its head and bumped against him.

"Good boy, good Neptune, I've missed you, too," he said softly. "But it'll be all right soon. Everything will be back to normal."

He heard the footstep just before Pengorren spoke.

"Nathaniel."

For a moment he was too shocked to turn, and then he swung around, disbelieving. It *was* Pengorren, there could be no mistake. He was standing in one of the empty stalls and he looked the same. A little disheveled, perhaps, without his shirt, and with only half of his handsome face lit by the lantern. His blue eyes mirrored Nathaniel's shock, and then they narrowed.

"You shouldn't be here," Nathaniel said, knowing even as he spoke it was a ridiculous thing to say. "It's too soon."

Pengorren frowned. "Too soon?"

"This is the summer of 1813."

Pengorren's face cleared and he laughed. "Oh dear. And here I was thinking it was *you* who shouldn't be here."

Nathaniel felt the anger building inside him. "You don't belong at Ravenswood," he said quietly, dangerously. "I want you out."

Pengorren's mouth thinned. "Interfering with time, boy? Didn't the sorceress tell you about the pitfalls of that? I'm sure she did. You're only going to make it worse, Nathaniel, just like you did last time. But you can't help yourself, can you? Just have to rush in and play the hero. Is that why you're here? To save your family? Or is it to kill me?"

"You seem to know everything, you tell me."

"I think I already know."

Pengorren smiled, his blue eyes glittered. Then he moved, pushing at something at his feet, where Nathaniel's view was hidden by the stall door. There was a soft squeak, and then the sound of a voice he knew. "Is it morning already?" Pengorren, watching him, caught his dismay and gleamed with malevolent enjoyment.

Touseled dark hair appeared, and then two bare arms and a smooth naked back, as Sophie stretched sensuously, tangling her fingers together with a little laugh. "Is it morning?" she murmured. "We don't have to go back yet, do we, Hew? Stay, please."

Pengorren was unmoved by her invitation. "Your brother's here," he said.

Sophie froze, and then slowly she turned. She was white, her face slack with shock. And then she gave a whimper and clapped her hands over her eyes.

"I said, *it's your brother.*" Pengorren gritted his teeth as he struggled to pull her hands away. "Look at him, Sophie."

Her eyes rolled wildly. "No, no, it can't be! Nathaniel's dead!"

"Sophie," Nathaniel whispered, his throat aching with sorrow.

She screamed shrilly, and Pengorren let her go with an expression of disgust, so that she fell to the ground, weeping. "It seems she doesn't want anything to do with you, Nathaniel. Could that be because you were buried last month? This is the summer of 18*14*, after all."

Nathaniel felt a wave of despair settle over him as he realized he'd rushed in without consideration yet again. And then despair gave way to anger as he read the victory in Pengorren's eyes. Neptune must have felt it, too, because the horse began moving restlessly, stamping his feet.

"Do you know, Sophie will do anything I ask of her?" Pengorren went on. "She follows me about like a little pet, don't you sweetheart? I've taught her all sorts of tricks—"

"Leave her alone," Nathaniel growled.

"But she's still fond of her big brother. Do you know what she did? Shall I tell him, Sophie?"

"No, no, don't tell him!" Sophie's voice was a high-pitched wail. For a moment she looked directly at Nathaniel. "Get out of here! Run, run . . ." And then she was screaming as though she had lost her mind.

Nathaniel backed away, shaken, his heart pounding.

"Yes, run while you can," Pengorren hissed. "Don't think I won't come after you, though, and destroy you forever."

Nathaniel stumbled at the door but caught his balance. Behind him he could hear Neptune's high-pitched whinnies mingling with Sophie's screams, and then a crashing and splintering as the horse broke through the door of his box. A moment later Neptune galloped by him.

Instinctively Nathaniel reached out and grasped the

horse's mane, pulling himself up and onto Neptune's back. He bent low, finding some comfort as Neptune took him away into the dark night, knowing there was nothing else he could do.

For a long time he rode, the image of Sophie in his head. He was a fool, a blind and impulsive fool. He'd returned to try and stop Pengorren, to save his family and Melanie, and instead he'd made things worse. Pengorren was right, he'd tried to play the hero again and instead he'd put at risk the past and the future. When would he learn he could not accomplish his task through reckless actions? When would he learn that he couldn't do this on his own?

He must learn to think about the future, to set aside instant gratification in favor of the benefits of waiting for the perfect moment. And he must learn that it was better to cloak himself in the cold and deadly anger of a man rather than waste his energy on the hotheaded impulses of a boy.

Gradually, as Neptune's fluid movements soothed his misery, he became aware that he was near the woods on the Truro Road.

It was here that it all began, the night he'd seen Sophie and Pengorren together, the night his mother died. And it was here it ended, when he was fatally shot and lay dying on the road.

As he remembered, he felt himself slipping away, losing touch with the here and now. He saw the moon in the dark sky, heard the cry of a hunting owl, and felt the cold air against his face. There, in crowded trees, he had stood waiting for the coach to come along, and all the time the pain inside him bit into him like something corrosive. He was thinking of his mother, dead, her neck broken, her eyes blank and dulled. He was thinking of Pengorren in Sophie's bed.

The memories washed over him now, so vivid and real, so painful. He couldn't stop them taking him back through time, he didn't try, as Neptune galloped on.

Nineteen

Nathaniel was standing in the shelter of the gnarled trees, a mask covering the upper part of his face and a neckerchief over the lower half, while the old tricorn hat was pulled down on his head. He was gripping a pistol in his hand, one eye on Neptune, hidden back in the woods out of sight, and the other on the road.

He could hear the coach and horses.

It was closing on him—Pengorren coming home to Ravenswood after his trip to Truro to make arrangements about the estate. Nathaniel's estate. He should have gone with him, he should have insisted, but all he could see in his head was Sophie and that man, in bed together, and his mother lying dead at the bottom of the stairs.

Nathaniel was in mourning, half-crazed with grief and suspicion, and in no state to be rationally discussing the future. When Pengorren had denied being in Sophie's bed, and then offered to go to Truro in his stead to "handle matters" for him, Nathaniel said nothing.

"He's lost his wife, and he still wants to lighten your load," one of the callers come to pay his respects had spoken in wide-eyed admiration. "You should be grateful for the assistance of such a man, Nathaniel."

Grateful! They didn't understand, and if they did, they wouldn't have believed it. Pengorren could do nothing wrong, while Nathaniel could do nothing right.

All day long his anger had been gathering force and focus. He needed to bring it to a head one way or another. He was sick of Pengorren's lies, sick of feeling disloyal because he couldn't trust the man. Sick of feeling like he was losing his mind. He needed to know the truth, whatever the danger to himself. He couldn't wait any longer.

As the coach rounded the corner, Nathaniel fired his pistol into the air, and it was a blessed relief to do something at last.

The ensuing din was very satisfying. The horses were rearing and screaming, the driver of the coach was shouting curses, and the coach itself was creaking and rattling as it came to a shatteringly abrupt halt.

"Get down!" he ordered, waving a second loaded pistol, his hand amazingly steady. But then he found it was always so in times of crisis. When the coachman refused to obey, he raised the barrel and sighted it upon the hapless man.

"What the devil is happening?" Pengorren roared from inside the coach like a caged animal.

"Major, if ye wud be so kind as to step outside."

He'd altered his voice, made it deeper and with a stronger Cornish accent, while the cloak concealed most of his tall, familiar form. The coach door swung open and the steps dropped down and an elegant leg in stocking and pantaloon planted itself on the top stair. Pengorren was wearing a black coat over his satin waistcoat—a small sober concession to Felicity's death—but other than that he was no widower.

"I can have you hanged for this," he hissed angrily.

Nathaniel smiled behind his mask. The risk he was taking made him feel more alive than he had since he left the army. But there was more to it than that. He was up against Pengorren for the first time; he was rejecting all that Pengorren was pretending to be. He was finally doing something, and it felt good.

Pengorren was furious. In the wan light of the coach lamp, his skin was flushed and his blue eyes glittering. The beringed hand at his side was clenching and unclenching, as if he wished it was fastened around Nathaniel's neck.

"I am the magistrate for this district," he said through his teeth. "You won't get away with this, you bastard. I'll have you hunted down."

"Well, we'll see about 'at," Nathaniel said softly. "Give me your purse, sir." He held out a hand. "An' I'll have your rings, too, while ye be at it."

Pengorren looked at him, and something in the major's expression made Nathaniel wonder whether he was being entirely sensible. He hadn't really planned *this out after all. As usual he was acting on impulse, on instinct. But it was too late, he wasn't going to turn tail now. It was done, and in truth he couldn't feel sorry.*

Pengorren was tugging at the rings on his fingers, tossing them contemptuously at Nathaniel's feet, before reaching for his purse.

"There's little enough in there," he said, throwing the small leather bag. "Hardly worth dying for."

Nathaniel caught it in one hand, the pistol steady in the other. "Enough for an ale or two," he replied pleasantly. "I'm very grateful, sir. Ye can go now."

But Pengorren didn't scurry back into the coach as he was supposed to. He stood staring at Nathaniel, cold-eyed, and then he said in a voice so low only Nathaniel could hear it, "You'll regret this, my friend."

When the coach had gone, Nathaniel stood alone in the darkness, the rings at his feet and the purse in his hand. His head was throbbing, as if he had just fought a vicious hand-to-hand combat, but there was a sense of elation, too. He had seen the real Pengorren tonight, the man who lived behind the amiable exterior, and he knew for certain that Pengorren was his deadly enemy.

The road shivered beneath his feet, and he stumbled, taken by surprise, attempting to stay upright. A part of his mind was telling him this wasn't right. It didn't happen like this. Pengorren had climbed into his coach and driven away. But now here he was again, standing in the road right in front of him. Just the two of them.

And it was no longer like a dream, it seemed real . . .

"That's right, Nathaniel," Pengorren said, his voice soft and seductive. "You stay right here with me in the past where I want you. You enjoyed that memory, didn't you? Make the most of it, because it will be your last. Did you really think I'd let you just ride away? I'm going to have to kill you all over again, and this time you won't be coming back."

"You can't," Nathaniel said, but it was a whisper, and he felt dizzy. Pengorren's face was wavering in and out of his vision. There was a thudding in his ears, like horses' hooves, and his face was wet with salt spray, and yet the sea was miles away from the Truro Road.

"Haven't you learned yet," Pengorren retorted arrogantly, "that there's nothing I can't do?"

Nathaniel! A woman's voice in his head, breathy and terrified. Nathaniel spun around, almost losing his balance, but there was no one there in the dark woods. Then, louder, closer. "Nathaniel!"

Pengorren cursed, and said, "Melanie? Where is that interferring bitch? Why can't she mind her own business and stay in her own time?"

"Melanie," Nathaniel whispered, "I need you. Come to me."

The salt stung his eyes, and he shook his head, trying to clear it. He could feel Neptune beneath him, he could hear the pounding of the sea against the cliffs. The cliffs? What in God's name was happening to him.

And then Pengorren grabbed Nathaniel's arm, his fingers pressing painfully deep into his flesh. His face was so close that Nathaniel could see the pores of his skin, and suddenly he was back on the road again, darkness all around him.

"No, you don't," Pengorren said. "No wandering off. You stay right here with me. I have you now, and I won't let you go."

Melanie was all alone in the darkened house. The storm had come over with terrifying swiftness, the wind howling around Ravenswood while overhead lightning flashed and thunder growled. The electricity had flickered once or twice and then gone out. She'd lit some candles, and she had her flashlight, but still the house seemed dark and dangerous, like a heavy weight around her.

Where was Nathaniel? When he left her he hadn't said he was going away. There was something very wrong, she could feel it. He was too rash, the sort of man who dived headlong into battle without considering the consequences. She feared for him.

An extraloud crack of thunder came from overhead, and she shivered. She wasn't certain if the surging noise she could hear was the sea against the cliffs or the trees blown by the wind. Melanie ran to the window and stood, fingers gripping the sill, peering out. It was as black as night out there, the rain thudding all around, puddles already forming on the driveway. Lightning slashed across the sky, dazzling her and making her blink.

Melanie . . .

"Nathaniel?" She turned, thinking he must be here in

the room with her, but she was alone in the dark house. And then she realized his voice was in her head, coming from that part of her she had kept locked away for so long.

Melanie, come to me.

He was fading, leaving her. Trembling, Melanie closed her eyes and concentrated. She drew his image into her mind, so real and vibrant and alive.

"Nathaniel, where are you?"

The room spun and the sound of the sea surged in her head. Melanie cried out as she felt a part of her breaking away, splitting in two. One half remained in the darkened room, grounded, while the other slipped backward into time, like a roller coaster on a hairpin bend, fighting it all the way.

It was night and cold. Melanie saw that she was approaching the woods, the dark trees leaning together like whispering widows. Nathaniel stood on the road, the moonlight shining eerily across his features. Pengorren was before him, eyes strangely aglow, as the two men faced each other.

Melanie stepped closer, not feeling the chill night, seeming to float above the ground. Inside, her soul, her spirit, was humming, so strongly, so powerfully she no longer felt like herself.

"Nathaniel?" she called.

His eyes flicked toward her, and for a moment she saw into his heart. He was angry, but he was also shaken. Things, she thought, hadn't gone as he wanted them to.

The contact seemed to anchor her, for now she

found herself standing firmly on the road. She came to stand at his side, aligning herself with him, and watched as Pengorren's mouth twitch in a scornful smile.

"Melanie," he said, "what a pleasure."

But Melanie wasn't fooled. It wasn't a pleasure. He didn't like her invading his past, any more than she liked him stealing into her present.

"What are you doing?" she demanded.

"I'm showing Nathaniel how he died," Pengorren said.

"You killed him," Melanie retorted, "and then made it look like an accident."

Pengorren smiled. "Far too simplistic, Melanie. I'm capable of a great deal more than that."

"What are you?" Nathaniel demanded. "What evil demon spawned you?"

"Ask the sorceress," he replied.

"The sorceress?" Melanie glanced from one to the other. "Who's she?"

"The self-styled queen of the between-worlds," Pengorren sneered.

"Do you—" Melanie began, but she was interrupted.

A cry sounded from the woods. "Hew?"

Nathaniel started forward. "Sophie?" But Pengorren held out his hand to stop him.

"She can't hear you," he said. "She's not really here. What you can see is the essence of Sophie, her ghost, if you like. I've brought her here so that she can replay her part from the night you died, Nathaniel. Don't you want to know what happened? I mean, what *really* happened?"

Sophie was in sight now, a dark cloak covering her from head to toe, except where the lighter strip of her gown showed between the fastenings. For something that was a "ghost" she seemed very solid. She gripped one of the tree trunks, peering around her. "Hew?" she whispered again. "Where are you? I don't like this place . . ."

"I'm here," Pengorren called. Then, to Nathaniel and Melanie, "Don't worry, she can't see you."

Sophie stepped out of the woods, sighing with relief, her eyes big and a little wild. "Why did you want me to meet you here, Hew? I don't understand. Is this another test of my love?"

"Yes, Sophie, this is another test," Pengorren said, taking her hands and placing the pistol in them.

She looked down at it and tried to pull away.

"No, Sophie, this is what I want you to do. Your brother has lost his mind. He is no longer responsible for his own actions. You do know that, don't you?"

Sophie stared up at him, white-faced. "I know he is playing at being a highwayman," she whispered. "But he's not like that, Hew, he's not!"

"I know, I understand," Hew assured her, "but I am the magistrate, and I am bound to act and soon. I will have to arrest him, and he will hang. You know that, Sophie. He will suffer. There is only one solution. End his life swiftly, and save me from the pain of being the one to sentence him to the gallows. You know how fond I am of the boy."

Sophie shook her head, but her eyes were fastened on Pengorren's.

Nathaniel groaned. Melanie reached for his hand, to comfort him, but couldn't seem to grasp it.

"You have to do this," Pengorren went on. "Sophie?"

For a time she continued to fight against it, but Melanie could see her weakening before Pengorren's greater strength.

"But Hew?" she breathed. "There must be another way. Can't we get him out of Cornwall, onto a ship for the Americas?"

"I'm afraid not, my dear. It's gone beyond that now. No, he must die, Sophie. A good clean death, what more could a soldier ask for?"

Soon she fell silent, listening to him, and then she gave a little sob and nodded.

"When?" she asked, and her voice had lost all color.

"Tonight."

"He will not suffer?"

"No. Not if you aim true."

"You bastard," Nathaniel whispered. "You evil bastard!"

Pengorren laughed. "Poor Sophie, she'd do anything for me."

"Hew?" Sophie whispered, not understanding.

Furiously, Nathaniel flung himself at Pengorren, but the other man moved back, fumbling at a chain about his neck and lifting some sort of medallion. The next instant, Nathaniel was gone.

Melanie spun around, searching the road, but Nathaniel had vanished. Sophie was gone, too. It was just herself and Pengorren, alone on the road.

"Where is he? What have you done to him?" she cried in a panic.

"He was never really here, Melanie. He was like Sophie. I captured his mind, his essence, but his body is elsewhere. It was a trick. While I kept his mind occupied, his physical body has been moving closer to its death. Maybe it's already too late. I'm sorry, I know you were fond of the boy, but perhaps I can make up for his loss."

Fear squeezed at her heart, but Melanie refused to let him see. "I doubt it," she said. "You're not my type."

"But I am, Melanie," he purred. "That's just it. I am." He lifted the chain again and swirled it in his fingers. She could see now it wasn't a medallion but a locket, silver in color and oval in shape. "Do you see this? This is a key."

"Key, what key?" she asked impatiently. Her heart was thudding. She clenched her hands into fists. Where was Nathaniel? She had to find him. She didn't have time for this.

"A key to time. But you don't need a key, do you, Melanie? Don't you realize how powerful that makes you? I almost feel a sense of familial pride. A shame I'm going to have to kill you eventually, but I have no option."

"I don't understand!" she backed away. "Tell me what you've done to Nathaniel."

"The stronger you become, the stronger I will become. When you reach your zenith, then I will harvest your essence, my dear. I will take your soul."

Melanie turned, searching the dark road with wild eyes. "Nathaniel!" When she looked back, Pengorren was fading into the shadows, vanishing before her eyes.

"Why?" she shouted at him. "Why do you want my soul?"

"Because I want to live, Melanie. I want to live forever . . ."

He was gone, she was all alone. Melanie began to shake. "Nathaniel," she whispered, "where are you?" What had she done before to find him? She tried to order her thoughts, calm herself. She'd pictured him in her mind. That was what she must do now.

Before it was too late.

Twenty

It only took a second, and she found him again. One moment she was on the road, and the next she was clinging to Nathaniel, riding pillion on a horse. Even though she knew she wasn't really there, it was terrifying. She didn't even have time to scream.

There was a full moon, and Melanie saw clearly the edge of the cliff and the dizzying drop to the black, heaving waters below. The horse trembled, wild with terror, but he did not stop. A wave crashed against the rock, sending up salt spray and drenching them, stinging her skin.

"Nathaniel," she shouted. "Stop, you have to stop. You're going to go over . . ."

There was something wrong with him. He should have heard her but he made no sign. He was here, or at least his body was, but his mind was still held fast in Pengorren's grip. In desperation she began to scream at him, pulling at his clothing, pounding her fists against his back, but he still didn't acknowledge her. He was going to ride into the sea.

Melanie wondered wildly whether she could jump down to the ground and pull him with her? It was a drastic solution—he might still be killed—but if she couldn't make him hear her, if she couldn't make him stop, then that would be his only chance.

"Nathaniel! Please, please . . ." It turned into a sob. She felt bleak, shattered, desperate. "Listen to me, Nathaniel . . ."

Nathaniel.

Nathaniel blinked, confused, wondering where the hell he was. He had been on the road with Pengorren and now he was . . .

"Nathaniel!"

The voice came from behind him. Melanie? She sounded husky, frantic, as if she had been calling his name over and over. Her arms grasped him so tightly he was finding it hard to breathe, and his back was hurting . . .

They were on the cliff path. His eyes widened. The edge of the cliff was only feet away, and after that the sea.

He felt her grab hold of him and knew instinctively she was preparing to jump and take him with her.

"No!" he shouted, and with a superhuman effort wrenched Neptune away, sending him galloping along the cliff edge rather than over it. Clods of earth and pieces of vegetation scattered into oblivion, but a moment later Neptune's hooves gained purchase. He began to murmur to the frightened stallion, urging him to be calm. Neptune was still trembling, his eyes rolling, as Nathaniel eased him to a stop.

He could feel Melanie's fists clenched in his shirt, feel her body shaking as she tried to regain her own control. He risked turning his head to look at her over his shoulder. "Melanie? I'm sorry, I'm so sorry. Are you hurt?"

She made a choking sound. Her face was sickly in the half-light, and her eyes were like dark pools, the lashes wet and clumped together, while her hair slicked to her head like an otter's fur.

"Pengorren," he said starkly. "He wouldn't let my mind go. He planned to kill me. Again."

She shuddered and pressed her cheek against the soaked cloth on his back. "I was trying to make you hear me, but you couldn't. I hit you . . . I'm sorry."

"A few bruises are the least of my worries," he said. "But how can *you* be here?"

"I can travel in time. Like Pengorren. God help me . . ." She shivered. "I'm not really here, Nathaniel. This is my essence. The real me is back at Ravenswood."

"You look real. You feel real," he said, touching her cheek.

"So did Pengorren. Don't ask me to explain, I don't understand it anymore than you." Her eyes narrowed. "Why did you go off without me? When I got back from Eddie's you were gone. I thought we agreed we would work together."

Nathaniel glanced at her over his shoulder, his smile rueful. "I thought I could handle it on my own. I know what Pengorren's capable of, and when you told me how he seemed to be following you through time, I just wanted to end it."

"So you set off to play the hero again," she said, her voice not quite steady. "I can't keep saving you, Nathaniel."

He laughed angrily.

"She's right. Have you learned nothing in two hundred years, my Raven?"

The voice was harsh, and Nathaniel jerked his head around in surprise. Standing in front of Neptune was the queen of the between-worlds, wrapped in her scarlet cloak, with her hair like licks of flame against the sullen sky. He'd forgotten how intimidating she was, especially when she was angry, but now it came back to him full force.

"Your Majesty."

"You have disobeyed me. I warned you against such a thing, and yet you went ahead anyway. You tricked Teth into taking you through the door."

Tricked Teth? Nathaniel opened his mouth to dispute that, and then wisely decided to keep quiet. He deserved to face her anger; Teth didn't.

"Well, have you nothing to say? No excuses? No charming denials?"

"No, Your Majesty. I wouldn't insult you with anything other than the truth. I know I acted impetuously. I thought I could strike quickly and save—"

"Impetuously?" she snorted. Her scarlet cloak flapped about her, catching the wind like wings. "You are a fool, Nathaniel. You have learned nothing. Why do I bother with you? I may as well return you to the between-worlds right now and save myself further trouble."

Melanie had been quiet until now, but Nathaniel heard her draw breath. "Your Majesty, he did it for me. He believes Pengorren wants me for some reason of his own, and just now . . . well, Pengorren admitted it. He spoke of you, too, as if you know each other. Do you?"

"You presume too much, mortal," the queen said stiffly, and the air about her crackled.

"Please, Your Majesty, forgive me," Nathaniel spoke with quiet and bitter sincerity. "It's true I wanted to save Melanie and that Pengorren is threatening her. I was rash and stupid. I won't do it again. But if you know anything that can help us defeat him, I beg you to tell us."

The queen fixed him with a stern look, and he forced himself to meet her eyes. His head began to swim, his stomach felt queasy, and his hands shook. Beneath him, Neptune shivered as if he had a fever, but he stood perfectly still, as if he was afraid to move while the queen blocked his path.

She spoke at last, and now she sounded considering rather than angry. "Pengorren is not a man you will defeat easily, my Raven. Yes, you have courage and daring, but it will need more than that. Patience, consideration, planning. Do you understand at last? Will you listen to me now? Or must I take away your chance to rewrite your history?"

"Please, don't do that. I understand . . ."

"Then do not travel through time again without my permission. I will not allow it. As it is, you have made changes that will affect your sister's life, although fortunately they are minor in comparison to the harm Pengorren has wrought."

"What do you mean? What will happen to Sophie?"

"You have compounded her misery," the queen replied. "She believes your ghost is haunting her, seeking retribution because of what she did. After her son is born she loses her mind completely and is locked away in a prison for the insane. You see what your interference has done?"

"Oh dear God." Sophie, in one of those dreadful places. He could hardly bear it, felt sick and furious at the thought that he had caused this. "I'm sorry," he whispered wretchedly.

Melanie's warm hand squeezed his arm. "We will fix it," she murmured for him alone.

"How?" he said bitterly, and shook his head. "I wish I had killed him the first time I saw him instead of making him my friend."

At that moment Teth appeared, bounding up to the queen and wagging his tail. She gave the hound a fond look. "Ah, Teth, there you are. Nathaniel, I gave you Teth as your companion because he wishes to attain a higher level, and I thought you would be a good teacher. Was I mistaken? Will you trick him and lead him astray again?"

Nathaniel tried to concentrate. "No, I won't do that." A quick glance at Teth showed a suspiciously innocent expression in the black hound's eyes. "I'll certainly be more respectful of Teth's abilities in the future, Your Majesty."

The queen smiled her cold smile. "One day, when I think he's ready, Teth will become a mortal."

The black whiskery face beamed.

"I look forward to it," Nathaniel murmured.

"As you have Neptune, I will allow you to keep him in the present. For now. Once you have completed your task, he can return with you to the past. But if you fail, he will fail with you."

"Thank you, Your Majesty."

She sighed. "Now I will return you to the present, where you are meant to be. This is your last warning, my Raven."

Hastily, Melanie cleared her throat. "Your Majesty, Pengorren was wearing something he called a key to time. What is it? How does it help him? He said I didn't need one to travel. How can that be?"

The queen gave an impatient sigh, tapping one of her talons on the ground. "So many questions, mortal."

"But how else are we to defeat him if we don't understand?"

"I am not here to do your task for you."

Nathaniel realized that her cloak was turning into feathers and the feathers into wings. "Pengorren isn't a mortal," he said, and it wasn't a question. "He's like you."

"No one is like me," she shrieked. In the next breath she changed into an eagle, soaring past him. At the same time Neptune came out of his unnatural calm and rose up onto his back legs with a shrill scream. Nathaniel lurched forward to grasp his bridle.

The air fizzed and spluttered, and was split asunder as

time shifted. It was no longer summer and the night was no longer still. As she had said she would, the queen had jumped them forward into the present, into the full raging force of the spring storm.

Melanie felt her body stretching, as if her essence was being pulled violently, and then there was a popping sound in her ears and the two—body and essence—reconnected. She was whole again, but she wasn't inside Ravenswood; she was here, with Nathaniel, on Neptune.

Lightning splintered the sky, followed instantly by the deafening growl of thunder. The rain was at their backs and the storm directly overhead. It was deafening. Neptune snorted, trying to outrun his own terror, but Nathaniel held him just on the verge of bolting, using all of his skill to keep them safe as they pounded their way toward Ravenswood.

"This is madness!" cried Melanie. "We must be crazy!"

But it was an exhilarating sort of craziness. Adrenaline was pumping through her, and she hardly felt the cold bite of the rain. The horse quivered as another bolt of lightning lit the sky, but Nathaniel held him. He was strong and in control and unafraid. Melanie had never known a man like him.

Ravenswood was visible through the rain, dark and brooding against the threatening sky. Melanie could see the trees in the park waving wildly as the gusting winds ripped through them. They passed Eddie's grey cottage, huddled in the pounding rain, and she thought she saw his white face through one of the upper windows.

The vegetable garden was flattened, the overgrown plants a sodden mess . . .

Suddenly there was a terrible rending, like someone in agony. Melanie jerked up her head and saw it through the rain. Rippling like a tidal surge, through the trees in the park, one of the biggest, oldest trees had been struck by lightning and now it was falling. Crashing down. And because of its sheer size, it was taking others with it.

The noise was horrendous. The earth shook.

Melanie stared numbly. It was happening just as she'd known it would, and nothing she'd done to try and ignore it, or lock it out, had made the slightest bit of difference.

They reached the safety of Ravenswood and Nathaniel was off his horse, reaching up for her, rain dripping into his eyes and running down his face. His teeth flashed white as he grinned; he was enjoying every moment.

She wanted to hit him again, she wanted to scream at him, and at the same time she wanted to grab him and never let him go. She'd never felt so confused in her life.

"Melanie," he said, his hands heavy and warm on her shoulders.

She rubbed a hand over her eyes, and then she put both hands over them, as if to hide herself from him. With surprise he realized she was crying—Melanie, the strong and the stubborn—and didn't want him to see.

"Melanie," he whispered, "I know it's difficult to trust me again, after what just happened, but you must believe me. I won't let him hurt you. Word of a Raven. I know what he's capable of now, and I'll be ready. Whatever the cost to myself, I will not allow Pengorren to harm you."

"Don't," she gasped. "You need to get back to the past to save your family. I don't expect you to put me first, Nathaniel, I don't want that. We're working together, remember? If we work together, then maybe we'll be strong enough to defeat him. Isn't that the whole point?"

He slid his arms around her and she didn't even resist. She relaxed into him. It felt so perfect, so right. As if she belonged there. "You saved my life," he whispered. "Thank you."

For a moment he just held her, soothing her shivers, murmuring words that made no sense. He could feel her warm breath against his wet shirt and the wetter skin beneath, and despite the situation they were in it felt amazingly sensual. But she was cold, and in the end he held her gently away, and said, "You need to go inside."

"What about you?" Even when she'd been crying her eyes were a striking blue.

"I'll see to Neptune. I examined the stable earlier when I was searching for Pengorren's portrait, and it looked as if it had been repaired not very long ago. He'll be warm and safe in there."

"The tree," she blurted out, giving another violent shiver. "I knew it was going to fall. And I found you, Nathaniel. Twice! I traveled through time and found you. Whatever is inside me is . . . is opening up. All these years I've kept it locked down, and now it's as if I can't hold it any more. It's got too strong for me."

"Melanie . . ."

Nathaniel bent his head and gave her a quick, hard kiss, as if he wanted to comfort her and brand her at the same time. Then his mouth gentled, and he held her away, leaning his forehead against hers so that he could remain connected to her as he spoke. "You know I want you." It wasn't a question.

Her breath was warm on his lips. "I want you, too," she said.

He kissed her again, he couldn't help it. "We'll come through this," he said firmly, and at this moment he believed it. Believed in himself. "Now go inside." His fingers slid over her wet hair, tucking it tenderly behind her ears.

She managed a smile. "Don't be long," she said, and gave him a look he could hardly mistake.

Nathaniel grinned as he turned away. Neptune was too weary to be much trouble, and he led the stallion around to the stable. He glanced back over his shoulder, watching as Melanie climbed the stairs to the front door. She was remarkable. She had saved his life. They had cheated Pengorren, and they were both alive—a sense of elation filled him—and just now it was enough.

Twenty-one

Melanie stepped inside the gloomy entry hall and the door shut hollowly behind her. She was freezing. Hugging herself, she ran shivering up the staircase, pausing briefly to glance at Nathaniel's portrait. Her lips twitched at the sight of him—the Gentleman of the Manor. Was that what he would have been if Pengorren hadn't come along?

Pengorren, he was like the rotten core in the apple.

Melanie reached the landing, her shoes squelching, and headed for the bathroom. With a prayer and cold, shaking hands, she turned on the hot water and almost sobbed with gratitude when steam began to pour into the big, chilly room. Stumbling, cursing, she peeled off her wet clothing and dumped it on the floor, stepped into the bath, and sank into rising water.

The water was only up to her hips, and her top half was still goose-bumped. She shivered, sliding down farther into the bath, trying to get warm. The combination of running water and the clanging of the old pipes was thunderous. The room was filling with so much steam, she could hardly see in front of her, but she didn't care.

Nothing could be worse than what she'd seen over the past days. Pengorren had found her, somehow, after all these years, he had tracked her down, and now it felt as if she would never escape him.

He came out of the steam like a ghost out of mist and Melanie shrieked, and then covered her mouth, her eyes enormous above her hands.

"Don't do that!" she gasped. "Don't you do that!"

"I'm sorry." Nathaniel hesitated, and then he sat down on the edge of the big old bath. "I was worried. When I got back, you'd disappeared. I heard the water running." He quirked an eyebrow at her, but wisely he kept his eyes fastened on hers. "What was I to think?"

"That I was cold? That I needed a bath?" Melanie wrapped her arms about her breasts and slunk down farther into the water. It was deeper now but still not deep enough. She wanted to sink under it completely and vanish, and take her troubles with her.

She felt his hand on her hair and looked up. He brushed the wet strands off her brow, gently, as if she was made of glass. Then he bent and kissed her warm, damp skin.

"Are you really here this time?"

"What do you think?"

"You're beautiful," he whispered.

Her heart began to thud.

"Nathaniel?"

"Hmm?" He pressed tiny, comforting kisses over her temple, across her cheekbone, moving with leisurely pace toward her mouth.

She could have stopped him at any time, but he was warm and real, and Melanie heard herself make a little sound of need. His lips caressed, moving over hers. For a moment the image of Pengorren flashed into her mind, but it was so far removed from Nathaniel and what she was feeling now, that it did not affect her, and she simply shut it out.

"You're wet, too," she said, drawing slightly away from him. "Aren't you cold?"

He met the look she gave him from under her lashes and smiled slowly. "Frozen," he assured her. "Do you mind . . . ?"

"Be my guest."

They were very polite, but their eyes, their mouths, were saying other more urgent things. His shirt was so wet it was transparent, outlining the curves and ridges of bone and muscle. He pulled it over his head, and Melanie reached out to touch him, trailing her fingers over his shoulders and chest and upper arms. His leanness was deceptive—he was all hard muscle. He pulled off his boots and tossed them across the bathroom, and then stood up and began to unbutton his breeches.

Melanie leaned back in the water, watching him through her lashes. She felt decadent, lying here naked, wanting him. Because she did want Nathaniel Raven, and for once in her life she wasn't going to deny herself just because she feared the consequences. Things had gone beyond that. They had experienced some dangerous and intense moments together; they had faced a common and deadly enemy. Who knew what the next hour would bring, let alone tomorrow.

Nathaniel wanted her, too.

The evidence was there as he wrapped his hands around her upper arms and lifted her body up against his, slowly, every inch sliding and touching. Water trickled over her flushed skin, glistening. She smelled the musky scent of him, felt his erection hard and exciting against her. Her breasts ached as they brushed against the hair on his chest, and she heard her own breathing quicken. She'd never been this hot for a man before, not like this. She wanted to twine herself around him, touch . . . no, *lick,* every inch of him.

His mouth, she couldn't get enough of his mouth. She clung around his neck, tugging his hair between her fingers. The dark ribbon slipped off, and she raked her fingers through the smooth shoulder-length strands.

They stood together in the bath, and their bodies moved together. He was exactly how she liked a man to be—she'd known that from the start—and she felt completely female, as if she could be as wild and wanton as she liked, and he would understand. He would accept her for what she was.

Nathaniel wound a short lock of her own fair hair around his fist, tilting her head up to his. His eyes were more gold than hazel, and his dark hair swung down to frame his handsome face as he gazed down at her intently. "You do want me," he said, and it was a growl of satisfaction. And then he claimed her mouth again.

Melanie lifted her thigh, pressing the sensitive inner

skin along the hard muscle of his, trying to get closer. She was hot, burning up, aching with need. It felt good as he gripped her, lifted her, and pressed her to the cold tiles on the wall. She gasped as her hot skin came in contact with the chill tiles, and then gasped again as he leaned his body in on her, his skin setting her on fire. He was cupping her bottom with his hands, stroking her, caressing her. And all the while he kept kissing her mouth.

And his mouth was hot. Nathaniel Raven was hot.

He lowered his head, and she felt his tongue on her throat, and then his mouth again, kissing, sucking. Melanie arched back, moaning softly, and felt his mouth against her breasts. He ran his tongue across the upper swell of one and then the other, and then he was covering her nipple with his mouth, sucking, rolling it with his tongue, tugging it with his teeth.

Melanie purred in her throat.

She clasped him with her thighs, and his erection pressed against the swollen folds between her legs. She wanted him inside her. She knew she had to have him inside her, completely. Melanie tilted her hips forward and felt him enter her that first little bit.

It was sensual heaven.

He groaned against her neck and reached down to adjust her thighs around his hips, but she realized he was holding back, keeping her prisoner between his body and the tiled wall, but not letting her end it. When he lifted his head she couldn't take her eyes off his mouth. She leaned forward and took his bottom lip between her teeth, biting down hard enough for him to feel her but not to break the skin.

"Now," she said, her voice husky with need. "Do it now."

He slid inside her, and she closed her eyes, feeling him, savoring it as he filled her. Already she was trembling, on the verge of climax. He must have known it, and, wanting to control it, he stopped. His chest was rising and falling as if he'd been running. He let his head fall back, and she licked at the arch of his throat, tasting him, wanting more. He slid out and then thrust into her again, harder, and the climax hovered nearer. She was balancing on the edge of the precipice.

"Melanie," he groaned.

Her name on his mouth was enough.

With a gasping cry she went over the edge, clinging to him, her hips moving frantically against him. Even while her body was soaring she felt him thrusting again, and then he cried out and followed her.

There were colors in her head, actual starbursts of color. It was like nothing she had ever known. She couldn't speak; speaking was beyond her. It felt more than sex, more than an orgasm; it was an experience she would remember for the rest of her life.

Melanie took a breath and wanted to ask him if he'd seen the lights, too. If he'd felt his body lifting and flying. But she was too weak, too sated. She realized he was taking her very carefully in his arms, holding her boneless body against his, and then he was lowering them both, down into the wonderful steamy water.

It sloshed, puddling on the floor, but she didn't care. For once in her life she didn't care about anything but the moment. She was content to lie lifeless in his arms. She sprawled against his body, supported by him and the water, her cheek on his chest, his arms wrapped about her, and she had never been more content.

Melanie could feel his heart beating. She turned her face and kissed his skin, tasting it, and then wondered at herself. Usually she had trouble turning her mind off when she was with a man, but this was different. She felt renewed. A new woman, she thought, with a smile.

"Are you all right?"

She could hear his voice inside his chest and wriggled closer. "More all right than I've been for a long time."

The colors in her head had receded, but there was still a strange echoey feeling in there, as if something had come loose. As if she'd gone to sleep and then woken up in a new body and now she had to get used to it.

Nathaniel liked her answer. He bent and kissed the top of her head. Melanie Jones had just succeeded in removing every other woman he had ever known from his memory. Who would have believed it? He was still trying to get his breath back. He cupped her breast, thoroughly enjoying the sensation of her smooth, full flesh in his hand. He'd wanted her since the moment he saw her; he'd felt the pull of attraction between them like the tug of a rope. Yes, he'd had reservations, but they had more to do with the fact that she was from now and he was from before, and that he had so little time to solve the mystery of Pengorren. He'd never doubted they would make wonderful love together.

He just hadn't realized quite how wonderful.

She tilted her head and looked up at him, and her blue eyes were so bright they were almost luminous. For a moment he found it impossible to look away from them. From her. He took a breath and closed his eyes, and when he opened them again, the intensity had dimmed a little.

"Nathaniel?" she whispered, and shifted against him. Wherever her body touched his skin seemed to tingle, his blood to heat up. He felt himself rapidly getting hard again.

"You're so beautiful," he said quietly, and bent his mouth to hers.

The spark ignited, turning into instant fireworks.

Melanie straddled him in the water, the tips of her breasts brushing his chest. With her short fair hair and slanting eyes, she looked almost otherworldly. An angel fallen to earth. Or maybe not, he decided, as her smile turned wicked and sensual. She reached between them and stroked the hard length of him.

Nathaniel groaned. He hadn't had a woman in almost two hundred years, but he'd be perfectly happy if he never had another one. Apart from Melanie. As she slid down over his body, using her tongue and her mouth, he just hoped he could survive what she had in mind for him next, without dying of pleasure.

Mr. Trewartha wasn't a sentimental man, far from it, but he had a few keepsakes from his past. A few mementoes. He had loved few people, but he loved his collection of antiques, and he loved his life.

There was one watercolor miniature he was particularly fond of. Awkwardly, he opened the case, holding the portrait up to the light.

She had really captured the look of him. She had talent, certainly, but as with most women it had been frittered away with self-destructive behavior. Time had taken care of the rest. Sadly, he'd fallen out of love with her quite soon after they'd met.

No use feeling guilty about it, it was just the way things happened.

Mr. Trewartha closed the metal case and slipped the chain back over his head. He shut his eyes, suddenly feeling very tired. So much to do. He'd have to ring the Jones woman again and let her know when he was coming. There were things she needed to hear, things he needed to tell her.

Before it was too late.

Twenty-two

Nathaniel was still sleeping. Melanie smiled.
Raven, the infamous highwayman, the daring and reckless heir to Ravenswood, was in her bed.

His face was turned from her so that she could only see the line of his cheek and his jaw, where his stubble was growing through more gold than brown. Ruefully, she felt the whisker burn on her own face and decided the most important thing Nathaniel needed to do this morning was shave.

There was a scar, high up in his hairline, almost out of sight. She hadn't noticed it before, but now she gently pushed back his hair and examined the white and puckered evidence of a serious injury. This must be the head wound he'd received in Spain during the ambush, in which he had been incapacitated so badly he'd had to return home to England.

His hand was resting on the white sheet, and Melanie touched the silver signet ring with her fingertip. She tried to make out the design, but the ring was worn, and the early-morning light in the bedroom was dim.

What was the time?

After their bath last night, they'd gone downstairs to the kitchen, and she'd made omelets with whatever could be found in the Eddie-stocked fridge. Then they'd opened a bottle of wine and complemented it with a shared chocolate bar she'd brought with her. She remembered his lips had tasted of chocolate and almonds when he'd kissed her. Soon after that, they'd gone to bed and made love again, lighting up the darkness with the colored lights in her head.

Melanie sat up, trying not to wake him as she moved from the bed, and began to dress. Outside, yesterday's storm was long gone and there was a breathtaking line of gold across the horizon as the sun came up, like a celestial apology.

As she pulled on her hip-hugging black jeans, she caught a glimpse of herself in the mirror and froze, startled. Despite the shadows in the room she seemed almost to . . . glow. As if she was lit from within. Skin, hair, her eyes, somehow everything was more . . . Well, just *more*.

Melanie stepped closer to the shadowy mirror, touching her cheek, frowning into her own eyes. She certainly looked very healthy. The lines that had begun to appear over recent years seemed to have suddenly vanished. Her lips were fuller, her hair glossier, her body more curved, and yet she was as slim as ever. She looked like some sleek, dangerous jungle cat.

"Don't be stupid. I know he was good, but that wasn't the elixir of life he was injecting into you. Or maybe it was . . ." Even her voice was different, pitched slightly lower so that it sounded huskier, sexier.

Swiftly, Melanie turned away from her reflection, dragging a black sweater over her head and running her fingers through her hair to comb it. She remembered at the last moment not to let the door slam, closing it gently behind her. Once outside on the landing, she took a deep breath, and then another. All her doubts and fears came rushing back.

She had never been like that with a man before. Not that she regretted what had happened between them, far from it, but she didn't understand it. And Melanie was someone who wanted to understand, who needed to understand, in order to feel secure.

For instance, how was it that she was suddenly feeling like a different person? Was buttoned-down, control-freak Melanie breaking out? Or was it just that the real Melanie, the Melanie who had been waiting inside her all these years, had finally decided to take her turn at the wheel?

Or, more frightening still, was this something to do with Pengorren? Was he changing her? Remaking her in his image? The idea was terrifying and made her sick to her stomach.

She stumbled down the stairs and found her cell phone in the kitchen, and with trembling fingers she rang Suzie's number.

"Be home, please be home, please . . ."

It was answered on the second ring.

"Hiya?"

"Suzie. Oh Suzie."

"Melanie?"

"Yes, it's me."

There was a pause, then a strangely cautious—for Suzie—"What's up?"

"Nothing. That is, everything, but I wanted to ask you . . . I thought you might know . . . Oh God, you'll think I'm a nut."

"Try me."

"You used to go on those crazy weekends to Glastonbury and . . . and Avebury. You must have heard about things . . . strange things, out-of-this-world things. Time travel and possession and spells and—"

"Whoa there, hang on. You're covering a lot of ground. Why are you asking me to tell you this, now, after all these years?" And then she spoke again and her voice was deeper, more serious. "What's happening down there in Cornwall, Melanie?"

Melanie forced herself to calm down, to *think*.

"I've started seeing things," she said slowly. "Things that haven't happened yet, or that happened a long time ago. I don't know. Things that aren't really, physically, there."

I can travel through time.

"You're having visions, you mean? Premonitions?"

"I don't know what they are."

She could hear her own breathing over the phone, as if she'd been jogging, and tried to control it. She wiped her palms on the thighs of her jeans, one at a time, changing the phone from hand to hand. "I don't know, Suzie, that's why I'm asking."

"You'd better tell me exactly what you *did* see."

"A tree in the park falling down during a storm, and then it did fall down. There was a storm yesterday and it—"

"Hang on, slow down . . . There was a storm," Suzie said encouragingly.

"There's a man. No," she said, before Suzie could interrupt, "not like that. At least, not that man . . ."

Major Pengorren and his strangely dazzling appearance, drawing people in, making them love him despite his repulsive actions. He had convinced everyone, apart from Nathaniel, that he was handsome and trustworthy, and even Nathaniel hadn't been all that suspicious at first.

"People find him irresistible. But he's not, Suzie, he's horrible. He's cruel and manipulative. He's so good at getting his own way, and he seems to be able to make them see what he wants them to see rather than what's really there. It's like he's wearing a mask, and behind it he's laughing. How can he do that, Suzie?"

"Go back in history and take your pick, Melanie. Some people have such a powerful aura that they can blind others to their real selves, and they're just naturally good at manipulation."

"I know what you're saying and . . . and . . . I know you're right. But this is different, Suzie, it really is. I almost feel as if he's able to cast some sort of, well, magic spell on everyone around him."

She'd said it again. *Magic spell*. Now Suzie would pronounce her completely insane. She could hear herself breathing heavily again, as she waited for the laughter.

"Well, that *is* a possibility," Suzie spoke at last,

thoughtfully, as if this topic of conversation were nothing unusual to her. "There are spells. Magic has been used before to control people although how effectively I can't say. I don't know enough about it."

Melanie was the one who covered her mouth and tried not to laugh hysterically.

Suzie went on, a little dreamily now, "Hmm, I'd have to have a think about it. It's a long time since I was going through my mystic period, remember."

"How could I forget?" But Melanie had tears in her eyes. "You must think I'm completely off my head, and though it's a possibility, I don't think I am. And that's what's really scaring me."

"This is the first time you've asked my advice on anything since you were five. No, make that nine, when that creep came onto you at the beach."

In the silence Melanie could feel her heart beating hard, and now she could hear Suzie breathing over the phone.

"What made you say that?" Melanie finally asked, and her voice was small.

"I don't know. I was thinking about it the other day. It just popped into my head. Is it . . . relevant? Melanie . . . ?"

But she knew it was, Melanie could hear the dead certainty in her voice. Suzie already knew exactly where the problem lay.

Pengorren.

"Melanie, it was after that creep at the beach that your imagination started to become a problem."

"Was it?"

"Yep, I remember. The night we arrived home from the beach, you woke up screaming because someone was standing at the end of your bed. Then you learned to stop the visions, didn't you? That's when the headaches started coming instead. You know, I'm not surprised the visions are coming back. Cornwall is a strange and mystic place; there are some very old sites down there. Maybe you've tapped into one of them . . ."

"I can't talk anymore." And she didn't want to. She'd already said too much, involving her sister in things she should not be involved in. Maybe even placing her in danger.

"Why not?" Suzie sounded surprised and a little annoyed. "What have I said, Melanie? You can't shut me out now."

"No, I . . ." Melanie cast around for a reason, gabbling in a very uncharacteristic way. "Someone's coming, and I don't want him to hear me."

"Someone? Who's there? Not the man you were just talking about?" Suzie said in a hard voice, sounding more like her big sister than she had for years.

"No, not him. Nathaniel."

"Nathaniel?" Suzie repeated, the name rising at the end. "Who the hell is Nathaniel? Sounds like the hero in a BBC costume drama."

Melanie choked back laughter. "If only you knew. Look, I'm sorry, I'll ring you back. Soon. I promise."

"Melanie—"

But she'd already ended the call. For a moment she stood, staring at her cell phone, listening to the words replaying in her head. Spells. Magic. Two men who

could travel through time—Nathaniel and Pengorren—
one who was a dream and the other the stuff of night-
mares. But Melanie had traveled through time, too, and
she was still traveling. They were linked together, the
three of them. *Chained* together. And Melanie was beginning to believe it was she who held the key.

The key to time?

"Who were you talking to?"

Melanie jumped. Nathaniel's voice came from close
behind her. She took a moment to steady herself, arrang-
ing her face into a smile, before she turned to face him.

He had retied his hair with the ribbon, and she could
see that beneath the stubble his handsome face was pale
and taut, with dark shadows beneath his watchful eyes.
Didn't he trust her? After last night? After all the words
he'd spoken? Or was it just her prickly manner that was
making him suspicious.

They were in this together, Melanie reminded herself.
There was no need to keep anything from him. It was
just habit that was making her so cautious now, a habit
she was going to have to break where Nathaniel was
concerned.

"My sister," Melanie said, with a shrug. "She's a bit
fey, and I thought she might be able to help, in a general
way."

"And can she?"

Melanie smiled. "Maybe. It was strange, but she mentioned that day on the beach, the one I told you about,
when I first saw Pengorren. We've never talked about it,
not since it happened. Why would she suddenly mention

it now? How did she know I was thinking about it, now?"

He didn't move, watching her.

"My sister believes in all the things I used to scoff about. She has no trouble accepting paranormal events. Seeing a ghost, or walking ley lines, or pagan ceremonies on hilltops during midwinter, they're as everyday to her as strolling down to the shops for milk and bread. Or at least, they used to be. She's more conventional now. Not like me. I was born conventional, and I always wanted it that way. I hated anything supernatural, anything I couldn't explain. I hated thinking there might be things I couldn't see, watching me from the shadows. Ironic, isn't it? Since I've been here all I've done is chase shadows."

He let her wind down. "Sometimes we avoid those things that we know are a threat to us. If you have the ability to see visions, and it frightens you, then it is understandable that you dislike the supernatural and that you wish to avoid it."

"Yes." She sighed.

"Melanie, did you tell your sister about me?"

"Why?"

Nathaniel gave his half smile. "I am averse to being locked up."

"Oh. No, I didn't tell her. At least, I mentioned your name, but not what you are . . . *who* you are." That was true, anyway. Maybe Suzie would forget about him. Yeah, thought Melanie, and Pengorren was a faery godfather come to grant her every wish.

Nathaniel held out his hand. "Come. I want to see the big oak tree that fell in the park."

She had work to do, she had a job and commitments, she had a future with the firm of Foyle, Haddock and Williams. But even as she automatically listed her priorities, Melanie accepted that they were no longer important to her.

She was caught up in a genuine struggle for life and death, and it put lists of chipped crockery and possible sightings of a Chippendale chair in the shade. Nathaniel needed her, and she needed him.

Melanie placed her hand in his and felt his fingers close possessively. He was looking down at her, and although he said nothing, his eyes did. They said: *We belong together.*

Twenty-three

Her skin was warm and soft, and there was a vibration that ran up his arm as he made contact with her. Nathaniel was uncertain just how much of this was sheer physical attraction and how much was something else. Something new. Something he should be concerned about.

She was dazzlingly beautiful. Her eyes burned like lanterns, and when he looked at her he actually felt breathless with his desire to possess her. Utterly. Not that he hadn't wanted her before, because he had, but now it was so strong it was almost like a separate force outside them both. He'd lusted after women in the past, but not like this. Never like this.

The sun was shining when they stepped outside, and her hair seemed to capture the light until it sparkled. Even her eyelashes shone as if they had been tipped in gold.

His mouth went dry, and Nathaniel forced himself to look away. Instead, he focused on the devastation wrought by the storm. Not that there was much he could do about that; Ravenswood wasn't his anymore, and the days when he could order his servants about were gone. He should have appreciated what he had when he had it rather than throwing it all away in an act of impulsive insanity.

Pengorren had been too strong for him, too cunning. Nathaniel understood that now, and he was also beginning to understand that if he was ever to go back and relive those moments again, he would first have to learn how to defeat Pengorren. He'd have to learn what made Pengorren weak.

Water dripped on them from the drooping foliage, and the soft ground was littered with the sticks and small branches that had been shredded by the wind and rain. A thrush began to sing, and a rabbit stared at them from the protection of some bracken before vanishing into the shadows. They picked their way cautiously through the devastation.

The fallen tree was ancient and as enormous as Melanie knew it would be. In its death throes it had taken several smaller trees down, too, as well as numerous branches and a blizzard of leaves. The tree lay broken and blasted, the black scorch marks from the lightning clearly visible upon the trunk—the pungent smell of burning was still in the air.

Melanie's hand tightened painfully on his. "This is exactly as I saw it," she said. "Exactly."

Nathaniel cast her a quick look, and even that was enough to stir in him the urge to let his eyes linger, to possess, before he dragged his gaze away once more, back to the tree. "You said that when you were a child you also had strange visions."

"Yes. I didn't like it. I stopped myself from doing it."

"How could you stop yourself, Melanie?"

"I shut it out. I concentrated on the present. I worked harder at school, I spent every waking moment busy. Soon it got to be easy—apart from the headaches. Until I came to Ravenswood. Now nothing I do seems to stop it."

"You saved my life, Melanie. I can't regret whatever power you possess."

Melanie managed a smile. "When you put it like that . . ."

He reached to take her in his arms, but the crunch of approaching footsteps stopped him.

"Someone's coming," Melanie said at the same time. "It's Eddie."

"You know this because you've had a premonition?"

Melanie gave him a droll look. "Who else would it be, Nathaniel?"

"Ms. Jones?" Eddie's voice drifted toward them. There was a muffled curse as he tripped on some debris.

"We're over here!" she called, and then whispered, her warm breath brushing his ear like a kiss, "He'll be curious, but don't worry, we can bluff our way out of this."

"I heard the tree fall yesterday," Eddie said, stepping around some fallen branches and into the clearing. He was looking at the mess. "Thought I'd better take a look, even though I won't be the caretaker here much longer. Still my job though, isn't it? For now?"

Melanie realized he was talking loudly to give them warning. He knew she had a man here—he'd seen them together on Neptune—and maybe he expected to find them stripped bare and making love in the wet leaves. She glanced at Nathaniel, but he still wouldn't look at her. He'd been acting oddly ever since he found her talking to Suzie. And yet he seemed calm enough as he faced Eddie. As always he gave the impression of being in total control of himself and the situation.

"Eddie," Melanie said, as the caretaker reached them. "I want you to meet—"

At the same time Eddie looked past her, to Nathaniel, and his genial face went the color of very old cheese.

Nathaniel smiled pleasantly, but there was a wicked gleam in his hazel eyes. "Nathaniel," he said easily, "named for my ancestor. Wrong side of the blanket."

"Yes, that's right," Melanie babbled on. "Foyle, Haddock and Williams turned up Nathaniel when we were searching for any legal heirs to the estate. His ancestor was illegitimate, but as you can see, there is a bit of a family resemblance."

"Bloody hell," Eddie muttered, gawking. "Thought I'd seen a ghost there for a minute, mate."

"I've already been told that by Melanie here," Nathaniel said easily, and she realized he was exaggerating his Cornish accent. "She looked as weak as a robin, the first time she saw me."

Eddie pulled himself together and held his hand out. But he was still eyeing Nathaniel uneasily, as if he thought that at any moment the other man might vanish in a puff of brimstone.

Nathaniel took the proffered hand casually enough.

"I'm Eddie," Eddie said. "I look after the place. You ride, do you?" he added, with a sideways glance at Melanie. But something about her seemed to catch his attention, and instead of looking away again, he fixed her with a frown.

"Ride?" Nathaniel asked, tucking his hands into his pockets.

"Yeah, I saw you during the storm. On that black horse you've got in the stable. I thought I was seeing things until I noticed Ms. Jones riding pillion. I didn't think *she* was a ghost." He was still staring at Melanie, without blinking.

She shifted uncomfortably, wishing he'd look away. "Yes, Nathaniel took me for a ride on his horse, but unfortunately the storm caught up to us."

Eddie, still staring at her, said, "It must have been some ride."

"Oh, it was. Nathaniel will be staying at Ravenswood for the next few days, Eddie. He's kindly offered to help me with the catalogue of the house contents. He works for an, eh, auction house." Eddie's gaze was making her nervous. She wondered, feeling panicky, whether she could remember all this stuff so that she didn't contradict herself next time.

"Ah-ha." Eddie seemed unimpressed.

But Melanie had enough. "Eddie! What is wrong with you? You're staring."

Eddie blinked, and color flushed his cheeks. He shook his head. "Sorry," he said, embarrassed. "I didn't mean to stare. You just look different, somehow. I was trying to work out why."

"Different?" Melanie demanded, upset and irritated. "How, different?"

But Eddie shook his head again, looking down at the ground now. "Sorry," he muttered again, just like a chastened little boy. There was something endearing about Eddie, and she couldn't be cross with him for long.

"It's all right." Melanie took a breath, and then let it out with a sigh. "I didn't mean to jump on you like that. I've had a lot on my mind."

"I suppose you have." He cleared his throat. "I took the portrait back to the house." Now he didn't look at her at all, his gaze directed somewhere over her head and into the trees. "I didn't know where you wanted it, so I put it in the library."

"This is the portrait of Major Pengorren?" Nathaniel cut in with sharp authority.

Eddie turned to him and fixed his eyes there.

"That's right, the good old major. Pity, really. Miss Pengorren tried to get it mended, but whatever's eating away at the paint just seems to be getting worse. She was told it'd cost a fortune to stop it, and even then the bits that are gone are gone for good. From what I've read the major was a very striking man, but now we'll never know what he really looked like."

"So his face is destroyed?" Melanie said gloomily. "Aren't there any other paintings? Sketches? He was an important man in the district, wasn't he?"

"Yes, but as far as I know, that's the only likeness known to exist. He must have been camera-shy, or whatever the equivalent was back then. Miss Pengorren told me that the portrait had been like that for as long as she could remember, with the face gone."

A blackbird landed in the trunk of the fallen oak tree, and then changed its mind and flew off.

"You know much about Major Pengorren, Eddie?" Nathaniel appeared relaxed, but Melanie thought his jaw was tense and his eyes half closed, as if to hide their intensity. "Have you read *The Raven's Curse*?"

Eddie snorted. "I have, yeah. Don't know if I believe it, though. Written in the 'forties. The author seems to have been completely blinded by Pengorren's good side. And he had a good side, I'm not saying he didn't, but he had a bad side, too. I can say that because I was also born on the wrong side of the blanket, Nathaniel. I'm related to Major Pengorren via one of his affairs with a servant girl."

Nathaniel smiled, as he was meant to.

"What about Nathaniel Raven? Did *he* have a good side?" Melanie asked. "That book didn't seem to think so."

Eddie began to turn toward her, and then changed his mind. Awkwardly, he turned his eyes back to Nathaniel. "Do you mean the stuff about him having to be insane to do what he did?"

Nathaniel's smile didn't waver, but Melanie could feel his increasing tension. He shifted his feet. "That's the stuff she means," he said quietly.

"Nah," Eddie was enjoying himself. "I don't think

Nathaniel Raven was insane. That's just rubbish. He was probably bored after his time in the army, and he was always a bit wild. But the truth'd be hard to sort out from the lies—too much time under the bridge since then. This *Raven's Curse* idea doesn't seem to have been around when Nathaniel died, not when you search through the records still existing from that period. It's a later invention. If you've read *The Raven's Curse,* then you'll know the author is trying to convince his readers that *he* knows when it all began. He says that Nathaniel Raven cursed Major Pengorren with his dying breath: *You and your descendants will never be happy at Ravenswood,* and no generation since has been safe from tragedy. If you take a look at the family tree, you can see there were an awful lot of deaths for one reason or another. But what that has to do with Nathaniel's state of mind . . ." He shrugged.

"He cursed him with his dying breath," Nathaniel repeated, and all humor had vanished from his voice. His eyes were bleak. "I don't remember hearing such a thing before."

"Oh yeah, it's common knowledge now, and your average visitor to the village doesn't bother checking his facts. Everyone believes what they read in *The Raven's Curse.*"

Nathaniel didn't answer.

"You really do know your Pengorren history, don't you, Eddie?" Melanie said brightly, uneasily aware of Nathaniel's silence.

Eddie looked sheepish, as if she had caught him out.

"Look, I should come clean," Eddie said abruptly.

"The book I'm writing . . . it's about Ravenswood, about the Pengorren family. I'm trying out a new slant on it. It's about time someone debunked that *Raven's Curse* nonsense. Before she left, Miss Pengorren agreed with me. Nathaniel Raven wasn't the villain; he was the victim."

Nathaniel shifted, and Melanie caught his eye. His face was haggard. "I'd like to read your book."

"Oh, it's not finished. I couldn't—"

"No, really, I mean it." Nathaniel forced a smile. "I've always wanted to know more about my family, but until now I haven't had the chance to find out. I agree with you, there was something, eh, skanky about the major. I'd certainly appreciate you allowing me to take a look at what you've got on him. You never know; I might be able to help."

Melanie watched with amused incredulity as Eddie's resistance crumbled beneath Nathaniel's charm. Maybe, she thought, that book in the library should have been called *The Raven's Charm*; it seemed more appropriate.

Eddie was nodding. "All right. I'll bring it up to the house. Tomorrow morning? I have a few loose ends I want to tie up first."

Nathaniel smiled again. "I'm looking forward to it."

Eddie seemed happy with that. He turned away, his eyes sliding over Melanie without really focusing, and after lifting his hand in a wave, he began to make his way back across the clearing and into the trees.

"I never spoke any dying words to anyone," Nathaniel said with quiet fury. "Edward's right, it's all rubbish.

Almost as if the whole purpose of the author was to blacken my name."

"Which is easy enough to do when your victim is dead and can't defend himself."

"Pengorren would do something like that," Nathaniel said. "I thought he was my friend, but it was all a pretense. Maybe he made up the last words story, and the author of that bloody book found a mention of it somewhere."

Melanie touched his cheek with her fingers. "Do you think Pengorren was jealous of what you had and what you were, Nathaniel? Maybe that was why he came to Ravenswood? Because deep in his heart he wanted to be you."

Twenty-four

Nathaniel shivered at her touch as much as her words. Was she right? He felt as if he wasn't quite as much in the dark as he had been, that the path was becoming a little less difficult to follow. He was on Pengorren's trail and soon he hoped to catch up with him and deal with him. Perhaps he wasn't doomed to wander forever the between-worlds with Teth after all.

"Nathaniel?" She was still stroking his cheek.

His gaze dropped to Melanie, and he tried to stop his breath from catching. She was dazzlingly beautiful. He felt his body go hard, instantly, and he couldn't do a thing about it. She was like a siren in a fable, able to lure men and ensnare them with a single glance from her glittering blue eyes.

She knew he was in trouble, too—he could see the knowledge in her face. She just didn't know why.

"What's different about me?" she asked with a mixture of irritation and worry.

Carefully Nathaniel rested his hand on her shoulder,

letting himself feel the warmth of her body through her sweater. The sensation was so intense he very nearly groaned. "Do you feel different?" he said, his voice gruffer than usual.

Melanie thought a moment. "Yes," she admitted. "I feel lighter, somehow, but also stronger. As though I'm more together than I've ever been. As if all the pieces that make me have fused into one. It sounds ridiculous, but that's how I feel. . . There's more, but I don't know if I should tell you about that." She looked at him sideways.

Nathaniel's hand was still on her shoulder and he brushed the skin of her neck with his fingertips, then slid them around to her nape, massaging the tight cords and muscles. She gave a soft sigh and tilted her head forward to give him better access. He moved closer, his body almost touching hers, and felt the iron control he had clamped on himself begin to fail him—like cracks appearing in a pane of glass just before it shatters.

"I thought we weren't going to have any more secrets from each other?" He stepped in even closer, until he felt bathed in the heat of her body. His fingers trembled with the strain, but he kept stroking her, caressing her. She leaned back into him, her bottom nestling against his groin. She must have been able to feel how aroused he was, but she just pressed closer.

"I feel sexy," she confessed. "I feel like I'm breathing sex. Like I'm suddenly one of those incredibly sensual women who just oozes it from her pores."

She turned, and she slid her arms about his neck and

clung there, gazing up at him with half-closed eyes, her pale skin flushed, her lips parted.

His mouth came down, but with an effort that was truly beyond human he stopped himself, held himself back, although every fiber of him was screaming with need.

Her breath was warm and sweet against his lips. "I've never been a woman who felt sexy about herself," she confessed. "I've always been too much aware of what was happening around me, too much in my head to really let go and *feel*." She nuzzled against him, licking the skin between jaw and throat, using her teeth to scrape the stubble. "But now . . . whenever I see you, whenever I touch you, I'm burning up."

She was on fire for him, that was true. He could feel her blood throbbing in her veins, and she was so alive, so desirable. Nathaniel knew he'd now gone past the point where he could stop himself again.

"Melanie," he groaned, and lowered his mouth to hers.

He felt her breasts through the thin sweater, swollen and peaked, and when he slid his palm underneath and cupped her full flesh, she arched against him.

She was breathing fast, reaching down to his breeches and forcing his buttons open with more brute strength than finesse. Before he could catch his own breath her fingers were on him, stroking him. When he tugged open her jeans, she didn't even seem to care, other than to push them down her long legs as quickly as she possibly could and kick them aside.

He slid his fingers inside her. She felt hot and slippery, and he'd barely flicked at her swollen nub when she came, shuddering and gasping, her body like a bow, so that he struggled to hold her upright. He gritted his teeth, cursing beneath his breath, trying to maintain some sort of control. He reminded himself that he was a gentleman, the son of a gentleman, and he was better than this. Where was tenderness, where was finesse?

But in truth he felt like an animal. Like a beast wanting to mate.

Hot waves of lust were rolling over him, and he wanted to explode. There was a primitive voice in his head. *Take her,* it was saying, *take her now, she's yours.*

Once again it was almost impossible to resist that primal urge, but he did. This wasn't how it should be—they were being manipulated. He threw back his head and fought against whatever it was that had been unleashed between them, and after what seemed a very long time he could hear the soft sound of her breathing and feel her lips, tender against the arch of his throat.

"Nathaniel," she whispered. "I need you now."

With trembling arms he laid her down on the ground where the leaves were thickest, and began to caress her with his fingers and his mouth. She was on fire again, insatiable for him, so he made her wait even though it was agony for him. But he needed to feel he was in control, he needed to believe he could stop at any time and get up and walk away.

Being with Melanie meant something more to him than just sex, and he wanted to prove that point to whatever was playing games with them.

In the end the waiting made it better for them both. When he thrust himself into her at last and came in an embarrassingly short time, he felt as if his head had been blown off by a French cannon. And when he was able to breathe again, think again, he realized Melanie was clinging to him, her face pressed to his shoulder, weeping hot tears that had soaked through his shirt to his skin.

"You're safe," he said.

"Safe from what?" she asked huskily, and wiped her face with a shaking hand. "Safe from who?"

Not me at any rate, Nathaniel thought with wry humor. He wanted her again. He should have been exhausted, but he wasn't. Nathaniel held her close to his side, feeling every contour, every inch of her, his own body stirring, readying itself for her again.

Eddie had seen the change in her, too, so Nathaniel knew it wasn't just him who was drawn to her. The poor bugger had hardly been able to keep his eyes off her—and whatever he'd been feeling had frightened him. Nathaniel wasn't frightened, but he was very aware of what was happening to him and very aware of his limitations when it came to resisting her.

This couldn't be natural. There was something happening here that was beyond the mortal world.

Pengorren.

He sensed his enemy's interference.

"This is your fault," Melanie murmured sulkily. She was watching him through her lashes.

Deliberately, he bent his head to look into her face. Aware of the raging need, the wildness only just kept at bay. It was like riding Neptune in the storm, with disaster only a hairbreadth away. For Nathaniel the risk taker it was sheer heaven.

"How can it be my fault?" he asked reasonably, as if they weren't lying half-naked in each other's arms in the middle of the park.

"My life was perfect until you came along."

"Your life was dull and boring, Melanie. I've brought excitement into it. You should be grateful to me." He found he had her breast in his hand, fondling, kneading.

"No, you're wrong," she went on, but there was a husky tremble in her voice, and she lifted her thigh across his.

He reached down and stroked her skin, and the strong, long line of her leg. He knew just how close he was to pushing her onto her back and taking her, again, and it was important to resist. To show himself he was the one in control here.

"My life was just as I wanted it," she protested. "I knew everything that was going to happen to me. There were no surprises, nothing out of the ordinary ever happened . . ."

"It doesn't sound like much of a life," he murmured, trailing his fingers over her hip and then over her soft belly toward the cluster of pale curls.

She held her breath, willing him to go farther, but he didn't.

"Nathaniel, please," her breath was ragged, squirming against him.

"Be patient, Melanie," he mocked, but the sweat was standing out on his brow.

She turned on him then, digging her nails into his hand, her eyes flashing like silver. Looking into them he felt light-headed and weak-kneed, as he did sometimes with the queen of the between-worlds.

Nathaniel jerked his hand away from her nails, feeling the sting where she'd cut him, and rolled on top of her. She was pinned beneath him now, and he didn't scruple to make use of his larger size and weight to hold her down.

"You can't live like that, Melanie." He was breathing fast, looking intently into her eyes. "That's not living. You were protecting yourself from being hurt, but where was the happiness? If you've removed all risk, then everything seems dull and bland. You need some spice."

"Oh, and you're the spice?" She was glaring up at him. He had hold of her wrists, and he could see her fingers clenching, wanting to get at him. There was a violence in her that had never been there before. He'd felt it himself, the wild animal beneath the skin, panting to get out.

"This is Pengorren's doing, isn't it?" she asked in a voice that shook. "He's making this happen. I've seen him having sex with a woman, brutal sex. Maybe that's part of what he is. Maybe he sees sex as something more than a physical act, maybe he needs it to stay alive. And now he's using us for whatever it is he gets out of it."

Melanie was angry, and she was scared.

"If we stay in control, then he can't use us," Nathaniel said, and licked at the tear that was rolling down her cheek. "We can defeat him."

"How? Look at us!" As she said it she deliberately

arched her hips, and he felt his cock brush the apex of her thighs.

He groaned, pushing her back down into the soft leaves. His voice sounded as if he'd stopped breathing. "Instead of having 'brutal sex' we make love. Then *we* win. Pengorren doesn't understand tenderness or caring or sacrificing yourself to make someone else happy. Melanie, he doesn't understand *love*."

Melanie's eyes filled with tears, and she closed them. Immediately Nathaniel felt his own strength returning. He began to kiss her, lavishing himself upon her. With a sob, her mouth opened beneath his, and they lost themselves in the sheer wonder.

Nathaniel slid deeply into her, felt her tremble, and began to move. She picked up his rhythm, slow and steady. Her hands were under his shirt, following the planes and curves of his back, caressing him with a studied gentleness. The effort made her shake, but he sensed she was back in control again. They both were. They were together in this, giving each other as much pleasure as they were taking.

Her body lifted against his, and she cried out, a moment before he reached his own climax. They lay gasping, rocked by the sheer force of their experience.

Melanie opened her eyes and smiled at him, and he felt that ache in his chest. "That was wonderful," she whispered. Her smile faded. "Do you think we'll be all right now?"

"I don't know . . ." he began, and then he groaned and covered her eyes with his hand. "Close your eyes,

Melanie, please. I can control it, I'm trying, but just for now I need you to close your eyes . . ."

She didn't try and push his hand away, but lay there obediently. "I felt like that when I first saw Pengorren," she said in a small voice. "I discovered that if I closed my eyes, or didn't look directly into his, then it was all right. Nathaniel," she went on in a rush, "I'm so sorry this is happening—"

He chuckled. "Don't be, Melanie. I promise you, I'm well up to the task."

Her mouth curled at the edges beneath his improvised blindfold. "I didn't mean that. I'm not sorry for *that*."

Nathaniel bent and kissed her smiling lips. "Good, because I don't think this is the end of it, Melanie. Not by a long way."

Twenty-five

Eddie had left the portrait in the library, resting against Miss Pengorren's desk. Melanie stood in front of it with Nathaniel just behind her, not touching her but close enough that she could feel the security of his presence. They were still disheveled, still shaken, but calm, too. Melanie knew what Nathaniel said made sense. Pengorren was trying to strip them of all that made them human, and they had to resist him. They didn't understand what he was up to, what drove him and why, but they knew enough to be able to remain safe from him.

For now.

"His face is gone," Melanie said, disappointed, although Eddie had warned her that the portrait was damaged. "I really wanted to see his face. I thought if I recognized him, then I'd be able to prove to myself he was the man I saw on the beach that day."

"You don't have to prove anything, Melanie. Pengorren is here, and we both know it."

"Are any of the other portraits affected like this?" Melanie asked suddenly.

"Not as far as I'm aware, and I've been all over the house. Do you think this is more than just bad luck?"

"I don't know." She dragged her fingers back through her hair, tousling it worse than ever. "That's just it, isn't it? No one knows."

He leaned closer, frowning at the portrait. Melanie tried to see what he saw. The face and a good deal around it was gone, and the paint and canvas had turned an unpleasant brown color.

"What's that chain around his neck?" she asked curiously. "Not a cross, surely."

"No, it was a locket. He always wore it. He said it was his mother's."

"The key?" Melanie murmured.

Pengorren's body was still intact. He was wearing clothing similar to Nathaniel's in his portrait, and the scene behind him was also very similar—Ravenswood and the trees of the park—but with the addition of a woman with dark hair and a child. They were both looking toward Pengorren, who dominated the scene.

It was meant to be Sophie, Melanie supposed, and their child. Before she was locked away? Or was this simply an artist's impression of the happy family that never existed?

"I imagine it wouldn't be polite to paint in Dorrie and the other women and their other children," she said dryly. "They weren't for public consumption, although everyone knew what he was up to."

"He used them all."

"Is that what Pengorren has planned for me? Bonking everything that moves?"

Nathaniel cupped her face in his hands and immediately the sexual desire began to stir. "I'm more than capable of keeping you satisfied," he said, with the sort of male arrogance she usually found so irritating but in him it was a turn-on.

"I'm sure you are," she whispered, the heat uncoiling inside her.

Abruptly he jerked his fingers away from her skin. Stepped back. "Close your eyes, Melanie," he said gruffly, "unless you want to spend the day in bed."

"Tempting," she replied, obediently closing her eyes and trying for a normal voice, "but I'm hungry. Peanut butter sandwich?"

Nathaniel was trying, too. "Cheese and pickle."

"Lovely."

They made their way downstairs to the kitchen, being very careful to keep their distance and not to touch each other.

The queen smiled to herself as she inspected the cave at the end of one of the narrower tunnels in the between-worlds. It was cramped and gloomy, and perfect for Pengorren. She'd be able to drop in and visit him as she was passing, just to remind him of all he'd lost by betraying her.

Of course he might escape her again, it was possible, but she didn't think so. His greed would be his undoing. He'd be unable to resist the bait. And he always underestimated her, believing himself to be cleverer and more cunning. A fatal mistake.

I am infinitely patient.

But then, she could afford to be. She didn't need to replenish her life force as Pengorren did.

The queen smiled again. Pengorren and she would have lots to talk about, and she would make sure she kept him alive.

More or less.

"No one makes a fool of me. Let that be a warning to you all!" Her voice rose and rushed through the tunnels like a windstorm. The creatures shuddered and hid, the waiting souls cried out in fear, and the doors to the between-worlds shook and rattled.

And far away, Pengorren lifted his head and listened, and knew he was running out of time.

Melanie was soaking in the bath. The water was warm, just verging on hot, but the truth was she felt too keyed up to relax. It was as if her metabolism had kicked up to high and she couldn't slow it back down. She'd never been lacking in energy, but this was different, and anyway she should be well and truly tired after all that had happened over the past few days. Any normal woman would be completely exhausted, but not Melanie—it was like she was on a constant natural high.

Or *un*natural, maybe.

She climbed out of the water and picked up the towel to dry herself. While she attended to her dripping hair, she let her thoughts drift back to Nathaniel. They tended to do that a lot, but this time they were bittersweet. She

had found a man who was everything she wanted—
although she'd always thought she wanted something
else, but now she knew better—and he couldn't stay. It
was going to be impossible for them to have a happy
ending together.

No long leisurely breakfasts in bed, no cappuccinos
at the local café and reading the Sunday papers, no
walks hand-in-hand and feeding the ducks, no sitting on
the couch watching movies and kissing when the com-
mercials came on . . .

She sensed the stirring in the air around her a moment before she heard it behind her.

Breathing.

The hairs stood up all over her body, but she didn't
turn. She had already pinpointed it; somewhere over
near the cupboard where the fresh towels were kept
folded. Heavy, labored breathing, as if whoever was over
there was sick. Or very old.

Slowly, reluctantly, Melanie lifted her gaze to the
mirror.

The steam had dissipated slightly, but the room was
still damp and cloudy. It blinded her. But there was a
darker shadow through the steam, something that looked
as if it was bent over. She recognized it. The thing she
had seen in the library was here in the bathroom, and
this time it was blocking her access to the door.

Just for a moment she was numb with horror, staring
at the reflection. And then the creature swayed forward,
and she could hear the dry rustling as it dragged itself
across the tiled floor. As it moved, the steam billowed
away from it, and she saw that the head was still bowed,

although the white tufts of hair were longer than before and there was more of it so that it almost completely covered the gleaming skull. Shocked, she saw that the body had expanded, too, bulked out.

Whatever it was, it was growing.

As if to prove her point, the creature began slowly to straighten up.

She screamed for Nathaniel.

She could not turn, she dared not turn, but in the mirror she could see eyes. Small, bright eyes that glowed like neon lights.

"Melanie." It spoke in a voice that was like the crackle of old parchment. "Do not fight me. You are mine, blood of my blood, flesh of my flesh . . ."

Melanie screamed again and stumbled forward against the washbasin and counter, scattering shampoo and cosmetics as she scrambled to climb on top. She slipped, bruising her hip, and fell to the floor. Quickly, she rolled over and pressed herself back against the drawers, not even feeling the metal handles digging into her flesh. Through her wet and tangled hair, she faced the thing that was shuffling toward her.

That familiar sense of evil, that sickening cloud of malevolence, wafted over her and filled the room. She could taste it, and for a second she thought she was going to retch. But there was no time to be sick.

"Go away!" she screamed, reaching above her to scrabble with her hand on the basin and finding the cake of soap. She threw it.

The cake struck the thing in the middle of the chest, but it didn't seem fazed. It came on.

"Oh God, oh God . . ."

Next she threw her tube of toothpaste, then the wash-basin plug, and then a bottle of expensive moisturizer. Nothing stopped it; it was as if it couldn't feel pain. Or maybe it was just so intent on getting to her that it didn't care what she did.

The creature's hand, more like a claw really, stretched out toward her, shaking as though it had some sort of dreadful palsy. Its face was so close now that she could not mistake it for anything other than a human face, but so old. Old beyond any possibility that it could still be living. The skin was yellowed and dried out, like something that had lain in the sun for decades, and the mouth was just a slit, without lips, without teeth. Melanie threw back her head and let loose another piercing scream.

She felt it touch her on the leg, the brush of brittle fingernails, and she jerked away in horror, crawling across the floor toward the door, sobbing for help.

The door was shaking. She hadn't realized, until now she hadn't heard the crashing and thudding as someone outside tried to break it down. And then suddenly the lock burst open, and Nathaniel was there. He had never looked more wonderful.

She clung to him, still sobbing hysterically, but deep inside where it was calm she knew that the thing was gone. That when she finally lifted her head and dared to look, the bathroom would be empty.

It took a very long time for Melanie to calm down.

Nathaniel found her description of what she had seen awful enough, but what really worried him were her stumbling efforts to explain to him the dark air of evil that clung to it like a cloak.

"It came for me," she said, over and over again, as he held her. "It called me by my name."

Nathaniel held her tighter, as if he could save her with the strength of his arms.

"It touched me."

She pulled away and pointed down to her leg and then froze. There was a mark on her skin, like a small burn, and it was red and blistered. It was similar to the mark on her hand—now gone—only more prominent.

Nathaniel swore. His fingers hovered over the injury but he didn't touch it. "Did you feel anything when . . . ?"

"No," she said, eyes wide with horrified wonder. "I . . . I think I was just too scared to feel anything. I was more intent on getting away. But now . . ." She leaned her face wearily against his shoulder. "Nathaniel, I feel completely exhausted. I just want to go to sleep."

It was understandable that she should be tired out, anyone would be. But Melanie wasn't anyone. She had told him that she thought this time the creature was stronger, looked bigger. More like a man.

Was it using her to fuel its regeneration? Was it feeding off her?

The idea made him sick and furious, but the more he considered it, the more he found it entirely possible.

Melanie could hardly keep her eyes open. Nathaniel lifted her into his arms and carried her to her bedchamber and tucked her beneath the covers. Then he stood by the window, keeping watch over her, while she slept. He didn't want to leave her. His time in the between-worlds had taught him that there existed beings far more dangerous than he had ever imagined, and they could, and did, prey upon the innocent.

And this being, whatever it was, wanted her.

Melanie.

Her leg had been burned, and now she lay exhausted in her bed. Nathaniel felt as if he should know what was happening, but he didn't. Was this something connected with Pengorren, or was it something else?

Melanie believed Pengorren had chosen him because he envied him and wanted to be like him. That Pengorren was consumed with jealousy and envy, and he wanted to take Nathaniel's life. But where did Melanie fit in?

Melanie made a soft sound, and he looked up sharply. She had turned her head toward him and her face appeared smooth and untroubled in sleep. Most of the siren glow had left her, but it was still there, pulling his gaze back to her again and again. He heard the voice in his head, soft but audible, telling him to climb beneath the covers with her, to use her as he had used other women in his brief and unimportant encounters that had nothing to do with the heart.

"I won't hurt her or deceive her," he told it. "She trusts me, and I won't put that in jeopardy. She's my woman, and I will protect her, from myself if necessary."

That he and Melanie had only met such a short time ago seemed remarkable to him. Could he really have fallen in love with her so quickly, or was their attraction to do with the change in Melanie? Whatever the reason, he wanted to stay with her forever, and yet that couldn't be. He would succeed and return to the past, or he would fail and be cast back into the dark tunnels of the between-worlds.

Either way he would never see her again.

Twenty-six

Melanie was propped up in bed picking at her toast and marmite, while Nathaniel sat in the chair watching her, narrow-eyed. He'd been watching her ever since she woke up, and she tried to ignore him. It was morning, and she'd slept the whole night through, but she still felt tired and weak. Yesterday she had been like a new woman, but today . . . she might as well be a hundred. The creature had taken all that from her, drained her of vigor.

Earlier, when she'd brushed her hair and looked in the mirror, she'd realized the strange aura had left her, too. The two obviously went together, because it was definitely gone; she was plain Melanie Jones once more. She admitted she was secretly disappointed about that—her goddess persona had some advantages—but it was a relief not to be ravaged by uncontrollable sexual appetites. Yes, she'd enjoyed sating them with Nathaniel, but the last time things had begun to get frighteningly, dangerously out of control.

"Eddie said he'd be over in a while," Nathaniel said quietly from his chair.

"You've seen him, then?" She pulled another piece off her toast, but couldn't eat it. She placed it with the other bits she couldn't eat, on the edge of the plate.

"He brought in some food. He said he'd arrange for feed for Neptune, too, from a local stable. Good man, that."

Melanie smirked. "Worthy of your patronage?"

"Very worthy." He stretched lazily, and Melanie found her gaze fastened on him. Maybe her sexual appetites weren't quite as depleted as she'd thought.

Making love with Nathaniel would rate among the best times of her life. When she was as old as Miss Pengorren, she'd be dreaming of her ghostly lover.

"Miss Pengorren was afraid, wasn't she? That's why she left Ravenswood."

"Whatever she saw over the last few months of her life, it made her want to replace Pengorren's portrait with mine, and it made her believe that I had been unfairly treated."

"So we assume she was seeing Pengorren and that he was threatening her . . . how? If he was like you were when I first saw you, a ghost, then she might be frightened, but she'd know he couldn't harm her. Why would she abandon her home? I wish she'd left a note."

"It would have been helpful, yes," Nathaniel said dryly.

Melanie pulled back the covers and examined the burn on her leg. The injury was healing remarkably fast. There was barely any sign of it left, apart from the fact that her skin was a little reddened and there was a blister in the center.

Nathaniel had wanted to take her to a "physician," but Melanie had refused. What would she say when they asked her how it had happened? Besides, it was nothing some painkillers couldn't ease. She'd had worse sunburn.

"So Miss Pengorren abandoned Ravenswood," she said thoughtfully. "Or did she hope Pengorren would follow her to London? Maybe she was performing her own exorcism."

"More marmite?" Nathaniel asked, but he was looking at her legs.

Melanie shook her head slowly. "I didn't think you liked marmite?"

"It grows on one."

"Hmm."

"Are you going to get dressed?"

Melanie glanced up at him from under her lashes. The way he smiled back at her gave her that warm all-over tingle. "Soon," she said, and did her own stretch, slow and thorough. "I don't feel like getting dressed just yet."

"You're doing that on purpose," he said in a mock growl.

Melanie laughed, and then grew serious. "It's gone, isn't it? Whatever I had yesterday has gone away?"

Nathaniel came and sat beside her on the bed and took her hand, entwining her fingers with his. She looked down at their hands, and they looked so right together it was uncanny.

"It has faded, Melanie," he said, "but it's still there. I

can feel it when I touch you and when I look into your eyes. It's even there when I'm in the same room as you."

"Perhaps you just fancy me rotten," she joked, but her smile went awry. "That thing . . . that thing last night, it told me I was blood of its blood, flesh of its flesh. How can I be? How can I have anything to do with something like that?"

"I don't know, my darling," he said, "but we will find out."

He bent toward her, and a loose strand of his hair fell forward and tickled her cheek. Then he began to kiss her, slowly, until she was drugged with need. He pulled off her pajamas and when she was naked, he pressed her back onto the bed and worked his way from her throat to her breasts until she was squirming. Only then did he move on, tongue warm and wet as he laved it against her stomach, and down. She clutched at his hair, holding him, as he settled himself between her thighs.

Sometime later, after the lights behind her eyes had burst and flashed like fireworks at night, he began to work his way back up again. By the time he'd reached her mouth, Melanie was on fire and more than ready for him to lay his long and graceful body upon hers.

"I'll bet you do this to all the girls," she said, but as she looked into his eyes she knew this was different, this was special.

"I've never had anyone like you," he murmured, kissing her.

"What will happen—"

He placed a finger against her lips. "I've been sleeping in the between-worlds for almost two hundred years," he said. "I may be there for another two hundred. I don't want to think about that. I want to think about you, how you feel and look and taste, the sound of your voice when we join together. I want to remember you, Melanie, when I'm gone."

"Nathaniel . . ."

But what could she say? Don't go? Don't fail? Take me with you? Her words wouldn't help either of them.

"You're right," she whispered, as he began to kiss her again. "We have to enjoy this moment."

They stayed in bed for another hour, and then they heard Eddie calling from downstairs. Nathaniel left Melanie to get dressed and went to head him off.

Eddie followed Nathaniel into the library, shooting quick, uneasy glances around him. "Melanie not here?"

"She'll be here soon."

Nathaniel smiled to himself. Eddie was expecting Melanie to pounce on him, and he appeared relieved to hear he'd be safe for a little while longer. "I brought my book," he said, trying to be nonchalant, but Nathaniel could see how nervous he was about letting him read it.

The "book" was actually a thick bundle of papers bound together with something narrow and stretchy. Eddie held the bundle out like a father offering his baby, and Nathaniel took it from him, carefully, and read the title.

"*Ravenswood Reclaimed.*"

"Reclaimed from *The Raven's Curse,*" Eddie explained in a self-important tone. "I wanted to redress the wrong done to the Raven, you see."

"I see," Nathaniel said quietly, looking at the other man with new eyes, "and I appreciate it. Please, Edward, won't you be seated?" He gestured to the chair opposite his own. *The Raven's Curse* was lying on the seat where Melanie had left it. Curiously, as if it might bite him, Eddie picked it up. He examined the cover with a frown, as if he'd never seen it before.

"Oh!" he said. "That's where I've heard the name."

Nathaniel had his head bent over the pages, already reading. "Name?"

"Trewartha. Melanie asked me if I knew a Mr. Trewartha who ran an antique business. I thought I knew the name, only I'd never heard it in connection with antiques. Now I know why. H. Trewartha is the author of this book." He held it up. *"The Raven's Curse."*

"Trewartha," Nathaniel repeated, stunned. "Antiques?"

Eddie nodded. "That's right. Melanie said she'd asked him to come and do a catalogue of Ravenswood's contents, for the auction. I hope she realizes she'll be listening to his theories about the Raven while he's going through the cupboards."

Melanie had asked Mr. Trewartha to come to Ravenswood to list the contents of the house? The same man who wrote that bloody book, claiming Nathaniel was insane?

The thought of *anyone* touching his things, going through the trunks of family belongings, reducing everything to lists, infuriated him, but he'd steeled himself to the reality of it. But for the author of that book to be doing it . . . It was too much! Nathaniel felt sick with anger and resentment. This was *his* house.

Eddie was watching him warily. "Are you all right, mate? You don't look too good."

"I don't like that book," Nathaniel said with quiet menace.

"No, but he wrote it with quite a bit of authority. I don't know the details, but it wouldn't surprise me if Trewartha was related to Pengorren, too."

"Everyone else seems to be." Nathaniel tried to swallow his anger.

Eddie laughed. "Couldn't seem to help himself. And the women didn't put up much of a fight."

"Act in haste, repent at leisure," Nathaniel said piously, sounding like his father.

"Do you mind me asking? You said your ancestor was born on the wrong side of the blanket . . . I am descended from Pengorren and Dorrie. Can you tell me something about yourself? I'm curious. I didn't realize there were any Ravens left."

Nathaniel removed the next page from the bundle on his lap. "A liaison between my fa . . . Nathaniel senior's brother, Oscar, and a woman of the town," he said, silently apologizing to his uncle Oscar, a respectable man who died wifeless and childless.

Eddie considered that for a moment. "I didn't realize. And I can understand why you're so annoyed about Trewartha's book. Family pride and all that. I'm a bit surprised you wanted him here at all."

"I didn't know he was coming," Nathaniel said dryly.

Eddie was finally silenced, and Nathaniel returned to his reading. Only to stop abruptly after a couple of sentences. He reread it, and then looked up at Eddie, his hazel eyes narrowed.

"What the hell is this?" he demanded. *"There is no record of Pengorren's birth, or any details of where he originally came from. His army records are incorrect, possibly downright lies, and lead nowhere. Historically, Pengorren never existed."*

"It's true." Eddie leaned forward with enthusiasm. "It's as if he stepped off a blank page. If you read on a bit, you'll see I speculate about whether or not his name really was Pengorren. When I checked the army records at Kew, I found a note written by a woman—a gentlewoman fallen on hard times—who said a stranger had paid her for the use of her deceased brother's name and address, and she'd heard afterward that he'd risen to be a major in the army. The brother's name was Hew Pengorren."

Nathaniel flicked over some more pages, reading here and there as he went. *"Mass murderer?"* He cocked an eyebrow. *"Serial killer?* Good God!"

"I'm writing a real-life historical murder mystery. I offer my own theory of what happened, and it's up to the readers to agree or not. This sort of stuff is very popular at the moment. What do you think?"

"I think you're probably right," he said quietly.

Eddie grinned. "I've done plenty of research, but I have to make assumptions when the records aren't there. Every criminologist makes assumptions, every murder investigator has to take a jump of faith."

"And you expect your book to be taken just as seriously as *The Raven's Curse*?"

"Why not? I think it's just as credible. At least I don't believe Nathaniel was insane, just gullible."

At that moment Melanie appeared in the doorway.

Nathaniel had expected to be angry with her, but all such thoughts flew out of his head because she'd dressed in clothing that made his eyes widen and his heart begin to race. She might as well have been wearing nothing—a garment that hung on her hips and barely reached to midthigh, and a tight shirt with no sleeves that clung to her breasts and showed her midriff. But it wasn't only her clothing that made his breath quicken. Her glow was coming back.

Eddie stared down at his shoes.

"Who was gullible?" she asked, looking from one to the other.

"Nathaniel Raven," Nathaniel said, when Eddie didn't answer. "Eddie forgot to tell us that he is writing the history of Ravenswood as a murder mystery in which Major Pengorren is the villain. You tell her your theory, Edward."

"Yes, please, I'm very interested." Melanie seemed to glide across the room toward them. Her eyes glittered like pale blue fire.

"I'm going for a different angle," Eddie told her, his enthusiasm tempered by the fact he was staring at the floor. "From what I've discovered, Pengorren was a bit of a mystery man from the start, but he and Raven quickly became friends, despite the difference in rank. I asked myself a couple of questions: What if Raven boasted about his home and his family? What if he made them sound so attractive that he caught Major Pengorren's interest? What if Pengorren was looking for somewhere to hide out, to make a new life for himself? Well, naturally, he'd look covetously at Ravenswood, wouldn't he?"

"But Eddie," Melanie began, awkwardly, glancing at Nathaniel.

"No, no, hear me out," Eddie insisted. "Pengorren saved Nathaniel's life, so naturally he is invited to Ravenswood to be thanked in person. He's a hero, why wouldn't he be? But as soon as he arrives things start to happen. First, Mr. Raven senior is killed in a riding accident, then Pengorren takes over the arrangements, making himself indispensable to the widow and family. They all seem to be completely under his spell. Even Nathaniel, the son, who doesn't seem to realize he's been targeted. Next, Pengorren marries the widow, and remember this is only a few weeks after her husband has been buried. Unheard of, a terrible scandal, but not one person stays away from the wedding. No one complains. And then his wife dies in mysterious circumstances, and the next thing he's marrying the daughter, Sophie, who's already pregnant with his child.

"By then young Nathaniel is dead. He'd taken to holding up coaches and running wild. Pengorren seemed inclined to ignore him for a while, but then Nathaniel started to irritate him, and Pengorren lost his temper. And he had a temper."

"I can believe Pengorren was a psychopath," Melanie said decidedly.

"Yes, exactly! Psychopaths haven't just appeared in

modern times; they have always been with us. Pengorren has all the traits."

Eddie was wound up, and in his enthusiasm for his pet subject he forgot to avoid Melanie. His eyes clashed with hers, and for a moment he didn't seem to know where he was. He shook his head like a bear waking from hibernation and cleared his throat, fixing his gaze on Nathaniel.

"Remember, Pengorren was a monster. He must have decided that Nathaniel wasn't worth the effort anymore. Anyway, by then he had what he wanted. He'd taken everything that belonged to Nathaniel, and now it only remained for him to get rid of the heir. So he had him shot."

You don't know the half of it, Melanie thought, feeling for Nathaniel.

"*The Raven's Curse* asserts Nathaniel was shot by Sir Arthur Tregilly's coachman," Nathaniel said without much passion. "Don't you agree with Trewartha?"

"Well, I know that's what Trewartha says," Eddie agreed, looking smug, "but I've managed to find some of the contemporaneous statements made by the witnesses at the scene. They were in the archives at Truro, mixed in with some other file, almost as if someone didn't want them to be found," he added darkly. "Didn't stop me, though. I've read the statement from Tregilly's coachman, and he denies he ever shot the Raven. He says he fired his gun when they were first held up, but only into the air. He knew it was Nathaniel, everyone did, and they didn't want to shoot him dead and face Pengorren afterward. He goes on to say that when the Raven fell, he was facing the coach, and the shot came out of the woods at his back. He died at the scene, and he couldn't speak at all, so there was no way he could have delivered any last-minute curses. It's all rot."

Nathaniel sat very still. "So you believe it was Pengorren alone who killed Nathaniel?"

"Definitely.

Melanie moved closer to his chair and rested a hand on the back of it, trying to offer what comfort she could by her presence without doing what she really wanted to do—curl up on his knee and give him a hug.

"It works, doesn't it? You can see what I'm getting at." Eddie was almost bouncing up and down he was so excited to be finally discussing his theory. "I think someone set him up. I think that when the robbery took place someone else knew what was about to happen and had already taken up position in the woods. I've read a couple of Sir Arthur Tregilly's diaries, and he claimed he knew the truth. Unfortunately, he pegged out before he could do more than hint at it."

He was serious, and he'd done his research. Melanie had to admire him for it. "So you believe it was a planned execution?" Her fingers crept over the back of the chair and touched Nathaniel's hair.

"Yes. Pengorren had a pretty good life afterward, didn't he? Did well for himself for a nobody from nowhere."

Abruptly Nathaniel got to his feet and tossed the manuscript onto his chair. His eyes met Melanie's and, despite the tension of the moment and the pallor of Nathaniel's face, she felt the attraction between them like yesterday's storm. Building. Images of naked flesh flashed through her mind, and she bit her lip. His gaze zeroed in on her mouth, and his eyes went dark.

He must have realized the inappropriateness of it, too, because he shook his head. But he managed a reassuring half smile before he turned to Eddie. His voice was measured and calm, although Melanie could hear the depth of emotion behind it. Nathaniel Raven was speaking from the heart.

"I think the Raven was confused. He'd been to war, he'd been wounded, then his father had died in an accident and his mother was planning to marry someone she hardly knew. He wasn't thinking clearly; he'd never had to be the man of the house before. Of course he acted impulsively. Of course he should have waited Pengorren out, played him at his own game. But remember, Nathaniel was an impulsive character, not used to waiting for the right moment or thinking too deeply. He went with his instincts."

Eddie pursed his lips. "Yeah, I can see what you mean. The Raven is a hero around here, or an antihero, anyway. I could write him as a tragic hero, a straight character who didn't work out the sort of creep Pengorren was until it was too late. Yes, I like it."

"Lovely," Melanie muttered under her breath.

"What about Sophie?" Nathaniel asked abruptly. "What happened to Pengorren's second wife?"

"Madhouse," Eddie said, with a grimace. "Went

totally bonkers after her son was born. They locked her up, and she died in there a few years later. By that time Pengorren had filled the house with his women and was more or less living the life of a sheik with his harem. And yet he was still respected, still liked, and still the magistrate for the district!"

"Everyone was blinded by Pengorren? You must admit, Edward, Pengorren had an amazing ability to persuade people to believe in him and to love him."

"Glamour," Eddie said.

"Glamour?" Nathaniel repeated, and frowned. He glanced at Melanie, but she shrugged, as confused as him. "Explain yourself, Edward."

"Glamour is the magical quality that faeries are supposed to possess. They wrap it around themselves like a cloak, and us normal human beings can't see through it. Instead, we only see what the faery wants us to see. In Pengorren's case, that would be a handsome and friendly man who is honorable and generous. A man everybody loves and admires. A man the women can't resist. That's your glamour in action."

"But Eddie," Melanie didn't know whether to laugh or cry. "You can't be suggesting that Pengorren was a . . . a . . ."

"I'm not. I'm just pointing out the comparison. Many psychopaths have charisma, glamour. They attract people to them and then—"

Downstairs a door banged. "Melanie!?" a voice drifted upward.

Melanie felt her mouth fall open and closed it.

"Melanie!" the voice was louder this time. Quick, light footsteps started on the stairs. "Melanie, where on earth are you . . . ? Oh!"

The voice had reached the door.

Melanie turned and said, with as much sangfroid as she could manage, "Hello Suzie. You made good time."

Twenty-seven

Suzie was thin and fair-haired, older than Melanie by about five years, but they were very similar in looks. Or they had been, Nathaniel supposed, until Melanie began to change . . .

Glamour.

He tried the word out. It made sense considering Pengorren's behavior and the way people responded to him. Eddie didn't know the full story, so he wouldn't realize that something like a magic spell was entirely possible when it came to Major Pengorren.

"I know, I know." Suzie gave Melanie a crooked but very attractive smile. "I shouldn't have come, and you're cross with me, but I was worried about you. After your phone call, I . . . I remembered something. I don't know why I didn't remember it before, but anyway I thought it was better to come down here and tell you face-to-face."

"You mean you were nosy and wanted to see where I was and what I was up to," Melanie retorted, but there was no animosity in her voice, just affection and a hint of weary relief. They were close then. Nathaniel remembered Sophie with an aching heart.

"That, too," Suzie admitted. She noticed Eddie, and tilted her head to one side as if she wasn't quite sure what she was dealing with. "Who's this then?"

"Eddie," Eddie introduced himself, holding out his hand. "I'm the caretaker."

Suzie took his hand, inspecting his bright shirt with the native girls in grass skirts dancing all over it, and then lifting her clever gaze to his good-natured face. Her smile said she liked what she saw. "Hello, Eddie," she said.

"And this is Nathaniel," Melanie went on, sounding stilted, as if this was an awkward situation for her. "Nathaniel, this is my sister, Suzie."

She felt very nervous, which was ridiculous. In the circumstances it shouldn't matter to her whether or not Suzie approved of Nathaniel or hated him on sight. It never had before. But this time it did.

Nathaniel gave her a smile, just a brief softening of his mouth and eyes. It's all right, that smile seemed to say. I understand.

She watched as he walked over to Suzie. He moved so gracefully, so beautifully, and—from the wondering expression on Suzie's face—he must have been wearing his most charming smile. Melanie was tempted to tell her sister that she could look, but she couldn't touch.

He's mine.

The thought was comforting and frightening at the same time.

"How do you do?" Nathaniel had taken Suzie's hand, holding it between both of his as he smiled down at her.

"Oh. Good," Suzie managed, with a glazed look in her blue eyes.

"Gets all the birds, does he? Not fair, is it?" Melanie jumped, as Eddie muttered in her ear. She didn't hear him sidle up to her

"You're not so bad yourself, Eddie," she retorted quietly. "And just so you know, Suzie likes a man who can make her laugh."

He gave her a doubtful look, as if he thought she might be having a go at him. But it was true, Suzie loved a joke, and Eddie's was the sort of easygoing, friendly personality she enjoyed in a man. The brooding, handsome ones always broke her heart.

Nathaniel let go of Suzie's hand, but she was still smiling up at him dreamily. Melanie decided it was time to ask some questions.

"Suzie, you said you had something to tell me?"

Suzie blinked, and then she was across the room in a gust of vanilla perfume. Her arms were thin, but they were strong, and she held Melanie tightly. Melanie closed her eyes, and for a moment she was safe, a child again, who believed Suzie could save her from all the monsters under the bed.

As they separated Suzie, held her away and frowned at her. "What have you done to yourself?"

"Nothing."

"There's something up," Suzie insisted, "and I want to know what it is. What's going on, Melanie?"

Melanie hesitated. "You first." She led her sister over

to the chair Eddie had just vacated. Suzie flopped down and surveyed the room.

"Wow, I'm impressed," she said, with a grin that made her look about fourteen years old. There was something familiar about her face and her windblown curls, but Melanie couldn't place it. And then her smile faded and she pushed up the sleeves of her jade green blouse. "All right, this is the thing. I remembered it after you rang, and it seemed important, too important to wait. Maybe I'm wrong, and if I am, then you can put me back in my Bug and send me home. But, Melanie, just hear me out first. Okay?"

Melanie realized that Nathaniel had come to stand beside her. His shoulder brushed against hers and fireworks went off in her head. She stepped away, concentrating on Suzie. "Okay. Tell me."

"Um"—Suzie looked at the two men—"are you sure? Do you want them to hear? Not that it's anything I wouldn't say in company."

"Just say it."

"Well, it was that name—Pengorren. It set off bells in my head. I knew I'd heard it before somewhere, and then I remembered. It was our mom. She used to talk about the wealthy Pengorren family down in Cornwall, with their great big house and their servants. When they lost everything, Mom and Dad, she used to say she'd go and see them and beg for her share. Dad scoffed at her, of course, said she was out of her head. "They won't give you anything," he used to say, "not when you're just some byblow from way back." You see, that was the thing. Mom said she was related to the Pengorrens, that we came from a bastard child born to a servant girl and the master. Happened a lot in the old days. No sexual harassment laws back then."

Melanie felt the room begin to rock under her feet.

Eddie snorted a laugh, then look embarrassed when the other two turned to him. "Sorry. I wasn't laughing at . . . It's just that there seem to be a lot of us Pengorren byblows about."

"What, you as well, Eddie?" Suzie asked, eyes shining. "Maybe we should form a Pengorren's Bastards Club—"

"I don't see what there is to be proud of," Melanie burst out, and swallowed. She felt sick. She put her hand over her mouth.

Suzie was on her feet. "Sis?"

"You're saying," Melanie went on, "that we're blood relatives of Pengorren? Is that what you're telling me?"

She was Pengorren's *blood of my blood, flesh of my flesh.*

This was it. This was the answer to the puzzle that the queen of the between-worlds had set them. She could help Nathaniel destroy Pengorren because she was intimately connected to him.

"Oh God . . ."

Her gaze found Nathaniel's, and she read the shock in his eyes, but she couldn't speak her thoughts aloud. She didn't want to give them that power.

"Melanie?" Suzie was talking to her.

And then Nathaniel's arms came around her. He was holding her, and Melanie could feel herself trembling, the shudders running through her, her legs shaking and weak, as the sexual attraction fought with her feelings of horror. And through it all, Nathaniel was holding her up.

Pengorren was in her head. Pengorren, grinning up at her, saying *Melanie*. Pengorren, who could make people love him despite his cruel and criminal behavior, just by looking into their eyes. *Glamour*. Pengorren, traveling through time, using her to . . . to what? Make himself young again? *Live again?*

"I see it now," Melanie whispered into Nathaniel's shoulder. "Coming here . . . I started it all up. This is my fault."

"No," he murmured against her hair, rocking her. "No, Melanie. It was meant to happen. You didn't start it up, you're here to put an end to it."

"Melanie, please!" Suzie's shrill voice broke through their private conversation. "What's the matter? Will someone tell me what's going on here?"

Melanie pulled away from Nathaniel, trembling, out of control. "You shouldn't be here," she said, her voice rising. "Suzie, you have to go. It's not safe for you here."

Suzie had Pengorren's blood, too. It explained her fascination with ancient sites and dancing in the freezing cold of midwinter solstice. She was part of that world, the world of magic and glamour and immortality. More so than Melanie had ever been or wanted to be.

Until now.

"If I leave, then you're coming with me," Suzie retorted, frightened but standing solid. "I'm not going anywhere without you. Now, come on, Melanie, tell me what this is about? You're scaring me."

"You should be scared," Melanie whispered. "My God, Suzie, you should be bloody scared!"

"Melanie—"

But Melanie turned and fled the room.

She ran toward her bedroom with the thought of locking herself in, like a child safe in the womb, where nothing bad could get at her. But the bad things were in her head, and she knew as she reached her door that she'd never escape them by running. She was so wrapped up in her own thoughts that she didn't hear the sounds at first. When she did her steps slowed until they stopped altogether, and she realized she was holding her breath. Listening.

Soft sighs and moans, rhythmic creaks and thuds. Just the same as before. Except that this time Melanie wasn't dreaming, she was wide-awake.

Pengorren.

Oh no, not again. Not so soon. Her heart began to stutter, and she felt light-headed. She didn't want to see, she didn't want to know. But at the same time she was angry, so very angry. Pengorren had hijacked her life, her mundane, ordinary life. She wouldn't let him frighten her with his tricks, not this time.

Before she could change her mind Melanie reached for her doorknob. Instantly, the sounds grew more intense, the moaning almost constant, as if the walls themselves were saturated with the sounds of the man and woman making love and were replaying the scene for her benefit all these years later.

"Hew," a female voice gasped from inside the bedroom. "I love you so, Hew . . ."

Melanie opened the door and stepped in.

This time Pengorren was more or less fully dressed as he lay on top of the woman. His face was buried in her bosom and her fingers were clutching at his shoulders as she climbed to her peak. Fair curly hair and young; it was Dorrie again.

Pengorren moved upon her steadily, almost mechanically, without passion. There was nothing erotic about the scene, nothing arousing, it was just sweaty and brutal.

Pengorren suddenly reared up, opening his jaws, and then bit Dorrie hard on her breast.

She screamed, twisting, struggling, but he didn't stop. He bit harder, as if her pain excited him.

"You'll hurt the babe, Hew," she moaned, tears streaming down her cheeks. "Please, Hew . . ."

"Stop it," Melanie whispered, then louder, "Stop it, you evil bastard!"

Pengorren let her go. He lifted his head, and there was a fleck of blood on his lips, but his ruddy and handsome face was calm and purposeful, while his blue eyes gleamed with awareness. He was looking *at* her, and then he grinned.

"This is what you have to look forward to," he said, as if Dorrie didn't exist, as if it was only Pengorren and Melanie. "Real power, complete power. Can't you feel it, Melanie? Growing inside you."

"No, I don't want that. I don't want to be like you. I'm not like you."

"But you are, my dear. *Flesh of my flesh—*"

"No!" There were an antique jug and basin on the table by the bed, the sort that used to be used for washing before bathrooms were invented. She reached for the jug, so furious she no longer felt in control of her actions, wanting only to strike out and destroy him.

He laughed, and his image flickered, fading.

By the time she'd swung the jug he was all but gone. It bounced harmlessly on the mattress. Pengorren hadn't even been here. It was just his essence. The real Pengorren was somewhere else altogether.

Tears stung her eyes. She felt no better for her loss of control, she hadn't gained anything. The worst of it was she'd seen the expression in his eyes, just before he vanished.

Satisfaction.

Twenty-eight

After Melanie had run out of the room, Suzie went to follow her, just as Nathaniel made the same move. They both stopped, and then Suzie changed her mind and turned instead to glare at the two men. "I hope someone here is going to fill me in," she said threateningly.

The shock of seeing her intelligent and conservative younger sister having a fit of nervous hysterics over a man who probably died before Queen Victoria, had deeply unsettled her.

Nathaniel shook his head. "No. I think it is up to Melanie to tell you what is troubling her."

He might be dreamy-looking, but Suzie didn't take that bossy tone from any man. "Obviously I think so, too, but she's not here," she said tartly. Frustrated, she turned her attention to Eddie. "What about you, Eddie? Got any opinions on what's troubling my sister? She's only been here a few days, and already she's a wreck. I haven't seen her like this since she was nine years old and . . ." Her voice trailed off. Something else had happened when Melanie was nine years old, and it had happened in Cornwall, not far from Ravenswood.

Eddie interrupted her thoughts. "Um, Suzie? I think Melanie is upset about my book." He gave a diffident smile, his kind eyes wearing a worried expression. A real sweetheart, this one, despite the shirt.

"Your book, Eddie? What book is that?"

"I've rewritten the history of Ravenswood and Major Pengorren's part in it."

"Oh? No, I can't see the connection yet, but go on."

Eddie cleared his throat. "Well . . ." and he launched into his theory.

Nathaniel watched Suzie concentrating as the rambling story unfolded, and thought again about following Melanie. But he knew she needed time alone to consider her situation. Her relationship to Pengorren was a stunning revelation, but it also made a terrible sense. He had noticed himself how Melanie's dazzling looks were so similar to Pengorren's. The glamour was something she'd inherited.

She must leave. She wasn't safe here, he knew that, had known it since last night. He just hadn't wanted to believe it. He wanted to keep her with him for the time left to him. But now he knew he had to persuade her to go home with her sister.

Nathaniel wandered over to the mullioned windows, and St. Anne's Hill stared back at him. The doorway into the between-worlds was silhouetted against the cloudy sky. Nathaniel narrowed his eyes—he could just make out a shadow by the stone, a hound-shaped shadow.

"So, you think that Pengorren had some sort of, eh, faery glamour." Behind him, Suzie sounded as if what she was saying was the most reasonable thing in the world. "Does that mean that I have it, too? And Melanie? And you, Eddie? How exciting."

Eddie snorted a dismissive laugh, but he was beaming, pleased by the comparison. "Maybe some have it more than others," he said, with painful honesty. "Your sister, for instance . . ."

His voice trailed off, and Suzie gave a thoughtful nod. "Yes. You're right. I wouldn't be surprised. I've always had some psychic abilities but Melanie is so closed down, so tightly reined in . . . There was a time when she used to see things. Then it stopped, and she used to get headaches, really bad ones. I always thought they were something to do with that shutting-down process, keeping everything confined."

"My old gran used to read the tea leaves," Eddie added helpfully, totally out of his depth.

Suzie laughed, and the atmosphere lightened. "And can you?"

Eddie smiled back. "Not really. But I can have a stab at it if you think it will help."

"No, thanks. I know as much about my past as I want to, and as for the future . . . I prefer to let it unfold as a nice surprise."

She looked up, catching Nathaniel watching them, and smiled as if she'd known all along that he was listening. Now she came to join him at the window, standing very close beside him. He wondered whether she was trying to intimidate him into giving her the information she wanted.

"Nice view," she said pleasantly, looking out over the park. When he didn't answer she turned to him, tilting her head back so that she could give him a thoroughly searching look. "And how do you fit in, Nathaniel? I think you know a lot more than you're saying."

Amused by her manner, he returned her look with a smile. "I'm related to the Ravens," he said truthfully. "Melanie asked me to come to Ravenswood."

"Hmm." She cocked an eyebrow, looking very like Melanie at her most skeptical. "I hope you're being nice to my little sister, Nathaniel."

Nathaniel's smile faded, replaced by a deadly seriousness. "You have my word that I am. She's more important to me than I can tell you. Which is why I want you to take her away from here. Now, today. She's not safe."

Suzie frowned, but her eyes stayed on his, as if she could see right inside his head. "If that's what *she* wants."

"She must go," Nathaniel spoke with urgency. "She must see sense. Surely you can persuade her, you're her sister?"

"Now," Suzie admitted, "that's where you might have a problem."

Melanie sat on the clifftop with her knees tucked up under her chin, staring down at the half-moon beach and the incoming tide. Tough little plants were growing around her, hardy enough to put up with the salt air and the wild storms and yet still scent the air with their perfume.

After she left the house via the servants' back stairs, she hadn't known where to go. She didn't want to return to the others, she needed to gather her thoughts. She needed to come to terms with what she was.

A monster, like Pengorren.

She looked down the cliff steps, longing to walk on the sand, but it was too dangerous. The tide was coming in, and she wasn't reckless enough to risk it. According to *The Raven's Curse* Ravenswood was a very unlucky house. Lots of deaths.

But Pengorren didn't want her to die just yet. He had plans for her . . .

There were voices. Crying out.

Startled, Melanie lifted her head to stare out to sea. Of course there was nothing. Just a haze along the horizon and some seagulls circling and diving, looking for their lunch. Maybe she'd heard a gull. But as much as Melanie tried to convince herself otherwise, she already knew that a ship was wrecked here long ago. Just as she'd known about the oak tree falling in the storm. She felt it, sensed the people who had drowned. She heard it again, the voices crying for help, faint but clear.

Melanie closed her eyes and gave in, letting herself go.

At once she felt cold. She was sitting on the clifftop in sunshine, but in her mind there was rain in her face and a gusting, savage wind pulling at her hair and her clothing. She smelled salt and spray, and her heart was thudding violently. Fearfully. There was death out there in the water.

It had to be done.

Pengorren's voice, in her ear.

Melanie started and swung around, ready to run. The adrenaline was pumping through her, and she was certain that if necessary she could have launched herself from the clifftop and flown like a gull.

But there was no one there. Pengorren was in her head this time, invading her thoughts. Just as he always would, as long as she stayed here at Ravenswood. Her gaze was drawn toward the old house and the opaque shine of the windows. Ravenswood was Pengorren's house, his essence was here. And his physical presence? What about that? Where was Pengorren hiding?

A movement to the side. Suzie was heading along the overgrown path with her usual brisk determination. Melanie turned away and leaned her head against her knees, closing her eyes. She hadn't decided yet whether she was glad or sorry that Suzie was here, but she was worried. Suzie was in danger and Melanie knew she would have to do her very best to send her sister home.

By force, if necessary.

Melanie waited until Suzie came up behind her before she spoke, her voice calm and faintly mocking. "You've taken your time. I was waiting for you to come and tell me you'd rung the funny farm and the van was on its way. Should I change, or will they bring the straitjacket with them? Hope they have my size."

Suzie laughed, bless her, but the hand she pressed to Melanie's shoulder wasn't quite steady. "You know I'm not going to do that, or at least I hope you know it. Anyway, if I did ring, they'd have to take me as well, wouldn't they?"

Melanie laughed back, surprised she could. That was one thing about Suzie, she could always make her laugh, sometimes at the most inconvenient moments. "I think out of the two of us I'm crazier."

"You're not crazy," Suzie said quietly, and sat down beside her. "You're a long way from that. Anyway, I remember when this happened to you when you were a child—you weren't crazy then, just frightened. I think the time has come for you to accept yourself for what you are."

"I hate what I am," Melanie whispered. "You know I've always had an aversion to everything to do with the supernatural. All that trance crap and talking to spirits and reading the future in the tarot cards. I've never wanted any part of it. And now I can't stop it from happening. The past is as clear to me as you, Suzie, and I've had visions of the future. I see . . . things I don't want to see. I know things I don't want to know. Oh God, you don't know the half of it!"

"Look, you just need to learn to control—"

"I don't *want* to control it. I want it to go away."

Suzie was silent for a moment, considering her words. "Melanie, let me tell you what I believe, and yes, I know it sounds trite. Everything that happens happens for a reason. Because it's meant to. Perhaps your, well, gift for want of a better word, was meant to return to you here at Ravenswood. Perhaps there's a reason you need it now when you didn't before. Have you thought of that?"

Melanie picked at her fingernail and then stopped herself, squeezing her hand into a fist. She hadn't bitten her nails since she was little, and she wasn't about to start again now. Suzie was right; Nathaniel had said much the same thing. She accepted that this was all part of some "meant-to-be" scenario. She'd been chosen as Nathaniel's companion in this time and this place *because* of what was inside her.

The voices interrupted her thoughts again, rising from the waves and calling out in mortal fear.

But Melanie refused to listen to them. She closed her mind, locked herself down. Always before such an action had caused her relief, but not this time. Now it felt claustrophobic, as if she was in a box in the darkness with only her own breathing for company.

"What is it?" Suzie asked sharply. "Melanie, you have to talk to me. I know there are things you haven't told me yet. You might as well, you know. I may even be able to help."

Melanie turned to her sister. Suzie's face was pale, the freckles standing out, and she looked worried and serious and more than a little cross. As if she was reprimanding one of her sons for being thoughtless. Was *she* being thoughtless? Suzie loved her, and it couldn't hurt to talk. Suzie might laugh in her face, but she mightn't, either.

"I should mention," Suzie added, "that Nathaniel has

told me he wants me to take you home. He was adamant. A bit scary, actually." She grinned. "Gorgeous at the same time, of course. Where did you find him?"

"He wants you to take me home?" Melanie repeated, and shook her head in disbelief. "How can he ask that? He knows he needs me here."

He was going to sacrifice himself for her, that was it. Return to the between-worlds for however long the queen wanted to keep him there, so that she could be safe.

If she was safe. Melanie sat up straighter. Who was to say Pengorren wouldn't follow her to London? Eventually. And Nathaniel would be gone by then, there'd be no one to help her. She'd be alone.

"No," she said abruptly. "I'm not leaving. I'll tell you why, Suzie, but keep an open mind, okay?"

Suzie snorted. "I always do."

"Then here goes. The abbreviated version. That man I was telling you about on the phone, with the dazzling allure, the glamour as Eddie calls it. It's Pengorren. Yes, Pengorren from Eddie's book, the man who's been dead for at least a century. Evidently he walked into the sea and drowned, but his body has never been found. Suzie, I keep seeing Pengorren in my dreams, waking dreams sometimes. A part of him is in the house and when I see him he's reenacting his past, except I'm not a spectator, because . . . he knows I'm there. He can see me, and he talks to me. He knows my name. And just now you told me I was related to him."

"Oh Melanie—" Suzie's eyes were round.

"No, listen, that's not the creepiest part of it. Pengorren is the man who was on the beach that day, the man who came up to me, and you pushed him over and dragged me away. He's the very same man, Suzie, I swear it."

Suzie was still staring at her. "I want to say you're making it up, but I know you're not. I *know* you're not, Melanie, because I've been thinking about that man again, too, probably because you are. *That* should tell you something about us. We're not like ordinary folk. We're fey, like Pengorren, only whereas he was a very bad man, as Eddie sweetly puts it, we are for the forces of good."

"Don't joke, and anyway I want to be ordinary." Melanie's voice was shaking on the verge of tears. "I've only ever wanted to be ordinary."

"Sshh." Suzie slid an arm around her shoulders and pulled her close. For a moment they leaned against each other like children, comforted by the warmth and closeness of each other's bodies.

Out on the sea the waves were rolling in toward the cliffs, the tide rising farther and farther up the small beach. A seagull shrieked as it flew past.

Suzie spoke again. "Does Nathaniel think Pengorren is trying to harm you, is that why he wants you to go home?"

"I don't know for sure what Pengorren wants and neither does Nathaniel. He's guessing, but going by Pengorren's past history I don't think anything he does would be very nice. Nathaniel believes Pengorren was responsible for the deaths of members of the Raven family back in the early nineteenth century. Major Pengorren gained a great deal from those deaths, but no one would have thought of blaming him. He was universally loved. And yet, looking at the facts coldly and rationally, he's the obvious suspect."

"Glamour," Suzie murmured. "There was a man I knew," she paused, her gaze far away.

"Go on."

Suzie shook herself. "It still upsets me when I think of it. I was traveling at the time . . ."

"With your New Age friends?"

"Yes. This man set himself up as the leader of a group, but I never trusted him. There was weird stuff going on. He seemed to have a hold over them that wasn't entirely natural, as if they were blinded to what he was really like. Sick stuff, Melanie. I think someone was killed, and then he was arrested. Those left behind still believed he was innocent, that if he hurt them, then that was okay because it was his right. A bit like Charles Manson. Some people are so charismatic they're able to manipulate their followers like that."

"Is that glamour, though? Or just plain evil?"

"Could some people use glamour as a cover for evil?" Suzie sat up straighter. "I've just had a thought. If Pengorren was alive in the early nineteenth century and we saw him as a flesh-and-blood man when you were nine, who's to say he hasn't been around in other time periods as well? What if he really is a sort of faery? A fey being. Theoretically, he could go on living for centuries."

Melanie's heartbeat quickened. Pengorren was alive. He'd been alive all this time, hiding in the shadows, changing his identity, slipping in and out of history.

And he was here right now, watching them, laughing at them, waiting for the right moment to put a stop to the queen of the between-worlds' plans to give Nathaniel another chance . . .

Nathaniel!

She didn't realize she said it aloud, or maybe she didn't. Suzie heard her, though, and now she was looking as if she was deciding how to phrase her next question.

"Nathaniel is in danger," Melanie said, anticipating her.

"Nathaniel thinks *you're* in danger."

"You don't understand . . ."

I will live forever. You will help me, Melanie . . .

"Oh God," Melanie gasped, turning sharply as Pengorren's voice whispered in her ear again.

Suzie was staring at her, wide-eyed. "What is it? Melanie?"

Melanie shook her head, locking herself down again, and then wrinkling her brow as a headache began its slow grind.

Suzie looked as if she was going to burst with frustration, and suddenly Melanie gave in. "There's more I have to tell you," she said, and immediately felt the relief of opening up. "Just be quiet and listen, and promise, if you do have me committed, it's somewhere nice."

Twenty-nine

Nathaniel looked up as the two women came toward him. He had gone out to the stable to see to Neptune, leaving Eddie engrossed in Miss Pengorren's diaries. He'd felt in need of some fresh air, as well as some physical exercise. It seemed sensible to allow Melanie and Suzie some time alone. Maybe they'd be gone when he got back?

But he knew he couldn't bear that. Painful as it was, he needed to say good-bye.

Pengorren had a lot to answer for. Like a squid, his tentacles reached far. He had to be stopped. Despairingly, he wondered how he was going to complete his impossible task without Melanie at his side.

Then he looked up and all thought left him.

Melanie was glowing again. The sunlight caught in her hair and reflected off her skin, as if she'd been dipped in liquid gold. When her eyes met his they sparkled, more silver than blue. He felt his blood throbbing through his veins. She was so beautiful, so captivating, and he was completely enraptured. Was this glamour? His heart gave a sickening lurch at the thought that none of what he was feeling was real, that it was Pengorren manipulating them.

"I'm sorry," she said, and now she was close enough for him to reach out and touch, but he bunched his hands into fists and didn't. Control, that was the thing. Self-control. He was beginning to enjoy restraining his impulses . . . well, most of the time.

"Sorry?" Her words finally penetrated. "You're leaving," he said bleakly, even though it was what he wanted.

She shook her head, then glanced at Suzie. Her guilty expression told him everything he needed to know. "You've told her about me," he said accusingly.

"I had to."

It was Melanie who reached out to touch him.

Something zapped between them so strongly that it hurt. He cried out, his head spinning and his body enveloped in heat. He wanted to lean down and kiss her. He could see the shine on her soft lips, he could taste her. He thought for a moment he was lost, that he couldn't stop himself this time, but somehow he found the strength.

"Close your eyes, Melanie," he said, hoarsely. "Please."

She blinked and took a step back. She didn't close her eyes, but she did look away, presenting him with her perfect profile. "I had to tell Suzie." Her voice was quiet, barely audible. "She needed to know, Nathaniel, she's a blood relation of Pengorren, too."

But Nathaniel didn't want to listen any longer. He wanted her out of here and safe. "You have to go back to London. Today. Now."

She shook her head, staring ahead.

He wanted to shake her, but he couldn't, he knew he couldn't touch her again. "You're in danger, Melanie," he said angrily, but he was pleading. "Pengorren wants you. He thinks that through you he's going to live forever."

"I know." She shuddered. "He's here in the present, he's alive, but he's grown old and feeble. He needs me so he can be strong again. When he touches me, he feeds off me like some sort of vampire . . ." She laughed, but it was more like a sob.

She was right, it was the only thing that made sense.

"That's why you have to leave," he told her. "He's going to kill you, Melanie."

Her chin lifted stubbornly. "And why is he trying to be strong again, Nathaniel? *So he can destroy you!* He knows you're here, he knows you've come for him, and there's only one thing he can do to stop you. I'm not going to leave you here to face him alone."

"You can't help—"

"I can. How do you know he won't follow me, anyway? How do you know that?"

"Miss Pengorren went to London, and he didn't follow her," Nathaniel said levelly. "I think that's why she went, to get away from him and to stop him from using her strength to keep himself alive. You're right, he feeds off people, he drains the life from them."

Melanie shook her head. "I won't go," she said stubbornly. "I'm not leaving you here to face Pengorren alone."

"Melanie . . ." Frustration made him want to shake her. Didn't she realize that her being safe was more important to him than anything else?

Suzie, who had been glancing between them like a spectator at a tennis match, put her hand on Nathaniel's arm. He frowned at her, not wanting her to interrupt, but she faced up to him. "I'm sorry, Nathaniel, but I think Melanie's right. Pengorren is still around, still alive, and he wants to get rid of you just like he did the last time. You need help if you're going to defeat him."

"I won't let him get rid of me this time," he said coolly. "I'm prepared. I know what to expect from him."

"But he's not a man, is he? He's something more."

"You need me," Melanie insisted, and she looked him in the eye, knowing how hard it would be for them both but needing to see his face and understand what he was thinking.

He sucked in his breath as desire enveloped them. "You know what you're doing to me, Melanie," he said on a groan.

"I know, but I'm Pengorren's flesh and blood. I see him, I talk with him, I am part of him, and he's part of me. He needs me, and we can use that to draw him into a trap." Melanie felt herself go cold at the idea of it, but she'd given it a lot of thought. If this was her reason for being at Ravenswood, then she must play her part.

Nathaniel knew she was right. His mind told him so, even while his heart was telling him to bundle her up in his arms and toss her into her car and send her on her way. He didn't want Melanie to be yet another sacrifice to Pengorren.

"Nathaniel?" she whispered, pleading for understanding. "I have to stay. You know I have to."

"You've made your decision, haven't you?"

She nodded.

He wasn't happy. "It seems as if I have no choice."

"I'll help you, too," Suzie piped up.

They both turned on her. "No!"

"I'm not leaving you to face this alone. Don't you dare try and get rid of me. This is the adventure of a lifetime . . . sorry, I know it's more serious than that, but I'm not going to leave you. I mean it."

"Yes, you will," Melanie retorted, unimpressed. "First sign that Pengorren has transferred his interest to you, and you're out of here. You have two sons who love you and need you. Promise me, Suzie!"

Suzie's mouth went mulish, but she gave a grudging, "Okay."

It was the best Melanie could get out of her.

Nathaniel was looking down at Melanie, at her mouth, and he was no longer smiling.

Suzie cleared her throat. "Well, I think I might go back and see what Eddie's up to." She waited, but no one answered her. With a sigh, she turned to go.

"Stay close to the house," Nathaniel called after her. It was an order.

Suzie turned and gave a smart salute, clicking her heels together, but no one was watching her.

"Stay close to the house," Suzie muttered. "Who does he think he is? The lord of the manor?" And then she chuckled, because that was exactly what he was.

After Suzie was gone, Melanie told Nathaniel what she had seen Pengorren do to Dorrie, the words sour on her tongue. "You know, when we were in the ballroom upstairs I thought there was something familiar about Suzie. Now I realize what it was. I could see something of Dorrie in her. God, I hate him! I can feel his inheritance inside me—the cruelty, the violence. I'm afraid I'll end up like him. Unless he kills me first."

"It won't happen," Nathaniel said quietly. "We have to get the key from him, Melanie. Once we have that, he won't be able to travel through time. He'll be trapped here, where his physical body is. He's still old and weak. We can destroy him."

"If we knew where he was hiding."

"It can't be too far."

"No, he needs to be close to me. I'm the bait, remember."

He shifted uncomfortably. "How could I forget?"

She reached out and brushed her fingers against his cheek, and they both felt the extreme flash of emotion mixed with sexual hunger. She gazed into his eyes, unable to tear herself away. "I feel as if you're a part of me, every fiber of my being aches for you. It hurts, Nathaniel."

"I know," he whispered.

"Is it real? Or is it all a lie?"

"I think the glamour has a lot to do with it . . ." His voice trailed off.

"But you wish it was real," she finished, with a sad smile. "Me, too. Everyone dreams of love like this, all-consuming, all-satisfying. I want so much for it to be true."

"We should enjoy it while it lasts. Who knows, once we've dealt with Pengorren, we might hate the sight of each other."

Melanie couldn't imagine it. This sort of love was the stuff of epic poems and romance novels—Tristan and Isolde, Lancelot and Guinevere. Sensual and all-consuming and achingly sweet.

It was a pity that with it came the darker emotions. Cruelty and violence and pleasure from pain.

"I wish you could hold me and take the demons away," she said. "But we can't even do that."

Suzie got on with Eddie like a house afire. They seemed to be able to guess what the other was going to say, which was a little scary. Suzie hadn't laughed so much for ages, and she felt somewhat guilty about that, considering what Melanie was going through. She should, she supposed, have been wringing her hands, but she'd never been the hand-wringing type.

Eddie told her about Miss Pengorren, and she could tell he'd been fond of the old woman. They examined the portrait of the major, with his missing face, which Suzie found creepy beyond belief. "So that hung on the wall for all those years? Yuk. No wonder she took it down in the end."

"I don't think that was the reason," Eddie said. "She knew Pengorren had done Nathaniel Raven out of his inheritance, and she wanted to make a statement. She had decided opinions, and she wasn't afraid to say them aloud, but you couldn't help but like her for it."

Miss Pengorren was also a descendant of Major Pengorren, and she must have inherited a little of the glamour, even if it wasn't enough to be noticeable to most people. *Like mine*, thought Suzie with a sigh.

"The Pengorren's were a tragic family," Eddie quoted. "Where's *The Raven's Curse*?" he muttered, and went to find it against the wall, where he told her Nathaniel had thrown it in disgust. When he flipped to the back, there was a family tree, abbreviated of course, but there were still an awful lot of early deaths in each generation. Far more than seemed normal despite the harsh times.

Suzie perched on the arm of Eddie's armchair, feeling very comfortable. "They can't have been a very healthy family," she said, running her finger down the list. "Look, in the end there was only Miss Pengorren left. She had two brothers . . . they both died before they reached adulthood."

"During the war she was a nurse for a time. When she came back there was talk of her marrying a man she'd met overseas, but it fizzled out. I don't know why. She never told me. But I don't think she regretted not having a family. Maybe she'd seen too much sorrow in her own."

"Was hers one of those wartime romances that went horribly wrong? Brave and handsome officer turns out to be a right cad."

"Women always go for the handsome ones," Eddie said, with a stoic look.

"Oh, I don't know," Suzie retorted.

She wondered what Eddie saw in her face, because he blushed. Romance blossomed in the strangest places, she reminded herself.

A phone began to ring, and Suzie saw that it was Melanie's cell phone, on the corner of the desk. She picked it up. "Hello? Melanie Jones's phone."

There was a pause. "Ms. Jones?" The voice was old.

"I'm sorry, she's not here at the moment, can I take a message?"

"Forgive me, but you sound very like her."

Suzie laughed. "Well, I am her sister. Who is this?"

"I'm sorry. This is Mr. Trewartha. I'm an antiques dealer. Your sister asked me to come to Ravenswood to help her catalog the items in the house. I've been trying to arrange some transport, but I'm afraid I haven't been able to manage it. I wondered, if it wasn't too much of an imposition, whether someone could pick me up from Launceston? She did mention her firm would be willing to meet my expenses . . . ?"

"Oh. Hang on a sec, will you?" She turned to Eddie and covered the mouthpiece. "Mr. Trewartha? He wants a lift out here."

"Say yes," Eddie said.

Suzie went back to the call. "Hello, are you there?

That would be okay. I'll have to check with Melanie, of course, but if there's a problem she can get back to you."

"Good. Shall we say eight then? I can't manage it any earlier. I'm at Number Six, The Close, Launceston. It's a new estate, on your side of the town, so you won't have to come far."

"Eight it is."

Suzie ended the call and rolled her eyes at Eddie. "I hope I've done the right thing. Evidently Melanie has been ringing him about cataloging Ravenswood's contents."

"Yes, the infamous Mr. Trewartha," Eddie teased.

"Huh?"

"Sorry. He's an antiques dealer, but he's also an author. He wrote this book." He held up *The Raven's Curse*. "His coming here could be tricky, but that's not our problem. Your sister will have to deal with it. So, don't worry, you did the right thing."

"I hope so. I can always go and get him. After all, I'm on holiday."

"I could come with you, give you directions," Eddie said airily. "Easy to get lost on these country lanes."

"There, then," Suzie smiled, "it's settled." Her smile slipped, and a crease wrinkled the skin between her eyebrows. "This probably sounds crazy, Eddie, but there was something about Mr. Trewartha's voice . . . I felt as if I knew him."

"Maybe he reminds you of your granddad." Eddie laughed.

Suzie's frown smoothed out. "Yeah, that's probably it. Anyway, I don't care what you say, he was a sweetheart, so old-fashioned and polite. A real old gentleman."

Thirty

"You don't have to meet him if you don't want to." Melanie was leaning her cheek against the cold glass of her bedroom window. "You can stay away until he goes. This will just be a preliminary look through the house, so it shouldn't take long."

Nathaniel sat in the chair, his legs stretched out in front of him, staring at his boots. As soon as they'd returned to the house, Suzie had told them about the phone call, and then dragged Eddie off to his cottage to give them time together.

That was a joke. Melanie was standing as far away from him as she possibly could, and she could still feel the power zapping between them like some electrical connection gone crazy.

"I'd like to meet him," Nathaniel said, showing his teeth in what was meant to be a smile.

"No, you'd be sure to say something to piss him off. I need him. I know what he wrote was horrible and wrong, but I don't want him here for his writing skills. I have a job to do, remember?"

"How could I forget?"

Melanie sighed. "I'm sorry. I know this is difficult for you."

Nathaniel uncurled himself from the chair. "I can't help wondering what things would be like, now, if Pengorren had never come to Ravenswood. Would the house still be full of my family? A living, breathing home instead of this dusty monument."

"We'll find him, Nathaniel. We'll stop him. You can go back in time and make everything right."

"But I won't have you," he said softly. "Will I?"

"If you'd seen what I've seen, you'd thank God for that!" she burst out, and moved toward the door. But as she passed, he caught her hand to stop her, pulling her off-balance. She tumbled onto his lap. It felt like a physical and emotional earthquake erupted between them. Disoriented, hurting, she couldn't breathe.

"Dear God . . ." Nathaniel gave an agonized groan.

Melanie struggled, trying to get up, to push herself away from him, but everywhere she touched his skin was warm, and she wanted to kiss him, lick him, suck him. "This isn't right," she protested huskily.

He wrapped his arms around her, the air fizzing and sparking. She lifted her face to his. The desire between them was so powerful there was no fighting it even if they'd wanted to. His mouth came down on hers, and they kissed mindlessly, wanting only the pleasure of their bodies touching and moving together.

She felt carnal, completely wild, and Nathaniel

seemed more than willing to accommodate her. She dragged at her clothing, pulling and kicking her shorts and panties down her bare legs, and ripping her top as she tugged it off. The clip on her bra wouldn't undo, so she forced it open. Naked, she threw herself against him, dragging his ruffled shirt up over his stomach and chest, planting openmouthed kisses against his warm, salty skin.

He leaned back in the chair, letting her have her way. She fastened on his nipples, tugging them with her teeth, only just stopping herself from biting him. Because she wanted to draw blood. It seemed important to taste his blood.

Fighting her own need, trembling with the effort, she clasped his face between her hands, pressing kisses to his mouth and his jaw. She could feel his erection through his trousers and straddled him as best she could in the confined space, fitting herself to him.

His eyes sprang opened, blurred with passion, and he lifted her, stumbling, and fell onto the bed with her in his arms. Instantly Melanie tried to climb on top of him, wanting him inside her, her nails raking him. But he pushed her off, back onto the mattress, holding her there with one hand on her midriff while with the other he fumbled to unbutton his trousers. His bootheel was caught in the covers, and he cursed, letting her go so that he could free himself.

While he was distracted she launched herself at him again. She felt so strong, so primitive. A sleek, wild animal. She began to lick at him, her hands sliding down his hard stomach, under the cloth of his trousers. He jerked when her fingers closed on him and groaned when she squeezed, just enough. He was looking up at her, dazed, a forest creature caught in the snare and unable to help itself. Not wanting to help itself.

Melanie smiled into his eyes and then with a snarl she bit him, hard, just below his collarbone.

Blood filled her mouth. And it tasted good. At the same time she felt her own blood singing and her body shaking with the power surging through her.

At first she didn't feel the pain and then her head jerked up, and she realized he'd taken a hank of her hair in his fist. He wrenched again, dragging her mouth away from his shoulder. He was hurting her, but she didn't care. There was power in making him do this, Nathaniel who had never voluntarily caused her pain. She smiled into his face, enjoying his hard, angry expression and the glitter in his eyes.

"Say it," she ordered him, her voice deeper and huskier than it had ever been. "Say you want me."

Confusion flickered in his eyes.

At the same time, deep inside, Melanie knew this wasn't right. Love wasn't meant to be like this. But she couldn't help it. She'd lost the ability to control herself, and if Nathaniel lost it too . . . She struggled to escape the dark emotions fighting for dominance inside her, but they were taking her over.

"End it," she growled. "You have to end it, now!"

"Melanie?" he said, but he knew what she meant. She could see it in his face.

He flipped her over onto her front on the mattress. He was so strong, and she reveled in his strength, in the possibility of violence. Because power and violence fed whatever was growing inside her, that part of her she knew wasn't mortal. Pengorren's legacy.

He was behind her, holding her down as she snarled and fought, her nails crooked like claws. She wanted to hurt him. And then the hard length of him was pressing against her, seeking entry. Blindly she lifted her hips to give him access, barely able to breathe because he was pushing her face against the mattress. He thrust in, almost brutally, except that she was so ready for him that he couldn't have hurt her. She heard his groan as he went deep, sheathing himself in her slippery heat.

She could lift her head. He was gripping her thighs now, holding her in place while he thrust into her. She clutched the covers with her fingers, pushing back at him with her hips. Mindless with a pleasure beyond anything she had ever known. All she could do was go with it. And then she came.

Her shouts were half-delirious, foul things she had only ever said before in anger.

Vaguely she felt him thrusting harder, faster, and she was peaking again, and then all coherent thought was lost in the explosion of ecstasy that ignited between them. Nathaniel collapsed on top of her. He was heavy, but there was something comforting in having him there. A moment later he was easing himself to one side and then he reached out an arm and dragged her limp body in safely against his.

She curled up in his arms, her pounding heart gradually returning to normal, the colored lights inside her head slowly extinguishing. She felt his warm breath on her hair and the rise and fall of his chest against her back. He kissed her nape, tenderly. The violence was gone, just like the storm, leaving them to wallow in peace.

But Melanie knew it was an illusion. The storm would be back again, and next time they might not survive it. This wasn't how it was meant to be. And then she tasted his blood in his mouth and could have wept.

"I'm frightened," she whispered. "I hurt you. Just like Pengorren hurt his women."

"I've had worse things done to me."

"Nathaniel, if I ever—"

But perhaps he knew what she was going to say, because he leaned forward and caught her earlobe between his teeth and nipped it, so gently. "There," he whispered, "now we're even."

"No, we're not."

"I love you," he said into her hair.

She gave a shaky chuckle. "It's the glamour, stupid."

He kissed her again. "Probably."

If things got worse, she vowed, she wouldn't stay here with him. She wouldn't risk doing to him what Pengorren had done to the women who loved him. She'd go away. Maybe she'd stand on the half-moon beach and let the tide come in and take her out to sea.

Nathaniel lay and listened to her breathing growing soft and relaxed; everything that Melanie wasn't when she was awake. His shoulder ached where she'd bitten him, but he didn't move to check it. He didn't want to wake her, and it was true what he'd said, he'd had worse.

He wished he knew what was going to happen to them. A slow anger was burning in him at the unfairness of it all. To find the woman you love and want to spend your life with, and at the same time to doubt every sweet moment of it. That Pengorren was gradually destroying them both for his own ends, turning their love into something dark and evil, driven by pain and suffering.

At least they now knew that Pengorren was living in this time. He was old and weak, and he needed Melanie to stay alive. He was vulnerable.

Nathaniel pressed his face to her hair, breathing in her scent.

"I'm going to find him," he murmured, "and I'm going to do what I should have done last time."

He closed his eyes.

"Kill him."

Melanie stood on the cliffs below Ravenswood. Through the storm she could see it. A ship, rolling sickeningly in a heavy swell. What remained of the rigging was tangled about her, and the hull was tilted at an impossible angle. This was a disaster, and everyone on board must know it.

The ship wallowed in the breaking waves and then she began to list to one side. All the time she was being battered by the storm and pounded against the rocks. There were voices, rising above the wind and rain, the voices she'd heard before.

Help us!

"Oh God . . ."

The ship was on the rocks! People . . . people were

drowning. And she couldn't do a thing about it.

Against her will, but needing to see, Melanie crept farther toward the cliff edge. The cold rain struck her face, and she had the mad urge to dive into the water and swim out and save at least some of them. Even though, deep in her heart, she knew they were already dead and what she was seeing was just a replaying of something that had happened who knew how many years before.

She stood and watched the old sailing ship rolling helplessly, already breaking up beneath the pounding she was getting, and the people running on the deck, slipping and falling, flailing in the water. They were drowning. Dying.

As she stared in horror at the scene before her, Melanie realized she could see their souls rising from their bodies. White and misty, like columns of smoke, they wafted upward. There were so many of them, they joined together until it was like a fog, growing thicker, until it all but obscured the scene of the tragedy.

The air crackled and zapped. She could feel the power, as if there was an electrical charge surrounding her. It was the same feeling she had when she touched Nathaniel. Her body began to grow stronger, taking in all the life essences around her. It was like being reborn, like being made young and strong again, only more so. She was a goddess, drinking in their souls. Or some sort of vampire.

Sickened, she spun away. She did not want this, she did not want to think she was capable of such a thing.

And that was when she saw Pengorren.

He was standing very still on the clifftop where the steps led down to the beach, watching the death and destruction taking place before him. And he was smiling. Because this was what he wanted. He had probably caused it to happen! A lantern burning in the wrong place, the warm light shining through the wind and rain and enticing the desperate ship onto the reef.

Melanie knew as if he'd told her that he wanted those people to die. More than that, he needed them to die, so that he could remain strong.

So that he could continue to live forever.

Just then he turned and saw her. His face changed, twisted into a mask of hatred. He came at her through the lashing rain, his eyes like burning lights.

"You!" he shouted against the storm, and reached for her.

At once Melanie felt herself spinning through the air, leaving the cliffs behind, until there was only sky all around her. A sweet young face filled her vision, framed by auburn hair, and with eyes so blue they hurt.

"Your Majesty?"

"Melanie, look. Look at what I'm showing you." The queen of the between-worlds waved an arm that was covered in feathers. Melanie could see a room, and in it was Pengorren. He was holding a silver locket in his hands and as she watched he opened it. There was a miniature inside, but he pulled it out and set it aside, and she could see something else in the case. A gold disk with strange writing all over it. Suddenly the room vanished.

"See?" the queen said, and when Melanie turned to

*her she saw that her face was narrowing and a beak
was forming and her eyes had become those of a predatory bird. "He has the time-traveling key. It belongs to
me. He stole it from me long ago. You must get it back
for me, Melanie."*

"How—?"

*But the eagle flapped it wings and rose above her,
hovering on an air current. "Get me the key," it shrieked,
"and I will give you what it is you wish for."*

*She watched it fly away, and then she was falling
through the sky, the ground rising up to meet her.*

"Melanie."

She was dreaming, muttering and twisting, as if
something had her in its clutches. Whatever the dream
was about she wasn't enjoying it. Pengorren again? Had
he drawn her back into the past with him?

Suddenly afraid, Nathaniel sat up and shook her
hard. "Melanie!"

She screamed.

Shocked, he pulled her into his arms, holding her,
rocking her. She wasn't crying, but every now and then
a shudder would run through her body, as if she had a
high fever, although when he felt her skin it was cold.

At last she drew a shaky breath and reached up to
touch the wound on his shoulder, her fingers very gentle.
"I need to bandage this," she whispered.

He tried to read what she was feeling in her face, but
she turned away and wouldn't allow it. "Melanie?"

"Don't," she spoke harshly, and pulled away altogether, sitting with her back to him. "I feel unclean,"

she said, and her voice was filled with disgust and horror. "We have to stop him, Nathaniel, for your sake, for my sake, for the sake of everyone in this world." And then she told him what she had seen in her dream, and what it meant.

Thirty-one

Mr. Trewartha lived in a town house in a quiet cul-de-sac. Lights showed through the windows as Suzie eased the Aston Martin car into the curb and switched off the engine. By now it was almost dark. "You may as well stay here," she said to Eddie. "I'll go and see if he's ready."

"Fine," he replied, leaning back in the squishy leather seat with a smile. Eddie had discovered luxury. Suzie was glad she'd persuaded Melanie to let her drive the boss's car.

There was a mock-Victorian streetlamp on the sidewalk, and she could see that the town house was built of a smooth dark red brick, with two windows top and bottom, and a steep pitch of grey slate roof. The garden appeared not to have been tended for a while. She walked along the path, flanked by an untidy box hedge, and rang the doorbell.

There was movement inside, and a wavery voice called out. "Come in! The door's open."

Suzie gave the heavy door a push. It swung open into a dimly lit hall cluttered with antiques.

"I'm sorry, I . . ." the voice dissolved into coughing.

Concerned, Suzie pushed past dusty chairs and a marble bust on a pedestal, down the hall. "Mr. Trewartha?" she said. "Are you all right?"

"I wonder if you wouldn't mind . . ."

He was coughing again. It sounded serious. As she reached the doorway and stepped inside the room, Suzie was trying to remember the basics of the first-aid course she'd done five years ago, but she'd been more interested in the good-looking instructor than what he was saying.

The curtains were drawn and all she could see was a shape, standing in the middle of the room.

"Mr. Trewartha?"

He moved toward her then, faster than she could ever have imagined, and the light from the hall spilled onto his face. "Suzie," he croaked, "it's so nice to meet you . . ." And his hand closed on her arm.

Nathaniel lounged in Miss Pengorren's old desk chair, swinging it gently from side to side, as he watched Melanie dart about, making notes, checking lists. She'd dressed in a dark skirt that stopped just above her knees, and a jacket in the same cloth, worn over a lime green blouse. She imagined she looked serious and professional, but the glamour was stronger than ever, and every time he glanced at her he had to remind himself to keep breathing.

"They should be here," she said. "Do you think there's a problem?"

"Maybe Trewartha and Eddie are fighting a duel over their respective theories. Pens at twenty paces."

"Very funny."

"I wonder if Pengorren has ever read *The Raven's Curse*? He'd enjoy it. It'd be like murdering me all over again, only this time it's my character and my memory being assassinated."

Anger was simmering below the surface, but he held it in check. Nevertheless, Melanie gave him a sideways glance—it was all they could manage at the moment. "You shouldn't be here when he comes, Nathaniel. This is business, that's all, nothing to do with his views on history. I want to get this meeting over and done as soon as possible. You know that."

He shrugged.

"I'm sorry." Her shoulders sagged in defeat. "I wish this didn't have to happen. I'm hoping I might be able to put him off doing the listing for a couple of weeks, so that you can carry on with your search. If I tell Mr. Foyle things are more complicated than we thought, he should let me stay on a bit longer, too. I mean, he trusts me, I don't see any problems."

She'd risk her job for him. He knew how much it meant to her, she'd told him. Determined to put aside his bad temper, Nathaniel pulled himself out of the chair and stood up.

"I'll go down and take a look at Neptune," he said. "Let me know when he's gone."

"Thank you." She smiled.

Alone in the room, Melanie tried to settle her thoughts. It wasn't easy. All the things she'd believed important now seemed mere distractions from the truly urgent task of finding Pengorren and putting an end to his evil. In a matter of days her priorities had taken a giant shift, her whole life had been changed irrevocably. Whatever happened next, Melanie knew she would never be able to go back.

Downstairs, the front door opened.

Annoyed that she hadn't heard the car arrive, Melanie hurried out onto the landing. In the dim light of the single bulb, she could see the man standing in the hall below her. He was wearing a hat with a brim, the sort that men like Frank Sinatra used to wear, and a heavy dark coat buttoned up to his chin.

"Mr. Trewartha?"

Even as she spoke she felt it rushing toward her. Strong, dark . . . evil. Creeping into her mind, over her skin, filling the house like black acrid smoke.

Pengorren.

He wasn't so bent anymore and although his face was incredibly wrinkled it was no longer just a skull. His eyes were shining like blue penlights, fixed on her as he shuffled forward with a rustle like dry paper.

"Melanie," he croaked.

She shook her head, but it was more of a denial of what he was, not who he was.

"You are mine . . . my blood, my flesh, my seed."

"I'm not yours!" her voice was shaking with revulsion. "I'm nothing to do with you!"

He laughed like a creaking hinge. He took off his hat and his hair wasn't quite so white anymore, more like pale blond, and he was bigger, bulkier, his body filling out. Right in front of her eyes he was growing as he moved toward the stairs.

She tried to steel herself as she stepped back. He needed her, so he wasn't going to kill her just yet. "Nathaniel won't let you win," she said, breathless. Dark flecks were beginning to spin at the edges of her vision, and she realized he must be taking her energy. He was sucking her life out of her because that's what he did. Fed off the lives of others.

Pengorren laughed again. He was gazing up at her as he came. "Nathaniel is easy meat. The dear boy rushes in and doesn't stop to think, he never has. You don't need him. You're far superior to him." His blue eyes gleamed with a warped paternal pride.

"I love him," she flung back at him.

"Love?" he sneered. "Our kind don't love, Melanie. We use and destroy, and we live on. Forever."

He stumbled, forgetting to watch his steps in his passion, and the chain about his neck swung forward. He was wearing something. The locket with the key inside it.

Get me the key and I will give you what it is you wish for.

Melanie could have run then, but she made a conscious decision to stay.

"How old are you?" she whispered, with a sort of horrified wonder. "Why aren't you dead and buried, where you belong?"

"I am older than you can imagine."

Suddenly Melanie felt her knees buckle, and Pengorren's face slid out of focus. Even if she'd wanted to run now, she couldn't. She shook her head, desperate to clear her sight. Pengorren was bulking up even more, and his cadaverous face was plumping out, the skin smoothing, becoming young again. His eyes still glowed eerily but now they were more like eyes, and they crinkled at the corners when he smiled. She was beginning to feel the effects of his glamour, like a meteor drawing closer and increasing in strength and brightness.

"Why do you do it?" she whispered. "Murder people, take their lives?"

He grinned, and he had teeth, white and strong. "Normal mortals are of no use to me. Their essence is puny. It is only if there are lots of them, if there's a mass death, then I can take power from them. I need the essence of those with my own blood to keep me strong. Before my children and grandchildren were born, I needed to bring a sailing ship onto the rocks to stay alive. But you know that, don't you, Melanie, my clever girl?"

His crooning voice lulled her. He'd almost reached her, and again her eyes were drawn to the locket. The chain looked strong for all its fineness, but one sharp tug might do it. She must reach out and grab it. She must try. He wouldn't be expecting her to do that, and she could take him by surprise.

"I have developed a way of farming the essences, the souls, that I need," he continued, as if proud of his perversion. "I create my own, with my own blood in them. I sired many brats on the women of Ravenswood, and then those brats had their own families. Plenty of fodder, or so I thought. But my plan wasn't quite as successful as I'd hoped. Some of my descendants didn't inherit much of my power at all, and that meant I had to take so many at a time that my line began to dwindle. I grew weaker. Lately I have been too weak to leave my home. You have no idea how grateful I am that you came to Cornwall, Melanie."

"You've killed your own flesh and blood to stay alive."

"Of course."

"You're a monster."

"I am a god!" Pengorren roared.

Melanie lunged forward, fingers crooked, but she was too slow and he easily evaded her.

"Don't be silly now," he scolded, steadying her with a hand on her shoulder.

She pulled away, staggered, and fell against the wall. And that was when she remembered something she should have remembered as soon as she saw Pengorren, alone, in the hall. Alarm made her voice more breathless than it was already, and she was filled with a sense of dread.

"Where's my sister? Where's Suzie?"

Thirty-two

Restlessly, Nathaniel kicked at the straw in Neptune's stall. The big horse was restless, too, ears pricked, skin twitching. Nathaniel tried to persuade him to eat, but he ignored the feed, lifting his head to stare at the door.

"Do you think that bastard Trewartha will stay long?" Nathaniel murmured, and Neptune turned to him, as if interested in the question. "I wish I could tell him what I really think of him. Pengorren and Trewartha . . . they make a fine pair."

Pengorren and Trewartha, they were both destroyers in their own way. Pengorren, who traveled through time and lived in different time periods, and was still here, somewhere. Trewartha, who was old and had lived in Cornwall for a very long time. Pengorren was old, too. He imagined that Pengorren would enjoy reading Trewartha's book, and gloating over the blackening of Nathaniel's memory. It was like something Pengorren would do himself. In fact, such a sly and underhand act was very characteristic of Pengorren . . .

"Oh God."

He'd been an idiot. How could he have missed the clues? Pengorren *was* Trewartha. And Melanie was alone in the house with him.

Nathaniel ran to the stable door and flung it open.

Just as something big crashed into him, sending him backward onto the floor. He hit the stone flags hard and lay there, helpless, with the breath knocked out of him. A shadow fell over him, and then a heavy weight pressed down on his chest, and he felt the warmth of his own blood on his face.

"Ah yes. Dear Suzie." Pengorren straightened up as he reached the landing. "Unfortunately she didn't have your power, did she? I'm afraid to say she was hardly worth the effort. Still, it was enough to get me this far."

Instinctively, Melanie edged along the wall, shaking, dizzy. "I hope you suffer for all eternity, you murdering monster," she said, her voice trembling with grief. It couldn't be. He was lying to her. Suzie couldn't be dead. Not now when they were just beginning to find each other again after all these years.

"Poor Suzie," Pengorren mocked.

He was towering over her now, and his shoulders were so broad, his feet planted apart. Imposing, terrifying, and almost completely regenerated.

She wanted to throw herself at him and bite and scratch him, to hurt him as he'd hurt her. But it was too late. She was sliding down the wall, her senses swimming. The end couldn't be far away. Her mind was fading. She realized, with a pang, that she'd never see Nathaniel again . . .

"Pengorren!"

For a moment she thought she'd dreamed his voice, but it was coming from the bottom of the stairs. Why was he down there? He should be up here, with her. And then she could hear the sharp click of claws on wood, the rush of something moving swiftly, and a deep angry growling.

His voice had the desired effect. Nathaniel watched as Pengorren spun around, staggering slightly—for all he looked like himself it was clear he didn't yet have a young man's strength. He climbed the stairs after Teth, and it wasn't until he was halfway up that he saw Melanie on the floor near Pengorren's feet. Her face was pure white, and she was slumped against the wall, her eyes sunk back into their sockets as if she had some terrible illness.

He shouldn't have gone away and left her alone. He should have guessed. As he'd lain on the floor, with Teth licking his face—the warm wetness hadn't been blood after all—he'd cursed himself for his lack of wits. Pengorren had bested him again.

Teth lunged, all demon. Pengorren let out a scream and fell back against a small table. They crashed to the landing, Teth on top, snarling, teeth fastened on the neck of Pengorren's coat. Cloth ripped. Pengorren rolled over onto his front, lifting his arms to protect his head, but Teth grabbed hold of his sleeve, shaking it and making terrible noises in his throat.

Nathaniel stepped hastily around them and bent down to pick Melanie up in his arms. She was weak, almost too weak to lift her head as he shifted her so that she could rest her cheek against his shoulder. He began to back away down the corridor, carrying her with him.

"The key . . ." she managed, hardly more than a whisper. "He's wearing it, Nathaniel . . . Take it . . . we must . . ."

He hesitated, glancing back at the writhing mass that was Pengorren and the hound. His first instinct was to take Melanie far away, to somewhere safe. But she was right. They had to have the key. He compromised, and carried her into one of the nearer bedchambers. It was a child's room, musty with disuse, and he set her gently down on the narrow, iron-framed bed.

"Suzie," she breathed, her eyes fluttering shut. "He has Suzie."

He felt a pang. If Pengorren had Suzie, then she was probably dead. Eddie, too. But Melanie looked so ill lying there, so different from the bedazzling woman he was used to, he couldn't tell her the truth.

"I'll find her," he said, and touched her cheek. "Stay here."

She managed a smile, her eyes fluttering closed. She trusted him. Leaving her was one of the hardest things he'd ever had to do.

Out on the landing, Pengorren was still shouting and cursing. Teth had drawn blood and torn a long strip from his coat. The locket was dangling outside his clothing. Nathaniel edged in closer and grabbed hold of it.

Pengorren, realizing what Raven was up to, snatched for his hand, but it was too late. Nathaniel gave the chain a hard tug, and it snapped. The locket was his.

Pengorren threw back his head in a shriek of rage, and at the same time Teth saw his chance and dived in to bite his cheek. The flesh tore. Pengorren roared and lashed out with his fist, knocking Teth off-balance. The hound gave a bloodcurdling howl as he struck the banisters. He rolled down several of the stairs and sprawled there, stunned.

That gave Pengorren enough time to get to his feet and stagger backward until he was hard up against the wall. His clothing was ripped, he was disheveled and hurt, with blood dripping from his hands and his face; but when he turned his gaze to Nathaniel, his eyes were the same gleaming, savage blue they'd always been.

"Call off your mongrel!" he shouted.

Teth was back on his feet again, growling, but he was limping badly. He made a feint at Pengorren, forcing him to take a step sideways down the corridor. Immediately Nathaniel thought of Melanie, lying defenseless in the bedchamber, and took a step of his own, toward the stairs. He held up the locket, letting it dangle from the broken chain, and Pengorren's gaze swiveled to him and narrowed.

"Want this, Hew?"

Pengorren swallowed, and pushed a swath of fair hair out of his eyes. The gash on his cheek was deep and brutal, and there was a long scratch on his neck. It was comforting to see he bled red, like ordinary mortals.

"Nathaniel," he said with soft menace, "you're making a terrible mistake. Give it to me now, and I might let you go."

Nathaniel laughed. "I don't think so."

He was moving away, down the stairs, and Teth came with him, hobbling on three paws. Pengorren hesitated and glanced behind him, looking for Melanie, but there was no sign of her. Nathaniel could see his indecision, but he hoped Pengorren would think she'd escaped down the back stairs.

"How does this thing work, Hew?" he said, twirling the locket chain so that the locket spun crazily.

To his relief, Pengorren turned to him at last and began to follow. He showed Nathaniel his teeth in what was meant to be a smile. "I'm going to enjoy killing you," he said.

The lights went out.

Melanie didn't know how long she'd been lying on the narrow bed with the worn, patchwork cover, only that it was dark and she was freezing and so very tired. Her bones seemed to ache, even her fingernails, and when she moved, she felt as if she'd aged a hundred years.

Gradually it came to her that she must get up, that it was extremely urgent she move. Pengorren was here— he could be standing outside the door right now—and both she and Nathaniel were in terrible danger. She didn't let herself think about Suzie and Eddie. Not yet, not now. Blame and grief would come later.

Slowly, she eased her legs off the bed to the floor and, gripping the iron railings on the bedhead, dragged herself upright into a sitting position. At once the darkness started to swim, and she dropped her head into her hands with a groan. It seemed to take ages for her vision to clear, and longer again for her to feel it was safe to get to her feet. The first step was the worst, but the next was better.

Her strength was returning. Slowly but surely, it was coming back. She really *was* powerful. She hadn't understood until now just how strong she was. As powerful as Pengorren? Perhaps. One thing was for certain, she wasn't going to let him destroy her without a fight. He'd had his way for far too long.

The corridor was so dark she had to stand a moment and let her eyes adjust. The whole house seemed to be blacked out, and she wondered if someone had done that on purpose or if it was an electrical fault. Maybe Nathaniel was trying to confuse Pengorren, or vice versa.

She hoped Nathaniel was okay. She didn't remember the fight very clearly, but from what she did remember it was Pengorren, not Nathaniel or Teth, who was getting the worst of it.

But where were they now? Everything was so quiet.

Suddenly she realized she'd stopped breathing and was feeling dizzy again. She gulped some air, but that was worse, so she forced herself to slow it down and take even, steady breaths.

As she grew calmer, her mind began to open up, tentatively reaching out beyond the corridor to the landing, then down the stairs and into the hall. There was nothing there, so she sought farther afield, her mind tiptoeing a little at a time, afraid of what she might find.

Despite her caution she landed herself right in the middle of it before she could stop. Dark, gooey, and unpleasant. Pengorren. Mentally she backed away, terrified, wondering if he could sense her as she was able to sense him. But after a moment, when he hadn't come after her mentally or in the flesh, she gave a sigh of relief.

Next time he found her, he wouldn't hesitate, she knew that. He'd kill her, and then spread his evil once more throughout the world.

The corridor was dark and airless. She'd have to move, but the thought of creeping through the black house was terrifying. She took a slow, cautious step, and then another, pausing to check it was safe. Soon she'd reached the top of the stairs.

Her eyes were adjusting to the dark now—better than they ever had, but she didn't want to think about that, or what she was becoming. She could see that the table on the landing was upended, one of the legs smashed, signs of the struggle between Teth and Pengorren.

Who had won? She didn't even know that. The fact that she'd felt Pengorren's presence meant he was still around, still alive. She could only pray that Nathaniel and Teth were, too.

Clutching the banister with one hand, Melanie began to descend the staircase.

Thirty-three

Had Nathaniel taken the locket from around Pengorren's neck? Surely he had the key by now? Melanie's hopes and dreams were resting on that key, and the favor the queen would grant her when it was returned. She and Nathaniel had just as much riding on the outcome of this night as Pengorren. More.

She reached the bottom of the staircase and halted. The faint echo of voices drifted from the direction of the kitchen. Melanie moved toward the sound.

Her strength was almost fully returned. She could feel the power settling over her like a mantle. If this was how Pengorren felt all the time, then she could understand his overweening self-confidence. She could almost believe herself to be invincible if she hadn't just received a painful lesson in her own mortality.

The door to the kitchen was just ahead of her when she heard Teth growl. Melanie froze. She didn't want to reach out with her mind again, in case Pengorren sensed her, but she knew he was in there anyway. Her flesh tingled, and the air sparked from his presence.

Nathaniel raised his voice. He sounded reckless. "Do you think it will melt?"

"You're being very childish, my boy." Pengorren at his most smooth and dangerous.

Melanie crept forward and peeked around the corner and into the kitchen. The shadows were lit by a strange blue glow, and she could make out Nathaniel with Teth at his side. Pengorren was several feet away, closer to Melanie, standing very still beside the bench.

"What will happen if you lose the key, Hew? No more traveling through time. No more escaping into the past. She'd find you, wouldn't she, the queen of the between-worlds? That's who you're running from. You stole her key, and she wants it back."

"I don't know who told you that, Nathaniel. I'm not afraid of anyone, most particularly not of you."

Melanie realized that Nathaniel had turned one of the gas rings on, the blue flame up as high as it could be. He was dangling the locket over it, swinging it back and forth. No wonder Pengorren wasn't moving any nearer.

Melanie held her breath. They needed the key to give to the queen. Surely he wasn't really going to destroy it?

"Why me, Pengorren?" Nathaniel sounded as if he really wanted to know. "Why Ravenswood, when you have the whole world to choose from?"

Pengorren shifted slightly, but Teth growled again and he remained where he was. "You made everything sound so inviting, dear boy. I couldn't resist. I began as a monk, did you know that? I wasn't a very good one, I'm afraid, but a monastery is a good place to hide. Then I founded a dynasty in France, and then another in Bavaria. To skip ahead a little, I was bored and wanted some adventure. I decided on the Napoleonic wars and changed my name and joined the British army—that was the winning side, after all. While I was in Spain I was fortunate enough to meet you. I think I've been in and around Cornwall ever since."

"So the drowning . . . ?"

"Just pretense. It gets embarrassing when the years pass and everyone else grows old and I don't. I had to think of some way to escape the questions, so I died. I changed my name again, traveled a little. I came back as Trewartha early in the twentieth century. I enjoyed being him, collecting my antiques and writing my masterpiece. *The Raven's Curse.* Have you read it, Nathaniel?"

"That's what gave you away, Hew. Only you could have written something so biased."

He chuckled. "Do you know, the old lady said that. I used to visit her, sipping at her essence, just enough to keep myself alive. I didn't want to take it all at once—she might have been the last of my line—and she was going to die soon anyway, I'd take it then. We used to chat, though, and if I have one fault, then I do tend to talk too much about myself. She wheedled the truth out of me. Next I knew she'd gone. Before I could track her down she was dead, and I was left with nothing. I thought I was a goner then. Strange how one's luck changes!"

"Your luck hasn't changed."

"Oh, I think you'll find it has," Pengorren said, and he half turned.

Melanie moved quickly back, out of sight. Did he know she was here? Should she declare herself or should she run?

Someone reached out from the darkness behind her and touched her on the arm. The only reason she didn't scream was because her throat closed over in terror. And then her heart nearly stopped as a face loomed up in front of hers.

"Melanie . . ." It was Eddie in a tremulous whisper. "What the fuck is happening?"

"Sshh!"

He tugged at her arm, pulling her away so they couldn't be heard. "I've got Suzie outside in the car," he said, and choked. "I swear to you, she was talking right up until the moment we got here. She told me she was all right. She promised. And she didn't want to go to the hospital . . . she said if I didn't bring her back here, she'd get out of the car and walk. But when we got here she just stopped. I think . . . oh God, I think she's . . ."

He caught his breath, held it, struggling not to break down. Melanie was numb, but she knew it was better that way. Numb meant she didn't have to feel.

"Is she still in the car?"

"Yes. Near my cottage. I thought she'd be safer there, out of the way, if *he* came. I didn't know he was already here. When I cracked open the door and saw him coming after Nathaniel, I ran to switch off the electricity, to help him get away."

"You did good, Eddie."

"What is he?" His eyes shone like marbles. "He can't be human."

"Have you heard about Dracula?"

"Yes."

"Then that's him, but without the teeth."

"I don't understand."

"Never mind. Let's go and find Suzie."

But before they could move, there was an awful crash from the kitchen. It sounded metallic, as if it was raining spoons and forks, and it went on and on. Teth was barking hysterically.

"What the—" Melanie spun around, but a bulky shape blocked her way. There was someone standing behind her. She sensed who it was even before he opened his mouth.

"Hello, my dear," Pengorren's voice was full of menace, "fancy meeting you here."

This time she did scream. He grabbed her shoulder in a brutal grip.

"Oh no you don't . . ."

Eddie gave a roar and threw himself at Pengorren, knocking him over. China smashed. She heard them struggling, and then Eddie was flung away as if he was made of papier-mâché. But by then Melanie was free. She began to run, blindly, knowing that in a moment Pengorren would be behind her.

Something else crashed to the floor. She slipped on water from a fallen vase and cut her knee on the broken porcelain. The stumble meant she didn't have time to get to the front door and had to turn to the stairs instead. She ran up them, feeling her way, heart beating in her ears.

Pengorren was closing. She felt him, the oily darkness that surrounded him. The suffocating sense of evil.

They headed down the corridor. *Take the servants' stairs,* she thought, but at the same time she knew that was what Pengorren would expect her to do. At the last moment she changed her mind, fumbling along the wall until she found the door to the attic. Opening it quickly, she darted inside.

She could hear him coming. Melanie breathed a sigh of relief as he ran past, heading for the servants' stairs, just as she hoped he would. She'd wait a little while and then she'd go back to the kitchen, collect Nathaniel and Eddie, then they could go to Suzie. Suzie . . . Maybe she should go now? There was no time to lose if her sister was as bad as Eddie thought.

But even as she reached for the latch, she heard Pengorren returning. Stealthily. Listening between each step.

The attic, a moment ago a place of safety, now felt like a trap. Fumbling along the edge of the door, she found the bolt, sliding it across as quietly as she could. It wouldn't stop him, she knew that, but it might slow him down.

Melanie climbed quickly up the stepladder into the roof space, knowing that after this there was nowhere left to go.

The attic wasn't just one big room. It consisted of several, built beneath the slope of the roof. And they were all full to bursting with the paraphernalia of people who had lived in the same house over several hundred years. So far Melanie hadn't time to do more than gaze in horrified fascination into the little, crowded rooms, frightened she'd break something valuable and happy to leave it to the experts.

Now she blundered her way past boxes and trunks and forgotten furnishings draped in dust sheets. When she knocked over a cane basket, old wooden children's toys clattered and rolled.

She was looking for somewhere to hide.

Behind her a grinding, splintering sound told her that the attic door had been kicked in. A moment later Pengorren's heavy footsteps were on the stepladder.

Melanie bumped her shin on the corner of a box, and she bit her lip to stop a cry of pain. It was a large box, and when she felt over it with her hands, she found the lid was open and it was half-full of old clothing. And then she realized she could smell lavender . . .

This must be the same box Nathaniel was talking about. It seemed like a good sign, and she needed to make a decision.

Melanie climbed inside, tucking her knees up under her chin and reaching up to close the lid. For a moment it stuck, and she thought it wasn't going to give, but then she gave it a sharp tug, and it closed with a muffled thud.

Inside it was sweet and musty. A buckle dug into her neck, and she wriggled, making herself as comfortable as possible. Nathaniel had said something about a cutlass, but she couldn't feel anything like that, no matter how her fingers probed and searched.

And then the air suddenly grew heavier. Oppressive. She could sense him before she could hear his steps. Melanie kept perfectly still, praying with all her heart that Pengorren wouldn't find her.

Thirty-four

"I don't understand," Eddie wailed for the dozenth time.

"And I don't have time to explain," Nathaniel retorted. After he and Teth untangled themselves from the drawers full of cutlery that Pengorren had thrown at them, they'd come across Eddie outside the door, struggling to get to his feet. There was no sign of Melanie. Eddie said that Pengorren—or Trewartha, as he knew him—had gone after her up the stairs, and there'd been a lot of noise.

"I blacked out for a minute, but I'm sure I heard them up there. Maybe she used the back stairs?"

Nathaniel moved forward and then tripped on something and nearly fell. He bent and picked it up. "What's this?" he demanded.

"Oh. I brought a flashlight from the car." Eddie took it from him and switched it on. The light shone directly into Nathaniel's face. "Sorry," he said, directing it elsewhere.

Teth growled low in his throat and showed his teeth.

"Nice dog," Eddie murmured.

"We need to find Melanie. If she's heading down the servants' stairs, then we can get to her more quickly by going around through the side garden."

Eddie followed him back into the kitchen. "Who . . . what is that man?"

"Trewartha. Pengorren. Whichever you like. He's one and the same."

"Is he really a vampire?"

Nathaniel opened the door to the garden. "A what?"

"Does he suck the blood out of people so that he can live?"

"He sucks the life from them, but he prefers those with *his* blood. Pengorren blood. Like you, Eddie, and Suzie and Melanie. Especially Melanie."

"I'm dreaming this, aren't I?" Eddie asked plaintively.

"Yes, Edward, this is all a dream. Now, come on!"

Nathaniel burst forth into the night, with Teth at his heels.

That terrible cloying sense of evil was everywhere, suffocating her, incapacitating her. She wished now she hadn't hidden in here. Another mistake. The feeling of being trapped, with nowhere to run, was worse than if she'd kept her options open.

And then the lid was flung open.

"Oh Melanie, Melanie," that hateful voice said, "did you really think I couldn't find you? I'd know your essence anywhere."

She pushed herself up, meaning to hit him in the face, but he caught her around the back of the neck with a grip that was excruciatingly painful, his fingers squeezing.

"It's all over," he murmured, helping her out of the box. "Accept it."

"Let me go." She could hardly speak, and the agony made it hard to breathe.

"Just think, with your help I can live for another hundred years!"

"I'd rather you'd died at birth."

He laughed, and then she felt him focusing on her strength, beginning to drain it from her like sucking a milk shake from a straw. He was going to kill her this time. Her head was already spinning.

"It's such a pity we can't both live," he murmured.

And she thought: *Well, why not? Not him, of course, but* me. Why couldn't she live instead of him? If Pengorren could do this to her, why couldn't she do the same to him? He kept telling her how powerful she was, how much like him she was . . .

His draining of her made it difficult to concentrate. She kept drifting away. If it went on like this much longer, she wouldn't even remember her name. Instinctively she struggled in his grip, and then slumped down, distracting him, causing him to rearrange his hold on her. The feeling of being drained halted, just for a moment, just long enough. Melanie focused all her remaining strength on Pengorren and imagined taking back her soul from him.

"Stop it," he hissed, giving her a shake. "I know what you're trying to do, Melanie. You can't win, I'm too strong for you. You'll only make it worse for yourself."

He might be right, but there was no way she was dying without putting up a fight. Melanie fixed her mind on him, picturing herself delving deep inside him, reaching into his pulsing living force and drawing it out, like a long, thin ribbon of light. She began to wind it around her own body, until she glowed with the beauty of it. The light was so bright it hurt her eyes, but she continued to draw it out of him and wind it around herself.

She like a burning comet illuminating the night sky . . .

She didn't notice Pengorren letting her go, not until he staggered and fell against the wooden box. Surprised, she turned to look at him. He was breathing strangely, harsh and chesty, like an old man. And then, as he lifted his head, she saw to her amazement that he *was* an old man.

She laughed, she couldn't help it.

"Melanie?"

Nathaniel was stooping beneath the low attic doorway, watching her anxiously from behind the glow of a flashlight. His gaze dropped to Pengorren and his eyes widened. "How . . . ?"

"The same way he does it. I can't believe I didn't try it before."

"Perhaps you weren't strong enough before," Nathaniel suggested, coming forward. He was holding a cutlass in his other hand, and he gave it to Melanie before leaning over Pengorren to examine him. Pengorren was too weak to do more than shrug off his hand. "Is he still dangerous? Can he regain his strength?"

"Not unless I let him," Melanie said arrogantly.

Nathaniel gave her a sharp look, and a crease appeared between his brows. The dismayed expression in his eyes caught her unawares, and suddenly she was ashamed. She sounded like *him*.

"I have the locket," Nathaniel said, reaching into his pocket. He flicked open the casing with his thumbnail and went still as he saw the miniature of Pengorren.

"Your sister painted that," Pengorren whispered, and gave a hideous, rotten-toothed smile. "Not long before they took her away to the madhouse."

"You evil bastard." Nathaniel lifted his hand as if to strike him, and then changed his mind. "I don't care what you say. I'm going to change all that. No one will even know your name when I'm finished."

"Is that so?" Pengorren taunted. "Haven't you forgotten something? If I no longer exist, then what happens to my descendants?" He laughed at the expressions on their faces, and then he began to cough.

"He's right," Melanie said. "If you take him out of history, then I won't be here, and neither will Suzie, or Eddie." She looked about. "Where is Eddie?"

"Gone to switch the lights back on."

"Nathaniel, I need to find Suzie."

He nodded, then gave Pengorren a nudge. He stopped coughing and glanced up, his eyes dull but still that same malevolent blue. "Come on, Hew. We're taking you for a little trip."

Pengorren struggled weakly and complained, and in the end Nathaniel picked him up and threw him over his shoulder. Melanie took the locket from him. By the time they reached the front door, Eddie had brought the Aston Martin around and parked it in the driveway.

"Where am I going?" Pengorren roared, as Nathaniel set him down.

Nathaniel ignored him. "Eddie, can you watch our friend here?"

Melanie was already at the passenger door, leaning over her sister. Suzie's face was white and drawn, but her eyes opened when Melanie brushed her cheek, and she managed a crooked smile.

"Sorry," she whispered.

"What have you got to be sorry about?" Melanie said gently, and her eyes filled with tears. "This is my doing. I thought you were dead . . . Can you ever forgive me?"

Suzie looked surprised. " 'Course I can," she retorted, with surprising vigor. "And it would take more than that to kill me."

"I'm so glad . . ."

Nathaniel leaned in, ignoring the zing as Melanie's shoulder brushed his. "Is she all right?"

"Yes, I think so." Melanie wiped her cheeks. "He must have been saving her for later, like he did with Miss Pengorren."

"For supper," Suzie murmured, and grimaced.

"We need to get you out of here," Nathaniel explained. "Pengorren is going on a little trip to St. Anne's Hill."

Melanie glanced at him sharply, but he didn't meet her eyes. As she stepped away, he was already easing Suzie from the car. Her sister held out her hand, and Melanie took it, glad to feel the warmth of her flesh.

"I don't know," Suzie whispered, "if I'll see you again.

I want you to make the choice that makes *you* most happy. And don't worry about me. I'll be all right. I think I've met my soul mate."

"Suzie!"

"Good-bye, Melanie. Enjoy your life. I'm going to. Now be quiet and let me make the most of being held in the arms of this gorgeous Regency man."

Nathaniel laughed, and carried her up the steps of Ravenswood. By the time he returned, Eddie was half-supporting and half-forcing Pengorren into the back-seat.

"She's all right," he assured them. "Just needs to sleep and get her strength back. Pengorren's inheritance can be a blessing as well as a curse." As he spoke he reached for the locket dangling out of Melanie's pocket. It was still open, and using his nail again, he lifted the minia-ture. Underneath there was a shining metal disc, just like the one Melanie had been shown by the queen in her vision.

"The key."

He nodded and stroked the strange swirling shapes that formed the pattern of the key. "Something like this is very dangerous in the wrong hands," he said softly. "Very tempting."

Melanie laughed, thinking he was joking, but his ex-pression was deadly serious. Did he really think she was turning into Pengorren? She supposed she couldn't blame him, after all that had happened, but still it hurt. Swallowing her emotions, she shook her head and looked him in the eyes. "No, it's not tempting to me. I'm going to give the key back to the queen and . . ." But she couldn't finish the sentence. He was so stern and uncaring that suddenly she didn't dare.

He cocked an eyebrow. "And?"

"Melanie . . . ?" Eddie's voice was faint.

Melanie shrugged. "And you can take care of it until then," she said, and went to walk away. But he stopped her, gripping her hand in his, ignoring the painful shock.

"You hold on to it," he said, tucking it back into her pocket.

She didn't know what to make of that, so she walked over to the car and Eddie. Pengorren was slumped in the backseat. Eddie gave her a sickly smile and passed the keys over to her. Impulsively, she gave him a hug, then climbed into the driver's seat and started the engine.

"Where are we going?"

"St. Anne's Hill," Nathaniel said as he climbed in beside her and closed the door.

"What? This is my employer's car!"

"Well, can you think of a better way to get Pengorren into the between-worlds?"

Melanie thought a moment, and then sighed. "No, I can't," she admitted, as she eased the car forward. A glance in the mirror showed Eddie, seated on the steps of the house, his head in his hands. Poor Eddie, it had clearly been too much for him.

Nathaniel was directing her to the stock gate, and he climbed out to open it. Once through and into open field, they found the ground hard going. Every time the car struck a dip or a mound, Melanie winced. Mr. Foyle was never going to forgive her. She should care more about that, but she didn't.

"I can't drive up there," she said, when they reached the base of the hill. "He'll have to walk."

It was easier said than done. Pengorren seemed in no state to do more than hang limply from Nathaniel's shoulder, and the slope was steep and slippery. With Melanie's help, and after several falls, they got Pengorren to the top.

Now Raven felt utterly spent, and lay down on his back on the ground, breathing in the cold night air. When he opened his eyes, there were stars wheeling above him. The change he'd seen in Melanie worried him; he couldn't pretend it didn't.

Pengorren's voice rose querulously. "You have no right to do this to me."

Melanie said something about shutting up or else.

Nathaniel smiled. Then again, only Melanie would talk to an immortal creature like that.

"Nathaniel!"

He jumped up, reacting to the panic in her voice. Pengorren was holding her, his arm around her neck as he dragged her backward toward the downward slope of the hill.

"Let her go."

"He's strong," Melanie told him, gasping as Pengorren's arm tightened about her throat. "He stole from Eddie . . . I should have seen . . ."

Nathaniel came at him, but Pengorren had let go, flinging Melanie away from him. She lost her balance, slipping on the slope.

"The key!" she screamed.

Pengorren had it. Nathaniel went for him, catching him in a tackle as he tried to run. They fought, desperation giving Pengorren renewed vigor. Nathaniel swung his fist and knocked him backward. His head jerked under the impact, there was a crack as knuckles collided with jaw, and then he sank into a heap by the standing stone.

"That's for Sophie," Nathaniel said, panting, and glanced over at Melanie. She was already on her feet, unhurt, so he turned back to Pengorren and hoisted him up by the front of his clothing. The locket had fallen onto the ground, and he reached down for it and tossed it back to her.

Pengorren muttered something, but he ignored him and began to slide him through the hole in the stone. Halfway through he woke up and gave a shriek like a banshee. He clawed for something to hold fast to, grasping Nathaniel's hands, and then he was slipping.

"Noooo!"

He was falling, back into the echoing darkness, and he was taking Nathaniel with him. Nathaniel fought for his footing, but it was too late. They were both being swallowed up. Tumbling through the door.

Into the between-worlds.

Melanie stood on shaky legs. The cold grey standing stone looked faintly luminous in the starlight. Nathaniel was gone. Pengorren had pulled him into the between-worlds.

She squeezed her hand, feeling the hard shape of the locket. At least she still had the key.

She approached the stone. Was she going to follow him? What if he didn't return, and she never saw him again?

Melanie knew she couldn't bear that.

Whatever problems lay between them were miniscule compared to the emptiness in her heart without him. She realized then that she'd already made her decision.

Thirty-five

Nathaniel woke, blinking in the darkness.
His first thought was for Pengorren, but when he sat up
he knew he was alone. Pengorren was gone.

He was probably trying to find a door out. That's
what Nathaniel would do. The trouble with the between-
worlds was that one tunnel looked much like another,
and you could wander in here for days, weeks, and
never travel more than a mile in any direction.

Unless you were very clever. Or very lucky.

Pengorren seemed to be both.

With a worried frown, he set off.

At first he saw little sign of Pengorren's passing, and
then he began to notice where, in his haste, he had flattened the scuttling creatures who lived in the tunnels.
After a time the direction of the tunnels felt familiar,
as if he'd been this way before, and he wondered if this
was where he'd followed Teth, thinking he was going
home to the Ravenswood he loved.

He quickened his pace. Pengorren mustn't escape, not again.

It was definitely familiar now. He remembered that dip in the roof, where he'd nearly brained himself, and the crevice in the wall where the orange thing with tentacles lived. And then he saw Pengorren ahead. He was shuffling along, dragging one foot. He looked as if he was nearly spent, but then he heard Nathaniel behind him and turned.

He was white and drawn, but there was a steely determination about him, too. He quickened his steps, heading toward the entrance with its tracery of branches. The way out.

Nathaniel wasn't going to catch him.

He knew it, even as he picked up his pace and ran. Pengorren would get away, and once out into the world, he wouldn't be caught. He'd find places to hide, he'd find souls to feed on. Nathaniel's dream of a new life would be gone forever.

Something pushed past him, and he stumbled and nearly fell. Black and powerful, it moved with supple grace, straight at Pengorren. He turned, saw it, and cried out. But it was too late. Teth brought him down.

By the time Nathaniel reached him, Pengorren was sobbing into his arms.

"Nathaniel?"

Melanie was only a few paces behind him. She staggered forward and bent over at the waist, gasping for air. She looked utterly spent, but her eyes were shining with happiness.

"You came," he said, sounding foolish.

"I couldn't let you go alone," she replied. "We're a team, remember? Teth came and I followed him through the stone and told him to find you. And he did."

"I couldn't let Pengorren get away."

"I know."

"Melanie . . . what are we going to do?"

She shook her head, her lips trembling.

"Do I have to choose? You or my family? Because that's what it comes down to, doesn't it, if I destroy Pengorren. Without him, I can have my family and Ravenswood back again. But without him, there will be no you."

"I don't want you to . . ."

"Melanie," he whispered, "I can't lose you."

Teth gave a sharp bark.

The tunnel was illuminating with light, light of an indescribable color. At its center it was so bright that it hurt the eyes. "The queen," Melanie breathed, moving closer to Nathaniel. She searched in her pocket and pulled out the locket. Her hand was trembling.

But the queen barely acknowledged them as she swept by in her scarlet cloak. She had eyes only for Pengorren.

"You've caused me a deal of trouble, creature," she said, standing over him, her eyes firing sparks.

"Oh?" He looked up at her, his face dirty and tear-streaked and full of reckless viciousness. "*Such* a shame, Your Majesty."

"Temper your tongue!"

"Why? I have nothing to lose."

"How do you know? I might be merciful."

Pengorren snorted. "When has a woman scorned ever been merciful? I still remember how you simpered and blushed when I told you I loved you. They say there's nothing quite as tenacious as a woman whose heart has been broken, don't they? And, my dear, you've been very tenacious in your pursuit of me."

The queen's eyes flashed blue fire. Her small frame seemed to grow and expand, and there was a sound like a thousand birds furiously beating their wings. Pengorren rolled over and dragged himself backward, and for the first time he appeared afraid.

"You will remain here in the between-worlds," she said, her voice rising and falling like the cry of a hunting eagle. "I have a special place for you, Pengorren. I want to watch you shrivel up and grow feeble, but I won't allow you to die. I want to keep you alive. Just."

"You can't do that to me!"

"Oh, but I can. I think I will eliminate you from history entirely. I'll wipe your memory clean from time, and no one will ever know you existed."

"Your Majesty!" Nathaniel came forward, dropping to one knee. "Please, I beg you not to do that."

The queen turned her face to him, stern and awe-inspiring. Melanie dropped her own eyes, unable to hold them on that shifting column of light.

"My Raven? You would have me forgive this creature? After all he's done to you and yours?"

Nathaniel shook his head and swallowed, clearly suffering under her attentions.

"It's not Pengorren. Melanie. If you make Pengorren disappear from history, then Melanie won't exist."

The queen smiled. "Ah," she said, "I see."

"Please, is there no other way?"

She was silent. "What if I said no, what then?"

Nathaniel sighed, his shoulders slumped. Melanie felt dizzy with the pain of knowing he could not choose her over all those he loved. She was nothing to him, a stranger from another time. He could not love her that much . . .

"Then I would let Pengorren live," he said.

"Nathaniel," she breathed. She came forward and dropped to her knees beside him, and tears were streaming down her cheeks.

"I love you," he said. "If I have to, then I will have to live without you, but I'll know you're alive in another time. I could never live if I thought my actions had ended your life."

"Are you sure it's not just the glamour?" mocked Pengorren, his face twisted with spite. "You'll never know, will you?"

Melanie looked up at the queen and held out her hand. The silver locket caught the light. "Your Majesty, you said if I brought the key back to you, then you would give me what I most want. Please, I ask you, will you let me live with Nathaniel at Ravenswood. I want to go home with him and be with him. I don't want glamour, I never did. I want to be an ordinary woman."

The queen nodded thoughtfully. Reaching out, she

plucked the locket from Melanie's hand, the touch of her flesh as cold as death.

"If you go into the past, Melanie Jones, there can be no returning. You know that, don't you? You will live and die in the nineteenth century."

Melanie glanced at Nathaniel. "I think I can cope with that," she said.

"Then you can't exterminate me from history!" Pengorren shouted gleefully. "I will live on."

The queen narrowed her eyes. "Not necessarily. I will take some of your essence from you, just enough to give your offspring a little glamour, nothing dangerous, and I'll channel it into someone else."

"Channel it into someone else?" he repeated, as if he couldn't believe she meant it.

"Yes. Your essence will ensure that Melanie and her sister do not change in the future, but the being who takes your place as their ancestor will not be as troublesome as you. He will obey my instructions."

"Who could take my place?" he roared. "There is no one like me!"

"Well, that's a good thing, isn't it? Your stand-in will be a protégé of mine who has been loyal and obedient and deserves the chance to step up to a higher level. Teth!"

Pengorren looked around wildly.

Teth came running up, tongue lolling.

"God, no." Pengorren was pleading.

"Don't you think Teth will make a fine sire, Pengorren? He couldn't do a worse job than you, and he will *be* you for all intents and purposes."

"She can't be serious," Melanie groaned.

The queen was bending over the hound, speaking some words in a low, harsh voice. The black hound began to shimmer. In the blink of an eye a tall, dark-haired man stood in his place. He was wearing the costume of a Regency gentleman, and he looked extremely elegant, with his black hair and lean, saturnine features.

"Did you see that?" Melanie gasped.

"I did."

Teth bowed low before his queen and spoke in a gravelly voice. "Thank you, Your Majesty, I am very grateful."

"And so you should be," the queen retorted. "Be good, Teth, or I'll turn you back. Now, do you know what you have to do?"

Teth grinned, his coal black eyes gleaming. "I think I have a fair idea, Your Majesty."

The queen gave an earthy chuckle. "Off you go then!"

Teth bowed again and strolled past her down the tunnel. He glanced at Nathaniel and Melanie as he passed, and winked.

"Your ancestor is still Pengorren," the queen assured her, "but I have just saved you from the nasty side effects."

"How boring a place the world will be without me," Pengorren muttered.

The queen turned to him, her eyes so brilliant that Pengorren covered his own. "Now for you," she said in a booming voice.

He screamed, but he was already gone. Vanquished to whatever prison had been prepared for him.

Nathaniel slid his arm around Melanie and drew her close. There was still a zing between them, a shimmer of sexual attraction and an ache of love, but not the painful experience it had lately become.

"I still love you with all my heart and soul," he said. "It wasn't the glamour."

"My Raven!" The queen demanded their attention. "I will miss you, despite your disobedience, but you have completed your task. Will you be satisfied, do you think, with a mundane life as squire of Ravenswood?"

"I will." He smiled. "If anything could be mundane with Melanie by my side."

"Then go. You know the way."

"Thank you, Your Majesty." It was heartfelt.

The tunnel opening lay before them. Nathaniel pushed through the lacework of branches, helping Melanie to climb out through the shrubs near the summerhouse. She lifted her head, blinking in the sunlight.

"I've come home," Nathaniel said, grinning like a boy as he surveyed the neat garden and the gleaming façade of Ravenswood.

Melanie looked at him and smiled back. "*We've* come home."

"Wait until you meet my parents, and Sophie." He paused, fixing her with a questioning look. "Do you really expect to be an ordinary wife, Melanie?"

"Of course," she teased. "If you will be a mundane husband."

"I will make you a promise then. During the day we will be both ordinary and mundane, but at night . . . well, that will be an entirely different matter!"

Melanie laughed as he took her hand in his, and they began their journey into their future.

Epilogue

The Sorceress strode through the great cathedral, enjoying the sense of space around her. Incense burned, flowers bloomed, and there was a deep ancient silence.

She smiled, congratulating herself. Everything had gone very well with her past two attempts at adjusting history, and she hoped for more success again.

She entered a white marble chapel, bleached by the light of many beeswax candles. The man in repose upon his tomb had once been called a giant among men—and his powerful arms and chest proclaimed him a warrior.

But Reynald de Mortimer had been far more than that.

With his white-blond hair and grey, almost colorless eyes, he was well named the Ghost. He was a brutal and powerful lord in the thirteenth century, and he'd had to be strong in mind and body to hold on to his lands despite all those who tried to take them from him. Yes, he was feared in his day, but even his enemies said of him that when the Ghost gave his word he kept it.

That was why it was so strange that he hadn't kept his word the day he died. Afterward his lands had fallen into chaos, with people dying in the slaughter that seemed to go on endlessly up and down the Welsh borders. The Ghost could have prevented that if he had lived.

But this was his chance now to make amends, and the Sorceress had found a particularly interesting mortal to help him out. She smiled. Yes, there'd be some fireworks between them, but that was all part of their journey.

She held her hand over his face, not touching him, but close enough to feel the stir of his breath. There was an ugly scar on one side of his throat where someone had tried to kill him, though the rest of his face was unmarked. Handsome, but it did not look as if he smiled very much.

"Your chance has come, Ghost," she murmured, and her voice caused the walls of the chapel to vibrate. She raised her arms and the heavy wolfskin cloak rose about her, the strands of her long red hair writhing like serpents around her face. She looked frightening, like a Welsh witch from the days of old.

She began to chant and the man on the tomb moved restlessly, as if he were fighting against some imaginary foe, and then his eyes sprang open. They were of the clearest, palest grey—almost the color of water. And he spoke one word.

"Run!"

**Want more of these
Immortal Warriors?**

**Turn the page and meet
Reynald de Mortimer in**

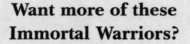

*Passions
of the Ghost*

Coming December 2006

Reynald stood perfectly still. Despite the darkness and the dank underground smell, the castle enclosed him, welcomed him, embraced him with familiar arms. One moment he'd been in the great cathedral with the redheaded Welsh witch and the next he was here. In the deep tunnels beneath his own castle.

Reynald bent low, awkward in his coat of armor—the garment was thick and heavy, made of steel plates and chain mail—only just avoiding knocking his head against the jagged ceiling. At first he'd thought he was back in the between-worlds, that fearful place he had inhabited before the witch took him to the cathedral for his long sleep. But this was different, this was familiar. This was home.

He realized he was still holding his long bow and a couple of arrows clasped in his hand. He was using the weapon when he died, had insisted that the task of striking down his enemy was his alone—and then he'd missed his mark at the vital moment. He shivered with a mixture of guilt and regret. He'd failed his people when they needed him most.

Reynald bumped his head and swore.

Moving about in the constricted space in his coat of armor and with his sword strapped to his side was difficult enough without the longbow. What use was it to him anyway? As he passed a niche in the wall, he paused to place the longbow and arrows within it, for safekeeping, until he sent someone back for them later.

Was it still 1299, the year of his death? Were his men still up above, in disarray and awaiting his orders? His servants would weep with joy when they saw him again. Somehow he would change history and turn defeat and slaughter into victory.

There were steps, narrow and dusty. As he climbed them he saw a light ahead, but it wasn't the uncertain flare of torch- or candlelight. This was brighter . . . steadier.

He paused to stare at the strange burning globe. The steps continued up, toward the armory, and he climbed on, refusing to listen to the increasingly uneasy voice in his head. Was the battle still going on outside? It was very quiet.

The armory wasn't there. No weapons cleaned and shining, no dented coats of armor or rusted chain mail. Instead there were some boxes and chairs stacked against the wall.

The door no longer had a latch or a bar, just a round knob, which he gripped in his big hand and turned.

Reynald stepped out into a world run mad.

All about him were colors, frenzied discordant colors. Yellow and red and pink. Everywhere his eyes rested they were assaulted by a rainbow of different shades and hues. How could his good stone walls have been so vandalized? A half-sized tree stood in an enormous barrel, its branches hung with many sparkling balls, while ropes of glittering gold were wound about and through them. As he stared eyes began to wink at him from the greenery. Many-colored eyes. Shocked, he forced himself forward and peered closer. The eyes were in fact small enclosed balls with colored lights inside them that flashed on and off.

"Jesu . . ."

His voice sounded deep and rusty from disuse. A moment later all thoughts left his head as a terrible whiny noise burst forth. He turned, and found himself confronted by a fat, bearded creature in a red gown.

"Jingle bells!" it shrieked.

Reynald lurched back as the creature began to swing its hips lasciviously at him, the reddened lips pouting as it sang. He drew his sword and brought it down on its head, splitting it asunder. There was a smell of burning, a whirring groan and the creature slumped into silence. Reynald could now see within the bearded head. This was no flesh-and-blood being but a man-made abomination, full of cogs and thin steel wires.

He backed away, sheathing his sword, bewildered and afraid.

This was his home, and yet it wasn't. Something was very, very wrong.

Striding quickly, ignoring the jarring changes—

perhaps if he ignored them they would go away—he made his way toward the thick iron-studded door that led into the training yard. Where were his men? Surely they were as keen to find him as he was to find them, he told himself, as he flung it open.

Outside it was nighttime, and cold. Fair colder than the air behind him in the castle. There was a flurry of snow, and he could see that white flakes lightly covered the surface of the yard and sparkled on top of the castle walls. There were winking lights here, too, stretching along the battlements, flashing on and off jauntily, and seeming to mock the blood that had been shed in this place.

Angrily, Reynald de Mortimer went to step outside, thinking perhaps to tear them down . . . and found he couldn't.

His body simply refused to pass over the threshold.

Frowning, he tried again, moving forward. And couldn't. It was as if there was some invisible shield between him and the outside world, something he could not feel or see, and yet it held him captive. He could not push through it.

He was a prisoner here in his own castle.

If it was even his, he thought bleakly. This place was very different from the world he had left behind in 1299. The witch had brought him back to life, yes, but it was not the life he knew and understood.

With a groan, Reynald turned and made for the winding stairs in the north tower. He needed fresh air. He needed to look out over his lands. He needed to think.

* * *

Amy Fairweather lifted the hem of her long gauzy skirt as she negotiated the narrow stone stairs that circled around and around to the top of the north tower. The castle was full of passages and steps, and it was easy to get lost. Stairs liked these certainly weren't made to be climbed in four-inch heels, but Prince Nicco had insisted. And the prince, she had learned, was used to getting his own way in all things. It was possible that in some men this might have been exciting and macho. In Nicco it just seemed spoiled and petulant. And when it came to Nicco, that said it all, really.

He'd made it more than clear that he expected Amy to accompany him to his private suite and into his luxury-sized bed. Not that she was averse to some hot quick sex. She wasn't a prude and Nicco would be far more pliable if she gave him what he wanted. Hell, the sex might even be good. But Amy couldn't bring herself to do it. Didn't want to.

No matter how much she owed Jez.

In fact—Amy paused as she stepped out of the stairwell and onto the roof of the north tower—she really didn't want to be here at all.

"Ah, magnificent!" Ahead of her, Nicco was making a grand gesture, sweeping his arms at the view.

As far as Amy was concerned there wasn't much to see. Cold, dark countryside and some bulky hills against an only slightly lighter line of sky. It was beginning to snow again, and as she picked her way over to the battlements, the roof felt slippery beneath her shoes.

She shivered, clasping the thin gauzy cloak around her. Jez said she was meant to look like a medieval lady of the manor, and although the costume was very flattering and feminine, Amy was pretty sure no medieval lady had ever worn something like this, unless she was the Barbie version.

For a moment the height made her she feel dizzy, and she reached out to clutch at the cold, hard stone before her. Down below the moat was frozen over. The sense that this was a big mistake and she didn't want to be here was suddenly so strong she felt sick. She should have told Jez "no" once and for all. But even now the thought of facing him, of explaining to him, made her flinch. She owed her brother . . . and he knew it.

"He likes beautiful women," Jez had told her. "Red-heads, in particular—so no need to color your hair, sweetheart. Women and jewelery are his top picks. He'd be putty in your hands, Amy. And I need to know where the Star is."

"Why wouldn't it be locked up safe and tight in a bank vault?"

Jez grinned. "The Star of Russia? The diamond ring of Catherine the Great? Come on, this bloke likes to feel it against his skin. Owning it isn't enough. He has to see it, touch it. The Star is hidden in one of his houses. I just need you to find out which one."

"I wish you'd stuck to stealing cars."

Jez laughed.

"Jez—" She tried to tell him, she really did, but the words stuck in her throat.

"Don't worry, it'll be a walk in the park. I trust you, Amy. You always come through for me."

But maybe I'm tired of coming through for you, she'd thought. Maybe I want to put the past behind me. Maybe I want to put you behind me.

"What have you been up to anyway?" he said. *"It took me ages to track you down. You've moved house, sweetheart."*

"I know. Sorry, I meant to tell you. I've been studying. I went back to school."

Jez laughed, just as she knew he would. *"You don't need to go back to school. How daft is that? What do you want to do that for?"*

For myself, Jez. For myself.

Nicco's hand closed over her arm, and Amy came back to the present with a jolt. She was standing on the freezing roof of a castle in winter in a dress more suited to a harem. Still, she was here now, and the sooner she got Jez the information he wanted, the sooner she could be gone.

Amy turned and gave Nicco her most brilliant smile. "I'm sorry."

"You were certainly far away, cherie. What were you thinking of?"

"Diamonds," she said truthfully. "Sapphires, pearls, emeralds, rubies . . ."

His smile was indulgent. She'd already told him of her passion for jewelry. Jez had got her a cache from somewhere or other to wear this week. It was all part of the character she was playing. The spoiled darling who was never satisfied.

"One day I will show you my Star," he said softly.

Amy felt her heart beat a little faster. "I wish you would," she pouted.

"I will place it upon your finger, and you will never be the same again."

"Is it very far? Perhaps we could go and see it tomorrow?"

Tell me, tell me . . .

But he gave her a secretive smile. He trailed his fingers up her arm and fastened them on her shoulder. It felt uncomfortable, as if he held her in a trap. His face was pressed close to hers, his breath panting against her frozen cheek. "You are very beautiful, my Amy."

I'm not yours . . .

She let him kiss her. He was an experienced kisser, she'd give him that, but despite his skill she was sickened by his touch. It was as if she was just another body to add to his list of conquests. She leaned back with a gasping laugh, pretending to be overcome with the heat of passion. He came after her, pressing his body to hers, pinning her to the battlements. Behind her the world fell away dizzyingly.

"Nicco," she said, trying to wheedle, but he ignored her. She'd kept him at arm's length too long, while making too many promises with her lips and eyes. He pressed his hips against hers, and she could feel his erection. "Please, I don't like heights."

"I will make you forget about such things," he said arrogantly.

Amy mentally gritted her teeth as he swooped in

again, all hands and mouth. She was going to have to stop him. Jez would be furious with her, but she couldn't stand this pawing another moment. Amy clenched her hand into a fist and prepared for a hard, sharp jab to His Highness's midsection.

A deep soft voice came out of the darkness, full of threat, and something more that made the hairs stand up on the back of Amy's neck.

"Unhand the woman, or I will split you like a pig."

Next month, don't miss these exciting new love stories only from Avon Books

A Duke of Her Own by Lorraine Heath

An Avon Romantic Treasure

The Duke of Hawkhurst is proud—and really rather, well, poor! To save his estate, Hawkhurst finds an American heiress to marry and hires Lady Louisa Wentworth to teach his betrothed about London society. Trouble is, Louisa is in love with the duke and now Hawkhurst has to make a big decision—before it's too late.

Finding Your Mojo by Stephanie Bond

An Avon Contemporary Romance

Gloria Dalton is beginning to regret her plan to move to Mojo, Louisiana. The town's residents definitely don't want her around. And to make matters worse, she runs into her first love, Zane Riley. Zane doesn't recognize the person Gloria has become, and she's determined to keep it that way. But the best laid plans . . .

The Earl of Her Dreams by Anne Mallory

An Avon Romance

After her father's death, Kate Simon disguises herself as a boy and hides at an inn on the way to London. Of course, she hadn't anticipated sharing her room with Christian Black, Earl of Canley. When circumstances force the two to join forces to uncover a killer, they both discover more than they ever dreamed.

Too Great a Temptation by Alexandra Benedict

An Avon Romance

Damian Westmore, the "Duke of Rogues," has more than earned his nickname. But when tragedy strikes, Damian abandons his carefree lifestyle to seek vengeance. He never expected to encounter Mirabelle Hawkins, the one woman who could thwart his plans . . . and heal his heart.

Visit www.AuthorTracker.com for exclusive information on your favorite HarperCollins authors.

REL 1006

Available wherever books are sold or please call 1-800-331-3761 to order.

Avon Romances

the best in
exceptional authors and unforgettable novels!

DISCOVER CONTEMPORARY ROMANCES *at their*
SIZZLING HOT BEST FROM AVON BOOKS

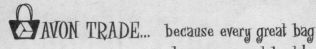